FIC   Hodge, Jane Aiken.
HOD
         First night

DATE		

First & Night

Also by Jane Aiken Hodge

Fiction

MAULEVER HALL
THE ADVENTURERS
WATCH THE WALL, MY DARLING
HERE COMES A CANDLE
THE WINDING STAIR
GREEK WEDDING
MARRY IN HASTE
SAVANNAH PURCHASE
STRANGERS IN COMPANY
SHADOW OF A LADY
ONE WAY TO VENICE
REBEL HEIRESS
RUNAWAY BRIDE
JUDAS FLOWERING
RED SKY AT NIGHT
LAST ACT
WIDE IS THE WATER
THE LOST GARDEN
SECRET ISLAND
POLONAISE

Non-Fiction

THE DOUBLE LIFE OF JANE AUSTEN
THE PRIVATE WORLD OF GEORGETTE HEYER

JANE AIKEN HODGE

First Night

G. P. PUTNAM'S SONS
New York

G. P. Putnam's Sons
Publishers Since 1838
200 Madison Avenue
New York, NY 10016

Library of Congress Cataloging-in-Publication Data

Hodge, Jane Aiken, date.
First night.

I. Title.
PS3558.O342F57   1989   813′.54   88-32249
ISBN 0-399-13453-0

Printed in the United States of America
1   2   3   4   5   6   7   8   9   10

1

The two young people stood facing each other on the wide stage of Lissenberg's brand new Royal Opera House. Behind them, an ornate set suggested the gates of hell. In the pit, the first few members of the orchestra were tuning up for the overture to Herr Gluck's *Orpheus and Eurydice*, but otherwise they were alone.

'Please, Max.' The black-haired girl put a pleading hand on her companion's arm. 'It's all to be sung in masks; no one need ever know. Just think what a joke for you to sing Eurydice! And Orpheus is perfect for me . . . I long to sing it. And you don't even care!'

'They'd find out, Bella. They always do. You don't know this court as I do. Why should you? You've only been here six months.' As dark as she, he had sparkling deep brown eyes, where hers were a surprising blue.

'Lord, Father was angry.' Momentarily diverted, she remembered her father's rage at what he considered his insulting appointment as Minister to the tiny principality of Lissenberg. 'Mr. Pitt came to dinner at Sarum House and spent all evening persuading him.' She laughed. 'They sent for me to sing to them. I was in bed! Such a to-do. Best muslin, my maid tying my sash while nurse worked on my ringlets – lucky they're natural – and in the end Mr. Pitt nearly wrecked the whole thing. Papa doesn't much like to hear my singing praised.'

'What do you mean?'

'I sang Orpheus' lament. I didn't think they were listening – Papa never does; he hates it. They were talking and laughing and throwing back the port-wine, taking no notice whatever, but when I finished, Mr. Pitt just said, "Well, that settles it, you have to go, Sarum. You know how set Prince Gustav is on this children's opera. That girl of yours will be the making of it, and we'll get all the troops we need for the war against

France."'' She stopped, suddenly anxious. 'You won't tell your father?'

'I never tell him anything. Least of all now.'

'I know. I'm sorry, Max.' They had become good friends in the weeks they had worked together on the Gluck opera with which Max's father was to celebrate his marriage to a princess of Baden. Max's mother, dead at his birth fifteen years before, had been merely noble, having married Gustav before he bought the tiny country of Lissenberg and became its Prince. 'Will she be kind to you, do you think, this Princess Amelia?' Cristabel asked now.

'Who cares? The one thing certain is that if she has a son, I'm out of the succession. Father gave himself the absolute right to choose his heir when he took over here. My mother was a plain Lissenberger; this Amelia is a princess, and three of her sisters have married royalty. I heard Father say she's plain as a boot, but no matter . . .'

'Poor lady.' Cristabel lost interest in her host's dynastic plans and returned to her own affairs. 'Dear, darling Max, say you'll change rôles with me! The tunics are almost the same.' Laughing. 'The Opera House cost so much that even your father had to agree to keep the costumes simple.'

'The first economy of his reign.' Bitterly. 'A drop in the lake of his extravagance. And that's only because he's been frightened by those mad revolutionaries in France. Your father, the Duke, has no need to fret; he'll get his Hessian troops all right, from Father's estates there. And the blood-money Father gets for them will help pay for this wedding. Sometimes, Bella, I wonder if the Jacobins aren't in the right of it.'

'Max!' Now he had really shocked her. 'You cannot be serious!'

'I don't know.' Slowly. 'Bella, I just don't know. I expect things are better in England. You don't have such poverty, such injustice there, do you? You're all one people; of course you are kinder to each other. My father doesn't care a rap for the Lissenbergers. He only bought the place because he wanted to be a Prince and an Elector of the Holy Roman Empire. For what that's worth these days! He looks on Lissenberg as his property, to be treated as he pleases. Your George III is answerable to his Parliament. Father cares for nobody. He's bled the people white in the sixteen years he's been here. Look

6

at this theatre!' An angry gesture swept the gilded ranks of boxes, cupid-infested ceiling and heavy velvet curtains. 'And the Palace, and Chapel Royal, where they are regilding vulgar gilt for this wedding. Real gold leaf, mind you! Nothing's too good for the bride.'

'Don't hate her, Max.'

'I don't.' Surprised. 'I'm sorry for her! Father will use her, as he does everyone else. I wonder if he married my mother because she was a Lissenberger, gave him some thread of a claim to the place. And killed her, establishing it.'

'Killed her?' Horrified.

'He insisted the heir be born in Lissenberg. Left it too late to make the journey. Busy hunting, I expect. It was almost winter. Well, you know what the road across the mountains is like. It's why Lissenberg has never been conquered. It was too much for my mother. I was born six weeks early, and she died of me.'

'I'm surprised he didn't marry again sooner,' said realistic Cristabel.

'You've not met the Countess Wunzinger. Nor her three daughters – my half sisters.' He threw it at her. 'If the Wunzinger had had a son, I really believe my father would have married her. She certainly hoped so. The oldest of the girls is older than I am.'

'Oh, your poor mother,' said Cristabel. 'Have you relatives on her side, then, Max? Aunts and uncles, cousins even?'

'I'm not allowed to see them. That's partly why father chose to rebuild the old castle above the town, so he can keep me shut away.'

'I can see why you don't much like him. So why should you care what he thinks? Besides –' she returned to the attack. 'No one need ever know we've changed parts. Just think what a lark it would be. To fool them all like that.'

'Not the kind of lark a prince should indulge in, Bella.'

'Oh, pfui!'

The Duke of Sarum had found life more pleasant than he expected at the parvenu court of Lissenberg. The hunting was good, the drinking hard, which suited him, and he had watched his daughter's growing friendship with the heir of the Principality, with amused surprise. When her governess had reported, with horror, that the children were on Christian name terms, he had shrugged it off. The father was an extravagant nobody, but the son was well enough. So long, of course, as no heir was born to the marriage he had come to help celebrate, and the Duke privately thought this unlikely, after studying his host at close quarters for six months. And Lissenberg was a long way from England. He flattered himself that he had done his best by the unwanted daughter of his disastrous marriage, but he was counting the years until her own wedding would take her off his hands for good. Then he might even look about him for some well-bred, biddable young creature who would give him an heir and help him forget his boyhood folly.

'No, no, let the young things enjoy themselves,' he had surprised Miss Jevons by his tolerance. 'Nothing wrong with the boy, and it's time Cristabel learned some conduct. She's a sad hoyden still.'

'She knows her own mind,' said Miss Jevons.

'Obstinate as be damned,' amended the Duke. 'Save your worry for Prince Maximilian. She'll have him dancing to her tune, you see if she doesn't. And, now, I must dress for this damned reception of the bride. And mind you see Cristabel doesn't disgrace me.'

'She won't,' said Miss Jevons. 'But she asks if she may ride. Prince Maximilian is, I understand.'

'Why not? That mountain road's the devil in a carriage. I shall most certainly ride. Mind the chit brings her own groom; I don't propose to trouble myself with her.'

Although Princess Amelia was the daughter of the neighbouring house of Baden, the short wedding-journey had had to be delayed until the slow spring of 1795 was enough advanced for the mountain road into Lissenberg to be passable. The Duke of Sarum and his daughter had arrived just before winter closed it, and Bella remembered the mountain drive, in a stuffy carriage and pouring rain as something of a nightmare. Now, riding out of the Palace gates with Max at her side, she breathed cold, fresh air with pleasure. The road down to the valley-town of Lissenberg had been open for some time and she and Max had ridden there to watch ice packs scudding down the swift river Liss, but the other track, over the mountains to the little landing-stage that was Lissenberg's only way out to Lake Constance, and the world at large, had been impassable up to now.

'It's a long ride,' Max warned her. 'And rough going.'

'I remember! Just look at the flowers, Max, it's really spring, at last. I wish we could stop.'

But the little cortège must keep up a steady pace to reach the landing-stage before the party from Baden, and she had to be content with Max's description of the way the seasons repeated themselves, backwards, as one got nearer and nearer to the snow line. 'I'll take you one day,' he promised, 'after the wedding.'

They came out of the trees at last, to see Lake Constance below them, brilliant blue in spring sunshine. 'And the royal barge of Baden lying off, waiting for us,' said Max. 'How like Father to be late to meet his bride! And she has sisters married to the Dukes of Hesse and Brunswick, *and* the Tsarevitch of all the Russias. It would serve him right if she turned round and went home to Baden.'

'She's very plain, they say.'

'So she'll wait? For Father! It must be terrible to be a woman, Bella.'

'Oh, Max, it is.' It was her chance, and she took it. 'That's why I want to sing Orpheus. To prove, at least to myself, that I can. That I can be a singer, not just a marriageable commodity. Please, dear, dearest Max, it makes so little differ-ence to you, and to me: everything.'

'But you couldn't! A career as a singer? A duke's daughter.'

'Worse luck. It will make it harder, of course. But you have no idea how he longs to be rid of me. I think, if I was sure I could make a living, I'd do something to disgrace myself. Something so dreadful, do you see, that he would cast me off. And then I'd be free! Venice, Milan, Naples . . . La Scala, the San Carlo! If I am good enough. I have to know that. It's a great deal to throw away . . .'

'All of this,' his wide gesture took in the mounted party, the heavy state coach rumbling along behind, the splendid prospect of lake and far mountains. 'Do, please, Bella, think hard of what you are planning. You have no idea, I am sure, of what life can be like for a woman.'

'For one who fails,' said Cristabel. 'I don't mean to fail. I

9

mean to have the world at my feet. Because I am me, not because I'm Sarum's unwanted daughter. Just give me my chance.' They had got a little ahead of the rest of the party and she reined in her horse to pause and face him. 'I may so well be wrong. How can I know what I can do, if I never try? It won't be an easy audience, after all the celebrations, all the drink. If I can hold them, if I get applause, for me, myself, Orpheus . . . Then I'll know it's worth the risk. If not, I promise you, I'll be a duke's good daughter for the rest of my life.'

He nearly said, 'Marry me.' But he was not yet sixteen, his position threatened by the bride they were come to greet. He reached out a hand as their ponies tittupped side by side. 'It's a bargain, if you will just promise to come to me for help if you should need it.'

'But of course!' She pushed back the plumed riding-hat to smile at him with enormous blue eyes. 'To whom else, Max?' And then, laughing, a hand setting raven ringlets in place. 'But, Max, as Prince of Lissenberg, or as composer of operas?' And, setting sudden spurs to her pony, set it scurrying down the last slope and across spring-green grass to the little landing-stage, where Baden's royal barge was tying up.

Hawk-nosed Princess Amelia, who had not been enjoying the enforced wait, now came out of the little cabin to see two laughing children reining in their horses at the water's edge, apparently so deep in talk that they had not even noticed her.

'Prince Gustav does not seem to be here yet, Highness.' The ship captain disliked the whole business.

'Never mind.' She smiled at him brilliantly and he thought she should always smile. 'His son seems to have come in his stead. I find that charming. I shall go ashore at once. Forgive me, Captain, but I find myself a little tired of your delightful ship.'

Prince Gustav, emerging in his turn from the trees, saw his bride standing between Max and Bella, laughing, holding a hand of each, while an appalled groom held the two ponies from which they had leapt to greet her. She turned, saw him, moved forward, still holding their hands. Then, dropping them, she swept into a regal curtsy, 'What a delightful greeting, Prince!'

She's not so plain after all, he thought.

It had taken all his architect's tact to persuade Prince Gustav that since the members of the orchestra must live in the town of Lissenberg, and much of the audience be drawn from there, his new Opera House must inevitably be built outside the castle precincts, below the last steep slope that made its position so secure. In the course of the building, the choice of site had been richly justified by the discovery of a disused tunnel which ran down from the castle, under the Opera House and so on to the little town below. The upper part of this tunnel had been cleared and made good so as to provide easy undercover access from the castle, while the burghers of Lissenberg were left to make the best of their way up by the mountain road.

'I suspect Father's Kapellmeister, Herr Franck, had more than a little to do with the choice of the site, in a quiet way,' Max told Bella as they made their way down the last of the steep cresset-lit flights of steps. 'He and Cuvilles, the Munich architect, were thick as thieves when Cuvilles was here. Just imagine what it would have been like rehearsing if the Opera House had been part of the Palace. Father would have been in and out all the time with his suggestions . . .'

'And some of them would have been good ones,' said Bella. 'He's no mean musician, your father.'

'And knows it.' Max turned and held out a hand to help her down an extra steep step. 'But you know as well as I do that no good ever came of divided command in the theatre. When I put on my first opera, I mean to be composer, producer, everything.'

'Just so long as I am prima donna.'

'It will be written specially for you!'

It was cloud-cuckoo-land and they both knew it. Kept increasingly busy with last-minute rehearsals, they had had little time to think that Bella and her father would be leaving soon after the wedding. Prince Gustav had contrived to stay sober enough, only the day before, to sign the agreement promising the British the Hessian troops they needed for war against the French revolutionaries, and the Duke of Sarum was eager to be off. 'He always shows himself at the Palace on the King's Birthday,' Bella explained. 'The fourth of June.' And then, returning to the subject nearest her heart. 'I do wish we could have contrived one rehearsal in our true rôles!'

'You know it would have been madness.' They had been forced to rehearse, in secret, wherever they could, on a remote terrace when the sun shone, in the never-used Palace library when it rained. 'And no need for you to fret, you really are going to be wonderful. I'm glad I agreed to change with you.'

'Oh, thank you, Max.' The blue eyes filled suddenly with tears.

Since all the performers were children, the performance of *Orpheus and Eurydice* had been scheduled earlier than the usual hour of nine o'clock, with the inevitable result that the audience arrived still elated with the toasts they had drunk to the newly-wedded couple. 'Heaven help the orchestra.' Max was listening to the rising volume of cheerful sound from beyond the velvet curtains. 'They never get much of a hearing, but tonight . . .' He took her cold hand. 'If they're still very noisy out there, when you have to begin, stand quite still, pick a spot high up at the back, look through it, count ten, as slowly as you can, then start.'

'Max, I'm frightened.'

'Do you want to change back?'

'No!'

The audience talked merrily all through the overture and the first exchanges between Orpheus and the chorus of mourners for the dead Eurydice. Max, peering out from the wings, feared the worst. He could see the royal party, and his father talking eagerly to his new wife. The Prince would be angry, afterwards, if his long-planned opera was a failure; for the moment, he had forgotten all about it. I'll never get drunk, so long as I live, thought Max, and saw his new stepmother put a hand on her husband's arm to hush him.

The unheard chorus fell silent. Cristabel stood, head up, gazing above and beyond the audience as Max had advised, waiting. But the clamour from the house went on, unabated, uncaring. Now his father had noticed, was stirring angrily, looking about him. Wondering what to do? And then, from the very back of the gallery, where the worst seats were thronged with Lissenbergers, came a single, clear cry: 'Silence for our Prince! Silence for Orpheus!'

For an astonished moment, the house stilled, and Cristabel seized it, took one step forward, plunged into song. Max listened, spellbound. She was his friend, Bella, who had laughed and played with him, teased and quarrelled with him. And she was also something quite else. She was Orpheus. She's right, he thought. She's a prima donna.

The audience felt it too, growing quieter and quieter as the performance continued. You could feel them sobering up, Max thought, caught, held and mastered by the singing. But when the curtain fell for the last time the roar of applause was deafening. Holding Bella's ice-cold hand, sharing that first surge of enthusiasm with her, he made up his mind. They had planned to take their curtain calls masked, but he knew now that he could not do it. As a musician, he could not accept the acclaim that was entirely hers. It would mean black trouble for both of them. No matter, it had to be done.

There were shouts for Orpheus now, for the Prince. It was his cue to leave the stage, to leave her alone to her triumph. He pressed her hand, in acknowledgment, in warning, took off his mask, bowed deeply to her, then more easily to the audience before he followed the chorus off stage.

At first, the audience did not understand. Cries of 'Unmask!' mingled with those for 'Orpheus!' and 'The Prince!' Bella stood alone for a moment on the huge stage, taking it all in. Then, with one slow step forward, she swept off mask, and wig and laurel wreath together and sank into the deepest, most formal of curtsies.

No mistaking her now; her dark ringlets had always stood out among the blond Lissenbergers. The audience gave a kind of universal gasp which merged into laughter, and clapping, and more cries of 'The Prince, God bless him.' They love him, she realised with a little shock of surprise. He's their Prince. And, inevitably, her eyes lifted for the first time to the royal box and Prince Gustav. Expecting anger, she felt his rage palpable across the gulf between them, was relieved to see his new wife's restraining hand on his arm.

Turning, she saw Kapellmeister Franck leading Max forward, the chorus following to form up behind them. 'You

13

wicked children.' Franck took her hand, still holding Max's. 'I've never been so frightened in my life. Forward now, bow and curtsy, not as we rehearsed it, but who cares? May I write an opera for you, Lady Cristabel?'

'I'll do?' She had to ask it, though in her heart she knew the answer.

'Oh, you'll do,' he said. 'No need to ask it.' And stepped back, leaving the two of them together.

'Bella!' Max bent to kiss her hand. 'I had to do it. Forgive me?'

'Forgive? But, Max, your father . . .'

'I know. Don't forget to smile for them, Bella. This is your night. As for tomorrow . . .'

'Let it come! Max, I do thank you! I know where I am going now.' Absent-mindedly, intent only on him, she bowed, instead of curtsying, and got a roar of delight from the audience.

'You have them in your hand,' he said. 'It's a great gift, Bella. And I'm going to write you your first opera.'

After that, the chorus surged round to exclaim and congratulate as the audience began slowly, reluctantly to leave. It was all confusion, laughter, delight and there was not a single moment alone with Max until they parted outside their dressing-rooms.

'Max, I do thank you!'

'Sleep well, prima donna. I'll tell you, in the morning, just how great you were.'

Miss Jevons was waiting in the dressing-room, her face chalk-white. 'Bella, how could you? He's most terribly angry.'

'The Prince? I saw. Poor Max. Wasn't he splendid, Miss Jevons?'

'Not the Prince.' Miss Jevons had hardly heard her. 'Your father. We're to leave in the morning. First thing. A figure of fun, he called you, a laughing-stock, a public show. All my fault. When I've got you safe home he says he never wants to see me again.'

'But that's not fair!' She was slowly taking in the extent of the disaster. 'I knew the Prince would be angry, but I really thought Papa would be pleased. After all, he made me sing in the opera.'

'But he didn't want you to,' said Miss Jevons acutely.

'I think a modicum of failure might have been more tactful.'

'Oh, darling Jevons,' with a quick hug. And then, 'But, tell quick, what about Max?'

'He's confined to his rooms. Until his father decides what to do with him. You'll not see him again, Bella.'

2

Martha Ann Peabody was so rich that London Society almost forgave her for being American, the daughter of a rebel. A close friend of George Washington, her father had worn himself out making arms for the revolutionary forces in his Philadelphia factory. He had made money too. When he died, in 1800, Martha found herself an heiress, surrounded by hopeful wooers.

They bored her. The Philadelphia businessmen had no manners, spat and smoked in her presence, and talked to her about their manufactures. And the plantation owners, riding north to woo, treated her like Venetian glass and talked to each other across her. About horses, mostly. Since what she cared for was music, she had soon had enough of this. On the day of her twenty-first birthday, in 1801, she sent for her father's man of business and told him she was going to England.

'Pray don't waste your time in protesting.' She silenced him with a gesture, and he thought her more and more like her father. 'I have it all arranged. I have been corresponding with my father's old friend, the banker, Thomas Coutts. He promises me his daughters' protection. They are very much the thing, apparently, all married to peers, for what that's worth. They will see me launched in Society. And you will see to it that I don't lack for funds, Mr. Jonas.'

'But, Miss Martha –' He had seen her grow up from a plain little girl to a neat, undistinguished young lady, had been awaiting the announcement of a suitable engagement. Now he gaped, as at a phoenix, rising. 'The war – You will be taken by a privateer!'

'Nonsense,' but she said it kindly, 'all the talk is of peace, as you well know. And naturally I shall travel on one of the Peabody ships, neutral and everyone's friend. And I shall take my maid, Deborah.' She laughed. 'I am promoting her to the rank of cousin. She hates it, poor girl, but I tell her one must suffer to be free.' She rose and held out her hand. 'I know I can count on you, Mr. Jonas.'

'You sound just like your father.'

'Thank you! Nothing could please me more.'

Reaching England at last early in 1802, Martha found the Coutts sisters friendly but elusive, busy with matrimonial problems of their own. But they gave her the basic advice she needed about clothes, and house, and, most important of all, Society. She opened her attack on it with a musical soirée at which she had persuaded no less a person than Michael Kelly to sing. Short of funds as usual, the famous opera singer found the immense sum she offered him irresistible. It was he who told her the story of the Duke of Sarum's daughter. Lady Cristabel had been kept immured at Sallis House, down in the country near Salisbury, since she had disgraced herself by singing a breeches part in Lissenberg, of all places.

'Not breeches, in fact.' Almost forty-two, Kelly had immense Irish charm, and made the most of it. 'A tunic, you know, classical stuff. She sang the part of Gluck's Orpheus and had the audience stuck like spellbound pigs in their seats. Her father was in a fine rage! Her mother was an opera singer, you see. Ran away after the girl was born. Preferred the stage to Sarum House. Can't blame her really. He never forgave her, of course.'

'What happened to her?' Martha asked, fascinated.

'Blessed if I know. Haven't heard of her for years. Dead I expect, poor thing. Her kind don't wear well.'

'And the daughter has been kept imprisoned in the country? It's monstrous! Is her voice really so remarkable?'

'So they say. And she's not precisely imprisoned. Comfortable enough.' Laughing. 'What the Duke doesn't know, because no one has told him, is that her mother's old teacher, Signor Arioso, went there, when he heard, offered himself as undergroom or something, been teaching the girl all he knows ever since.'

'Good gracious! Her father doesn't know?'

'Never goes there. He's going to remarry in the spring – the mother must be dead, come to that – everything may change then. The wedding's to be here in town; he can hardly leave the child out of that. Not a child really. Not much younger than the new bride, I believe. Eighteen, nineteen, something like that.'

'What an extraordinary business. If she does come to London, I'd dearly like to meet her. Could you manage it for me, do you think, Mr. Kelly?'

'For you, dear lady, I would do anything. But I warn you, it won't be easy.'

Martha was soon fending off English fortune-hunters, just as she had done American ones, and finding them different, but not much more interesting. Totally realistic about her own appearance, she knew that the fashionable high-waisted muslins did nothing for her. She was neither tall nor slender, and her hair remained mouse-coloured, however stylish its cut. 'I'm not an antidote,' she told her maid, and confidante, Deborah, 'but I'm no beauty. No sense flattering myself that they court me for my looks.'

She read the details of the Sarum wedding in her *Morning Chronicle* and noted that Lady Cristabel had indeed made an appearance as the senior among a bevy of bridesmaids. And when the Duke took his bride for a honeymoon tour of his Irish estates, Lady Cristabel was reported to be staying on in Sarum House.

'I long to hear her sing,' Martha told Michael Kelly. 'But how?'

'Nobody has, that I know of. The Duke has left her in the care of his dragon of an elder sister, and there seems no sign of her making an appearance in Society.'

'At least he's not sent her back to moulder in the country. That has to be encouraging. Tell me about the dragon-aunt.'

'Not a lot to tell. Younger than her brother. Never married; God knows why not, with her fortune . . . Must have a fortune.' He thought about it, added a qualifying, 'I suppose.'

'Does she go out in Society? Did she before Lady Cristabel joined the household?'

'Not a great deal. St. James's for the Birthday. That kind of thing.'

'That's not much help to me. Where could I meet her?'

'That's a hard one. Frankly, I don't know, Miss Peabody.'

'Think about it for me?'

'I'd do more than that for you.'

'Ah, don't you start! Tell me, Mr. Kelly, the singing master – what did you say his name was? Did he come to London too?'

'Blessed if I know.'

'Find out for me?'

'Delighted to.'

He called next day to report that Signor Arioso was indeed to be seen in his old haunts in town. 'He don't talk about the girl, but the word is that he's in touch with her.'

'Without the knowledge of the dragon aunt? I wonder how. Has he a voice still, Mr. Kelly? Could he perform at one of my evenings?'

'I don't know . . .' doubtfully.

'Unlike you to admit ignorance. Would you ask him for me?'

'To sing?'

'No, to call on me.'

Signor Arioso arrived a few days later. He was small, plump, anxious, in clothes that showed their age, and he was very much puzzled by the summons. 'Miss Peabody,' his English was accented but fluent, 'you wished to see me?'

'It's good of you to come so promptly. Mr. Kelly has told you about my musical evenings?'

'I have heard of them, of course.'

'I was hoping you might care to perform at one of them.'

'I?' His laugh had a savage note. 'Why do you think I became a singing-master, Miss Peabody? It was because I lost my own voice. After such a sacrifice! Mr. Kelly was doubtless embarrassed to explain to you. I have grown used to it! My parents had such hopes for me. And then, nothing, at seventeen, to find that one had lost everything that makes a man's life worth living! And all for nothing.'

'You mean, you're . . .' She had heard of the barbarous custom, but boggled at the word.

'A castrato, Miss Peabody, but without the voice. I'm no use to you, to myself, to anyone.'

'Mr. Kelly says you managed to be of much use to the Duke of Sarum's daughter.'

'Lady Cristabel! Ah, there's a voice for you. Better than her mother's because there is more behind it. Not a drawing-room voice, you understand, an operatic miracle. And all they'll let her do is sing to the company after dinner, if she is lucky. Her father and his new bride return from Ireland next month. Then we shall see . . .'

'It sounds as if you manage to keep in touch with her.'

'Oh, yes. I've not seen her since she came to town, but we correspond. All the servants love her, that's the kind of person she is.'

'You make me more and more eager to meet her. But how?'

Michael Kelly supplied the answer, calling to report that the Duke and his new Duchess were back in town. 'And it sounds as if his bride had talked some sense into Sarum while they were away. At all events, the girl is going into Society with them. A stunner, they say, in her own way. Raven-black hair and blue eyes. The Duchess is a blonde English beauty, maybe likes the child as a foil. Anyway, they are to be seen everywhere, hand in hand. "Like sisters," the Duchess says. But what I came to tell you is that Lady Cristabel is to sing at the charity concert in the London Rooms. Quite a concession by her father, you must admit, and absolutely as far as he is going to go, Arioso tells me. So if you are really so eager to hear her, I had better set about getting you tickets for the concert.'

'You think you can?'

'Did you not tell me you were President Washington's god-daughter?'

'I am certainly named for his wife. But that can hardly be a recommendation here, Mr. Kelly.'

'Among the Whig ladies who are patrons of this concert? I think it might do the trick. It's a pity Mr. Coutts' three graces haven't bestirred themselves a bit more for you.'

'Three graces? It's not what I'd call them.'

'Ah, the poor girls. You should have seen them when Angelica Kauffman painted them in their prime. They've all had noble husbands long enough now to know it's not roses all the way. English Society's a battle from start to finish, Miss Peabody. Never forget that.'

'Oh dear!' She sighed, shrugged, rose to her feet and prowled over to the window that overlooked fashionable Bruton Street. 'You've put your finger on it, Mr. Kelly. I came here with such hopes. Of a Society more interesting than ours at home, where a woman might be allowed some small part in the conversation, be listened to sometimes. But it's really just the same. Oh, they pretend to listen, because I am rich. Am I such a bore, Mr. Kelly?'

'Of course not.' He had risen when she did to follow her to the window. 'And you know it. A pity, really, that your talent is so general. If you painted just a little better, or had started to learn the piano earlier, you could set up as a *virtuosa*. Lead a life of your own. Like Madame Le Brun or Angelica Kauffman. As it is, you'll need a companion for the concert, you know.'

'I suppose so.' She had begun to recognise that Deborah was not taken quite seriously as a chaperone. An acute observer, she had noticed that the young and not so young men who thronged her elegant drawing-room did not treat her quite as they did their sisters and cousins. At first she had thought this a tribute to her American differentness, but as she became gradually more and more aware of a hint of freedom in their behaviour, she had begun seriously to wonder whether she ought not to hire some old tartar of a chaperone. Or was it already too late? For the moment, she smiled at Michael Kelly. 'I'm sure you must know some impecunious, starchy, old lady I could bribe to accompany me.'

He laughed. 'For you, anything.'

Martha refused an offer of marriage from a delightful young Irish captain that night, and found his reaction disconcerting. 'They said it was no good at the Club.' He had drunk a good deal of her excellent wine to bring himself to the point. 'Said you were hanging out for an earl at least. You could make my fortune if you'd just tell me, Miss Peabody. The bets are mounting up in the Club book. Be a sport, tip me the word. I can't begin to tell you how dead broke I am.'

'I'm sorry, Captain O'Shaughnessy.' Hard to know whether to be amused or angry. 'I'm afraid I can't help you.'

It took her a very long time to get to sleep that night. Bets on her at the clubs! Had she made the most appalling mistake in coming to England?

She woke next morning to the sound of bells, and talk of the charity concert gave way for a while to talk of the Peace of Amiens.

'Mr. Addington calls it the peace everyone's glad about and no one's proud of.' Michael Kelly had called with tickets for the concert. 'I've found you a companion, by the way, a Miss Chevenix. You won't like her, and I doubt she'll approve of you, but she has as many quarterings as I have notes, and for the evening, she'll do.'

'I don't know what I'd do without you, Mr. Kelly.' She held out an impulsive hand.

'Miss Peabody.' He took it in both of his. 'I'm old enough to be your father, but I've taken a real fancy to you. Just think what a life we could lead –'

'Oh, Mr. Kelly, not you too.' She shook her head at him and withdrew her hand gently. 'I'm grateful to you for not lying and talking of love, but if I ever do marry, that will be what it is for.'

'Forgive me?'

'Of course.'

Miss Chevenix was everything Michael Kelly had suggested, but she was also passionate about music, and she and Martha found common ground in this. The concert hall was packed when they reached it. 'Everyone is here,' Miss Chevenix looked round with satisfaction. 'Natural enough, since it's for such a good cause. Funds for men wounded in the long war with France. And the performers all of the most impeccable breeding. I am afraid you and I may have to make allowances for them, my dear Miss Peabody. They are used to perform for each other at Lord Guilford's home, Wroxton Abbey. A more tolerant audience, I imagine, than this will be.'

The concert opened with a series of songs from Handel's operas, sung with varying degrees of competence, solo and chorus, by groups of young ladies in white muslin and young gentlemen in elegant black. The audience was restless, some meaning to listen, some paying attention only when relatives of their own were performing, many still plagued with winter colds and unbridled coughs. Then Michael Kelly himself appeared to bring the house down with his famous solo from *No Song No Supper*.

'That will be a hard act to follow,' said Martha.

'I wonder who will dare,' Miss Chevenix hushed as a

black-haired girl appeared from the wings and the Master of Ceremonies bowed deeply, took her hand and led her forward.

'Ladies and Gentlemen, I have great pleasure in presenting Lady Cristabel Sallis, who has most kindly consented to sing to us, her first appearance on the London stage.'

'Not on any, however,' whispered Miss Chevenix. 'You know the story?'

'Yes.' Shortly. 'She's beautiful.'

'And knows it?'

'No, it's not that. It's that she likes an audience, I think.'

After a word with the accompanist, Lady Cristabel was standing, very much at ease, gazing beyond the audience as the Master of Ceremonies announced that she would sing 'He was despised', from Handel's *Messiah*.

'That's brave,' said Miss Chevenix.

'Hush,' said Martha.

But the audience was astir with curiosity, noisier than ever. The dark-haired girl stood for a moment, still gazing out over their heads, then turned to her accompanist, gave a confident little nod, took one step forward and swept a low curtsy. It got her the hush she needed. Then, as the golden voice wove its spell, whispers stilled, coughs subsided, even breath seemed suspended. And, at the end, pandemonium, clapping, stamping of feet, cries of 'encore'.

'I see now why they put her to sing before the interval,' Martha turned to her companion. 'Is she as brilliant as I think?'

'I never heard anything like it. And look how she holds the audience. We've seen a career start today . . . Would have, if she were not a duke's daughter.'

Martha did not remember much about the interval or the rest of the concert. Miss Chevenix introduced her to a great many people and she managed to make the right responses to the inevitable questions, sighed with relief when it was time to return to their seats, and sat hardly hearing the popular songs which made up the second half. Only when the audience rose for a spirited rendering of *God Save the King* did she sigh, and stir, and return to the present.

'You're very quiet,' said Miss Chevenix.

'How can I meet her?'

'There I am afraid I cannot help you.' Miss Chevenix knew

at once whom she meant. 'A duke's daughter is quite above my touch.'

'Then I shall write to her.'

But what to say? She was scratching away at draft after draft next day when her maid announced Signor Arioso. 'The very person.' She rose eagerly to greet him. 'Your Lady Cristabel is absolutely everything you said, and more so! But how can I meet her, Signor?'

'No chance, I am afraid. Her success and the talk it has caused have enraged her father. She's to be sent back to the country.'

'Medieval! How soon, do you know?'

'Tomorrow, they say.'

'So soon?' She thought for a minute. 'She'll travel in some comfort, I take it, spending the night on the way. Could you find out where, Signor Arioso? I have a great mind to make a little excursion into the country myself. Dare I ask you to accompany me, or would my reputation be gone for ever?'

'I'm afraid so, Signorina.'

'Pity. Oh well, I have managed so far with only the company of my maid; I shall just do so again.'

Arioso returned later in the day to report that the Duke always spent a night at the Angel at Guildford, when he drove down to Sallis House, and Lady Cristabel and her chaperone would doubtless do the same. 'Their departure is postponed until the day after tomorrow, by the way.'

'That's a blessing. Who is the chaperone, do you know?'

'I'm afraid it is Lady Helen.'

'The dragon-aunt! Well, I must be thinking how best to tame her. What do you know about her, Signor?'

'She's something of a blue stocking, I believe. A friend of the Miss Berrys, Horace Walpole, that set. But they are bound to have hired a private parlour at the inn. It's not going to be easy.'

'Nothing that is worthwhile is easy. But I am a very determined woman, Signor.'

'I begin to think so.'

It was the first time Martha had left London since the windswept, rain-sodden drive up from Southampton, and she was amazed all over again at the green neatness of England. Today the sun shone, birds sang in flowering trees, wafts of perfume from cottage gardens came in through the open carriage window. 'This is going to be something like,' she told Deborah. 'I'm just about ready for this after all those cramped respectable rides in town.'

'Yes, Miss,' said Deborah.

'No, Deborah.' Martha leaned forward to pat her hand. 'You've forgotten again. You're my cousin-companion, don't forget.' She looked at her watch. 'I wonder if we are ahead of Lady Cristabel on the road or behind her.'

'Ahead I should think.' Deborah had not enjoyed the ruthlessly early start. 'But how will you contrive the meeting, Miss?'

'Not Miss, Martha.' Patiently. 'And the answer is the Good Lord knows, and I mean to leave it to Him.'

It was still early afternoon when they swept into the yard of the prosperous coaching inn where Martha had taken the precaution of sending to engage lodgings. This, and the elegant hired carriage, ensured an obsequious welcome from the landlord. 'I'm rather hoping to meet a friend here,' she told him carelessly. 'Lady Cristabel Sallis. You do expect her, do you not?'

'Yes, indeed.' If he had bowed deeply before, he almost touched the ground now. 'I will see to it that your rooms are convenient for her Ladyship's, ma'am.'

'Thank you. They'll dine with me, of course.' She gave swift orders for the best he could offer. 'And if you will be so good as to let me know when Lady Cristabel arrives?'

'With pleasure.'

But the stir in the yard when the Sarum coach swung in was announcement in itself, and Martha anticipated the little boy who came tapping at her door. 'Thank you.' She stepped demurely downstairs after him, timing herself by the sounds in the yard, and reached the main hall just as the newly arrived party entered it. 'Cristabel!' She moved forward, hands outstretched. 'What a pleasure to meet you here!' She turned, gravely curtsying to the tall lady in black. 'This must be your aunt, whom I have never had the pleasure of meeting. Is not this a happy accident! I could not believe my good luck when the landlord told me he expected you tonight. You'll give me the pleasure of dining with me, of course. I took the liberty of

25

giving the orders. But I am sure Lady Helen is blessing me for keeping you standing here, when she must long for the comfort of her room. I've a million things to say to you, Cristabel. Bear with a savage of a tourist and come and look at the Castle and the Abbot's Hospital with me? My cousin Deborah is a devoted companion, but no sightseer.' She had taken Cristabel's hand in an apparently impulsive gesture as she began this breathless speech, now pressed it hard.

'I'd be delighted.' Cristabel took her cue. 'Lord, it's an age since we last met. I hardly know where to begin.'

'By presenting your friend to me, perhaps?' Lady Helen had been looking Martha up and down, unable to find fault with anything except the soft trace of a Philadelphia accent. 'I don't remember your mentioning . . .' The English good manners, on which Martha had counted, made it impossible for her to put her doubts more directly.

'Cristabel never spoke of me? Oh, now, I mind that! Of Martha Ann Peabody? You were surely never ashamed of your American friend, Cris? I may still call you Cris? But what are we doing, standing about in public here? Your rooms are next to mine, I asked the landlord specially. This way.' She had her by the arm now, leading her towards the stairway. 'Say you'll come walking with me as soon as you are settled?'

Half an hour later, the two girls were walking side by side, along Guildford's handsome high street, with Deborah keeping a respectful pace or two behind them. It had been market-day, and the street was still crowded with prosperous red-faced farmers. By tacit consent they kept silent until they reached the gardens of the Abbot's Hospital. Then Lady Cristabel stopped by a bed of gillyflowers, turned to face her companion. 'And now, perhaps, you will explain.' Generations of authority sounded in the cool, deep voice, and Martha felt a sudden qualm almost of fear.

'It's not so much an explanation as a proposition,' she plunged in. 'We can't stay out long, can we? No time for beating about the bush. I'm more grateful than I can say, that you caught on so quickly back at the inn. Briefly, the thing is this. I heard you sing at the London Rooms the other day. Michael Kelly had told me about you. You're all he said. More. You've a great future before you, if you want it.'

26

'Kelly?' Black brows lifted over the amazing blue eyes.

'He's a friend of mine. He has told me about you. But of course I had to hear you myself; see you. The way you mastered that restless audience. I was spellbound. We all were. You must have felt it. You must want to use your gift. On the stage, in opera, where you belong.'

'I've dreamed of it. Trained for it, thanks to Arioso. This is a very strange conversation.'

'Is it not? My fault. I have not explained myself.'

'I've heard a little about you.' The rich voice sounded amused. 'I may live immured but I'm not entirely out of touch with the world. You are the American heiress.'

'That's it. My father left me everything. With no strings attached. He trusted me, bless him, believed in my good sense. When I got to England and found things no better here, I began to wonder if he had been right.'

'No better?'

'For a woman. In Philadelphia, after Father died, I was surrounded by men who meant to marry me. Not me, my money. They hardly bothered to hide it. I amuse you?'

'Yes. You cannot seriously have thought things would be better here in England?'

'I thought the men would be more interesting.'

'And they are not?'

'Not the ones who want to marry me. They are dull about different subjects, that's all. They take it just as much for granted that I am lucky to be listening to them.'

'And so you are,' said Lady Cristabel. 'My father wants me to marry a man I have not even met. He's fifty. His lands march with ours down in Somerset and his first wife has just died. Childless, by which I mean leaving only daughters. I refused, and am going back to the country until I see the error of my ways, which means for the rest of my life, I think. How strange to be telling you this.'

'It makes things easier for me. To say what I want to. I hope you will listen. Do you know Michael Kelly?'

'How should I? You seem to know about me, know how my life has been until these last few weeks. I know of him, of course. But what has he to do with anything?'

'It was his idea, really. I was grumbling to him, do you see, about my dull life, women's dull lives. He said it was a pity I wasn't good at something, couldn't play, or sing, or paint. Then I could have been what he called a *virtuosa*, would be entitled to a life of my own, like Mrs. Billington or Mrs. Jordan, or someone I've never heard of called Madame Vigée Le Brun. That's what made me think of you. With your voice, and my money, I think we might be able to make a life for ourselves, if you would only risk it, only trust me. I've been thinking of nothing else since I heard you sing. Please, Lady Cristabel, don't say "no" before you have thought about it, slept on it.'

'Say no? Do you think me mad? But – Miss Peabody, I'm not ready. It would not be fair not to tell you this. I've been shut up: cloistered. Even Arioso, who is my dear friend, has told me I need experience of real opera, preferably in Italy, Venice maybe, to go every day through the season, eat and drink opera, breathe it, live it. Then, he thinks, he did say that he hoped . . . It's no use. I've given up. It's impossible . . .' The extraordinary voice faded into silence.

'Venice,' said Martha. 'What a delicious idea. I had been thinking of Naples, but it sounds a sad tatterdemalion kind of a place, not the thing for two ladies on their own.'

'Whether Venice would prove any better, now it is under Austrian control – Good gracious,' she broke off. 'I am talking as if it were a possibility.'

'Believe me, Lady Cristabel, it is. If you'll only venture . . .'

'You mean . . . You really mean . . .'

'I most certainly mean it. I've talked to Signor Arioso. Nothing would make him happier than to act as courier for us. He speaks all kinds of languages, he tells me. Now the peace is signed, we can go the easy way, through France. And that will be interesting too . . . Maybe a stop in Paris? The opera there?'

'You've really thought about it!'

'I've thought of little else since I heard you sing. I love music, Lady Cristabel, play well enough to accompany your practice, sing well enough to know how brilliantly you do. It would be a happy life for me, on the fringe of yours, maybe managing yours a little. My father was a keen man of business. Anything rather than this everlasting round of Society!'

'Which I have hardly experienced. But that wedding! My poor stepmother! To get away from it all! But, can we?' She looked at the little gold watch pinned to her habit. 'I must be getting back. Aunt Helen will be anxious . . . I'm fond of her.'

'I saw. It's a problem. I had meant to propose abducting you, here and now.'

'What?'

'Well, not precisely.' Laughing. 'But my carriage is ready, my things still packed, my rooms paid in advance. We could have left your aunt to eat the dinner I have commissioned, driven all night – there's a moon – taken ourselves some quiet lodging in an unpopular seaside resort and made our plans for the journey. I thought you would just leave a note for your aunt, but I see now that that is impossible. You have to tell her. We have to tell her. Explain. It means it's going to be harder for you, I'm afraid.'

'Better in the long run. I don't shirk my fences, Miss Peabody. Come,' taking her arm, 'let us go back to the inn and tell Aunt Helen. I owe her that. Not my father. A letter will do for him, but we must have his tacit agreement, or he could make things very difficult for us. And, Miss Peabody, I have to tell you, I am penniless. Entirely dependent on my father. And the most I can hope from him, I think is non-interference.'

'Never fret about that. A few years and you will be commanding a prima donna's fees. You can pay me back then, if you want to.'

'You really believe it!'

'So do you. Let us go and face your Aunt.'

'You are out of your minds,' Lady Helen had listened impassively as the two girls outlined the plan. 'Sit down, both of you, don't tower over me, it makes me nervous. You have known each other . . .' she looked at her watch. 'An hour and a half, and you propose to go gallivanting off together, to Venice, of all places, unchaperoned – I'm sorry, Miss Peabody, but that "cousin" of yours is neither here nor there – where Cristabel will become a famous opera singer and make her fortune. Just like that.'

'Exactly like that, Lady Helen.' Martha was beginning to respect the dragon-aunt. 'But I am sorry you don't think poor Deborah will do,' she went on.

'Of course she won't do. Couldn't say "boo" to a goose, poor girl. Well enough as your maid, which I take it is what she really is. So I am going to come with you.' Amused blue eyes took in their amazement and Martha, with time now to study her, was revising her opinion of the dragon-aunt. She had expected an old lady, but there was only a frost of grey in the black hair so like Cristabel's. And there was nothing old about the set of the neat head on elegant shoulders, or the snapping blue eyes that had moved from face to face as they told their story. 'That will take the wind out of Sarum's sails,' said Lady Helen with satisfaction. 'And I can pay my way, Miss Peabody. My brother endowed me with an adequate pittance when he finally gave up hope of my marrying. No chance he'll do the same for you, Cristabel. This is going to make him angrier than I have ever seen him. I must be a coward. I'd as soon be out of the way when he explodes.'

'You really mean it, Aunt Helen?'

'Indeed I mean it. I always wanted to see Venice. But it is up to you, Miss Peabody. I won't be a charge on you, but I'll alter the shape of your party more than a little. I'm not in my dotage, but I'm a short-tempered old maid, who likes her comforts.'

'And you shall have them.' Martha took a deep breath. 'When do we start?'

'First we write to the Duke. Both of us, I think, Cristabel. Not asking him, telling him. I think we had best do that from Sallis House, don't you? No need to start defying him, and spending Miss Peabody's money before we must. Will you give us the pleasure of your company there, Miss Peabody?'

'Why, thank you! But don't you think I would be better employed in setting about our arrangements in London? There will be a million things to do, and I want to see Mr. Kelly as soon as possible for advice and introductions. You won't mind if I tell him? In strictest confidence, of course.'

'It will be a nine days' wonder soon enough,' said Lady Helen.

3

Lady Helen's joining it made the mad scheme possible. The Duke fulminated in Sarum House, his young bride went about town looking as if the devil was after her, and the gossip columns were full of hint and innuendo. Martha was too busy to care, but she made time to go to Mrs. Billington's benefit performance in *Algonah* at Drury Lane, since some of the music was by her friend Michael Kelly. Calling on her next day to be congratulated, he told her that the opera had had to be largely revised because it was no longer possible to find a male soprano to take the part of the hero. 'My good friend Storace wrote the opera for a castrato, of course. A barbarous practice but we miss those extraordinary voices. I'd been thinking about that . . .' He took her arm and drew her away from her other guests into a window alcove. 'Had you considered how this will affect your brilliant friend's future? When I was young, we all wrote our operas for castrato heroes. Now there aren't any, and not many women who can take breeches parts either. Mrs. Jordan still gets away with them, but it's a miracle . . . Even Mozart had to rewrite his *Idomeneo* for tenor when they performed it at Munich. And Lady Cristabel started her career as Orpheus. The managers will be wild for her when she is ready.'

'Thank you. You're a good friend, Mr. Kelly. From time to time I get frightened; think our plan quite mad.'

'Oh, no,' he told her. 'It's enough to make a man want to live for ever. To see Lady Cristabel's career . . . You'll spend some time in Paris, I hope, on your way to Venice? I'm sure Lady Cristabel should see the opera there. I rather hope to go there myself, now the way is open at last.'

'Yes, we certainly hope to spend some time there.' But when he had left, she sat for a long time, hands in her lap, brooding. For the first time in her life, she was having trouble about money. Helpful Mr. Jonas had not sufficiently understood the intricacies of European banking, and cautious Mr. Coutts was proving gently unhelpful in the matter of the letters of credit and large advances she needed. He treated her like a child and pooh-poohed her insistence that, in paying for Cristabel's training, she would in fact be making a highly promising investment. She had come away from their last interview angry to the point of furiously-resisted tears at his bland, obstructive patronage. Little girls, he implied, should go away and play with the young men.

What could she do? Where could she turn? Borrow? Every instinct revolted at the idea. But she had promised Cristabel, and Lady Helen . . .

A knock at the door. Deborah. 'There's a very strange young man asking for you.'

'Strange?'

'Jewish, I think. Quite young. Very sure of himself. Says it's to your advantage. His name's Rothschild. Nathan Rothschild.'

'Rothschild.' Thoughtfully. She was remembering something her father had said after his last visit to Europe the year he died. He had gone to Frankfurt on business and been introduced to an amazing old man called Mayer Rothschild. 'He sits in a tumbledown house in the Frankfurt ghetto and holds the web of European finance in his hands. I never saw anything like it.' Not a common name. A son? 'Send him in,' she said.

Impeccable dark business clothes, dark red hair above the plump, round face, dark eyes that contradicted something obsequious in his manner. 'Mr. Rothschild,' she held out her hand. 'I believe my father knew yours.'

'Yes.' His hand in hers was moist. 'It's good you know that.' His English was heavily accented. 'I have a proposition to make to you, Miss Peabody.' He came direct to the point.

'Yes?'

'Mr. Coutts is being difficult.' Seeing her surprise, he threw out a hand in a curiously eastern gesture. 'Miss Peabody, we financiers must know everything about everything, or fail. I am come to offer you the funds Mr. Coutts has refused.'

'At a price?'

'Of a kind. I am glad to see you're enough your father's daughter to recognise there would have to be a price.'

'For my own money.'

'For making it easily available.'

'Unlike Mr. Coutts. So – what is your price, Mr. Rothschild?'

'Not money. A small favour. You plan to go to Paris, I believe, and then Venice.'

'You are well-informed.'

'I make a point of it. All I ask, Miss Peabody, is that you deliver a letter for me to an associate in Paris. I do not wish it to go through the usual channels. It is impossible, these days, to keep finance and politics separate. I am sure, as your father's daughter, you will understand that.'

'Oh, yes, but I think I need to know what kind of politics I would be involving myself in. It must be an important letter if it is worth an interest-free loan to you.'

'It is important, yes, but I can promise you – on the Torah, if you like – that you would entirely approve of its contents. Not that you would understand them. It would be written in code, of course, seem like a totally harmless bit of family correspondence. A letter to my brother James, that's all, introducing you and asking him to care for your interests in Paris. And, then, when you move on to Venice, he will charge you with another one, to our brother Salomon, introducing you once again.'

'And that's all?'

'Absolutely all, and they will be at your service as I am.'

'It's very tempting,' she said. 'It will make Mr. Coutts very angry.'

'Would you mind that?'

'I should enjoy it.'

'Then shall we consider it settled? I'll have your letters of credit drawn up today. The one thing I do ask is that you leave as soon as you possibly can.'

'The first letter is urgent? Well, that would suit me. I'll be out of the way of Mr. Coutts and his daughters when the talk begins.' She held out her hand. 'A bargain, Mr. Rothschild. And I thank you.'

Afterwards, she wondered what magic he had used to make her agree so easily. But the letters of credit duly arrived, and Lady Helen, coming to London for the King's Birthday was amazed to find her preparations so well-advanced.

'My brother has washed his hands of us, I'm glad to say.'
She had terrified Martha's other callers into flight. 'It's the
best we could hope for. Better than I feared. I begin to think
he is really enamoured of that new bride of his; glad to shrug
off his daughter. My going with you makes it possible for him.
I hope it does not appal you.'

'Nothing of the kind.' Martha was grateful for this plain
speaking. 'I agree with you; your coming makes it all possible.'
She laughed. 'It hardly needed the sight of my wooers in flight
before you today to make me sure of that. I can't tell you how
glad I was to see them go.'

'They will be back tomorrow.'

'And more of them. You have quite changed my position in
Society by coming to me like this.'

'As I intended. Ridiculous, is it not? But one might as well
make the most of it. This is what Cristabel does not understand
yet. She does not recognise, I think, quite what a stir she is
going to cause. A duke's daughter. On the stage. In breeches
parts.'

'You had worked that out?' Now Martha was impressed
indeed.

'I'm past my prime, Miss Peabody, but I'm not stupid. Yes,
I had worked that out. Cristabel has not. That is what I am
come to discuss with you. You two are of an age, more or less,
but do you, I wonder, realise how much younger than you she
is?'

'She thinks only of her career. It's formidable . . .'

'Yes. And what she does not understand is that there is
more to a stage career than being able to sing like an angel,
and hold an audience. That, we know she can do. But what
about life off stage? I found you here, Miss Peabody, entertaining a group of agreeable young fortune-hunters with only that
maid of yours for chaperone. You had them entirely in line.
Cristabel could not do that. She has never had the chance to
appear in Society, learn its ways. Would you think it wildly
extravagant of me if I were to suggest that we spend some time
in Paris on our way to Venice? Everyone seems to be planning
to go there, except, I am glad to say, my brother, who vowed
never to set foot in France again when they murdered their
king. He may regret it now, but he's a man of his word; he
won't go. I confess I quite long to! And Cristabel could make

34

a kind of unofficial début there, under my wing, and learn a little of your social sense.'

'Why, thank you.' Martha never blushed for a man's compliment, but she did now. 'Lady Helen, you have taken the words out of my mouth. I long to see Paris, and Mr. Kelly was advising just the other day that we spend some time there so that Lady Cristabel can go to the opera. Better there than here in London, don't you think?'

'Very much better.' With emphasis. 'I think she had best stay in the country until we are ready to leave. Life at Sarum House could hardly be called a bed-of-roses just now. My brother has not actually sworn at me, but he has hardly spoken to me either. It makes for an uncomfortable sort of household.'

'I should just about think so! Lady Helen, I can't begin to tell you how grateful I am!'

'Then pray don't try. Nothing to be grateful about. This is probably the most selfish thing I have ever done in my life, and I am beginning seriously to wish that I had started on an enlightened career of self-interest much earlier.' She pulled on her gloves, and rose. 'How soon do you think we can start?'

After neat England, France was untidy. Sheets were damp and postilions familiar. Martha rather liked being called *citoyenne*, but even she was surprised when their new post boy peered into the chaise and said, 'Well, they're pretty enough anyway.' But the combination of her money, and Lady Helen's idiomatic French and air of quiet command, got them good service all the way to Paris, where Signor Arioso had reserved them rooms in the Hôtel de l'Empire, formerly the home of a rich banker.

'I wonder what happened to him in the Revolution?' Cristabel had been admiring the silk-covered furniture and ormolu clocks that must have belonged to the previous owner.

'Best not ask, I think.' Lady Helen looked up from the note she was writing, the last of many. 'There, that should launch us. I don't know which is the stranger, to find so many old friends still here, or to remember those one will never see again. I was presented to the poor Queen in eighty-nine,' she told them; 'just before the trouble started. Who would have thought . . . ? And I believe there is talk that now he is on the

35

way to being First Consul for life, Bonaparte begins to dream royal dreams.'

'Only dreams, I do hope.' Martha had written some notes of her own, to Michael Kelly who was already installed in an hotel on the Rue Neuve St. Marc, and to her father's old friend M. de La Fayette, back in Paris after his long incarceration as prisoner of war in Prussian and Austrian fortresses. He was the first to call on her and shook his head when she told him their plans.

'I do beg you to be careful how you go on in Venice,' he said. 'I owe Bonaparte a great deal for insisting on my liberation under the Peace of Campo Formio, but what he did to the Venetian Republic in that agreement was a wicked thing. They surrendered to his army in good faith only to be handed over lock, stock, and barrel to the Austrians, in exchange for concessions in the Rhineland! A crying scandal. But what hope of honour, of principle in a parvenu like the Corsican? I must warn you to be aware, always, in Venice, of the ears of the Austrian secret police.'

She smiled at him. 'You don't fear the French secret police here?'

He threw out a hand, laughing. '*Touché!* But I am afraid the answer has to be, "Not yet". Besides, you would never betray me! I don't suppose you remember, but when I visited your new United States years ago you sat on my knee and did the most dreadful things to my epaulettes!'

Shortly after he left, the smiling servant announced M. de Rothschild and Martha greeted another short, stout, pale-faced young man and handed him his brother's letter. 'Thank you.' He did not open it, but asked how he could serve her and when they planned to leave for Venice. And, when she promised to let him know shortly before they left, uttered a warning not unlike M. de La Fayette's. 'You will need to be careful how you go on there, Miss Peabody.'

Michael Kelly, calling next day, had his own view of Venice. He had been appalled at the sight of the Lions of St. Mark, looted from Venice by Bonaparte's troops, and installed in the Place de la Carrousel. 'And gilded, Miss Peabody! As if their Venetian bronze was not good enough for these French robbers. What else can one call them? I hope you do not find tempers too high in Venice, but they are a happy-go-lucky, pleasure-loving set of people.' He sighed. 'How I wish I could come with you! But I am forgetting my errand, which is to urge you to get tickets for the Théâtre Français tonight. Talma is to act Orestes in *The Distressed Mother* and I am reliably informed that Bonaparte himself will be there. And Mr. Fox too. It should be interesting to see how they are both received.'

'Yes, I look forward to it,' she told him. 'Lady Helen's old friend M. Talleyrand has arranged seats for us in his box.'

'I should have known! You're lucky in your chaperone, Miss Peabody!'

'I should just about think I am.'

Since Charles James Fox actually got a heartier round of applause than the First Consul at the theatre that night, it was hardly surprising that Bonaparte was not in the best of tempers at his *grande levée* at the Tuileries next day. Lord Whitworth, the British Ambassador, had arranged for Lady Cristabel to be presented, and the three of them were near enough to young Lord Guilford in the reception line to hear the First Consul refer insultingly to his father, Lord North, as, 'the man who lost America for England'.

'Hardly the words of a statesman,' said Lady Helen afterwards.

'What a rude little man,' said Cristabel. 'He asked me where I got my dress! I told him the Pantheon Bazaar, but of course he was not listening.'

'And would not have understood anyway,' said Martha regretfully. 'What a cheap sort of place it is, I mean. A pity. He has no conduct, that man.'

'You could say that he does not need it,' said Lady Helen.

They saw Bonaparte again a few days later, when they went to see Paisiello's opera *Nina* at the Italian Opera House. 'He's very attentive to his wife,' Martha noticed. 'It puts him in a more attractive light.'

'She looks charming,' said Cristabel. 'Hard to believe the stories . . .'

'And best not to refer to them,' interrupted Lady Helen. 'Did you know that Bonaparte brought Paisiello here from Naples and established him in apartments in the Tuileries?'

'Setting up as a patron,' said Martha. 'Odd to think that

Paisiello spent all that time at the court of Catherine the Great of Russia. I wonder what differences he finds here.'

'I long to meet him,' said Cristabel. 'Could we, Aunt? Signor Arioso told me that they put on his opera, *The Barber of Seville*, at Malmaison the other night, with Hortense de Beauharnais as Rosina.'

'Josephine's daughter?' said Lady Helen thoughtfully. 'In that case I see no reason why we should not invite Paisiello to call on us.'

'He goes everywhere.' Martha already had her little court of fortune-hunters and was glad of the French lessons her father had had her given by an émigré viscount.

The Italian composer called a few days later accompanied by a blond, heavily bearded young man, whom he introduced as his pupil, Franz Wengel. 'You will not mind my bringing my young friend, Signora? He is to be the next Gluck, I think. A formidable talent. I found him working as a copyist, and starving a little, here in Paris. He has heard of your voice,' turning to Cristabel. 'And begged to meet you. He might write something worth your singing one day.'

'I should dearly like to.' The young man bowed over Cristabel's hand. 'I'm from Lissenberg, ma'am. They still talk, there, of the girl-Orpheus who held an audience in the palm of her hand and caused a small diplomatic incident.'

'You know about that!' Eagerly. 'Then can you tell me what happened afterwards? In Lissenberg? All these years, I have never known how much harm I did my friend Prince Maximilian. My father took me away. No one would tell me. Do you know, sir?'

'What everyone knows. He was in terrible disgrace for a while. Then that poor girl his stepmother failed to produce an heir. His star rose again. His father brought him back from the University, made him give up his musical studies and take what he called his "proper place" in the army. And then, just two years ago, the Princess Amelia had a son. Lord, what a to-do! Fountains running wine all through the country. Bankruptcy a step nearer. You'd have thought there had been no heir before. Well, Prince Gustav has absolute right of appointment, and Prince Max never would toady to him.'

'I remember,' Cristabel said. 'He wanted to write opera, poor Max, just like you. Does he still, do you know?'

38

'Everyone knows. That's part of the trouble. Prince Gustav looks on musicians as hired servants. To be bullied like his other underlings.'

'I remember. He frightens me.'

'He frightens everyone. Even his wife, poor lady. Nobody dares question the money he spends. They say Prince Max did, when he was summoned home and found the country groaning under more and more stringent taxes, the currency debased, the civil service corrupt . . . He spoke up, they say. His father had him locked up in the cells under the Palace. Cold as death. Bread and water. He was afraid for his voice. Made his submission, poor boy.'

'Boy? He must be about your age, surely?'

'In years, maybe. Not in experience.'

'You think not? Have you seen him ever? Heard him sing?'

'Good God, no. He doesn't get the chance to do that much. I told you. Prince Gustav thinks singers just a little better than the scullions in his kitchens. And as to seeing Prince Max, I come from the wrong end of Lissenberg, Brundt, the poor end, where the mines are. Prince Max did come once, when he was still heir, but I didn't see him. He went down the mines; no one could stop him. He was the heir. He was horrified by what he found. Said something must be done about conditions there. Meant it, I think. His half brother was born not long afterwards. So much for Prince Maximilian.'

'Oh, poor Max,' said Cristabel. 'It's strange how it all comes back, talking about him. Even then, when we were children, he was unhappy about the way things were: the money his father spent, the things he spent it on.'

'He's not managed to do much about it,' said Franz Wengel. 'But am I not to hear your voice? I have been told that it is something quite extraordinary. I came in the hope that I might have the privilege . . .'

The words were respectful enough; the tone was not. Cristabel flashed him a challenging glance. 'And if it pleases you, Monsieur the new Gluck, you will condescend to write an opera for me?'

'I might.' And then, 'Forgive me. For me, the world of music has its own ranks.'

'There is also the world of manners, Herr Wengel,' said Lady Helen.

*   *   *

39

'That's a very self-confident young man,' Cristabel said to Martha after their last guest had gone.

'Wengel? Yes.' It only struck Martha afterwards as odd that she had known at once who Cristabel meant. 'I wonder if he really is the new Gluck. Are you going to sing for him?'

'Oh, I think so. A hostile audience is just what I need.'

'You thought him hostile?'

'Well . . .' Cristabel thought about it. 'Patronising, maybe?'

'No proper respect,' Lady Helen had listened to the exchange with amusement. 'Very good for you, Belle. A taste of what your future holds. To be patronised by a miner's son.'

'An educated one,' said Martha. 'We talked a little, he and I. He's read a great deal. Put me right on a quotation from Rousseau.' She was surprised by one of her rare blushes. 'He was right. I looked it up just now.'

'Maybe all the miners' sons in Lissenberg go to the University,' said Lady Helen. 'You always made it sound like the Kingdom of Heaven, Belle. Except for the tyrant prince.'

'Who is worse than ever, from what Herr Wengel said. I wonder what I should sing for him.' She was moving towards her music-room when her aunt put out a restraining hand.

'I trust you are not thinking of giving that young genius a private audience?'

'Oh!' Now it was Cristabel's turn to blush. 'I had not thought . . . But, with Signor Arioso . . . Just one of my ordinary lessons . . .'

'No,' said Lady Helen. 'When we get to Venice, and you commence your career, you may be as Bohemian as you please, but so long as we are here in Paris you will behave as Lady Cristabel, a duke's daughter. I think we owe your father that.'

'I cannot imagine why,' began Cristabel mutinously, but Martha intervened.

'I've been thinking that we should give some kind of informal entertainment . . . A "thank you" to all the friends who have been so good to us. And then, what more natural than that Cristabel should sing for the company?'

'Herr Wengel among them, because he has been so good to us?' asked Lady Helen.

'No, because he might write an opera for Cristabel. I agree with you about the difference between Paris and Venice, so far as our behaviour is concerned, but we must still be taking the long view about Cristabel's career. If he is really as promising as Arioso says . . .'

'And so expert in the modern classics!' Lady Helen laughed. 'I thought Herr Wengel well enough, in his brusque way, but I can see there must be a charm to him that passes the elderly by.'

'You're not elderly, Aunt Helen,' protested Cristabel. 'Why, only yesterday I heard Talleyrand flirting with you in the most outrageous way.'

'Dear man, he always does. It makes one feel quite young again. So – this entertainment of ours . . . Tomorrow week, perhaps? Do you think we can organise it by then, Martha? And do you think Signor Arioso will permit it, Belle?'

Arioso was enthusiastic about the plan, only insisting that the actual singing be kept as informal as possible, but another problem presented itself. Too many people wanted to come. The gossip about the unusual trio of women had followed them from England, and they were soon at their wits' end as to how to accommodate their guests in their small, elegant salon. The problem was solved by Talleyrand, paying an unexpected call before their usual receiving hour. 'I had hoped to find you alone,' he told Lady Helen. 'I am come with a request which I hope, as an old friend, you will feel able to grant.'

'Yes?'

'This soirée of yours next week. Lady Cristabel is to sing, I believe. It has aroused a good deal of interest, as no doubt you are aware. It has been suggested to me that you might have difficulty accommodating the numbers in your charming apartments. Would you consider changing the venue to my house? I would be proud and happy to entertain your guests, if you would not mind my adding a few of my own.' He leaned forward, suddenly confidential. 'The truth of the matter is that the First Consul has heard the talk about your niece. He was struck with her when she was presented to him the other day. She made him a saucy answer, he says, and there are not many women who dare do that. An unusual young woman, and so is Miss Peabody, who is American, one of our natural allies. I do beg you to oblige me in this, Lady Helen. I am sure it can do your protégées no harm.'

'It would be . . . unusual,' she said.

'So is your whole situation. And, consider a little. Think what a friendly gesture it would be. I, a Frenchman, to give a reception for your English and American young ladies. I am sure you want this peace to last as much as I do.'

'I most certainly do. And you think it won't?'

'You were always quick.' He shook his head at her. 'I most certainly think it would be a pity if my master were to feel himself slighted in any way by you British just now.'

'And he would take a refusal as a slight?'

'He's not an easy man, madame.'

'I hardly felt I could refuse, when he put it like that,' Lady Helen told the two girls afterwards.

'It's hardly the informal little party we planned,' said Martha.

'I hope Herr Wengel doesn't decide not to come,' said Cristabel.

'Oh, he'll come,' Martha told her. 'He thinks the sun rises and sets in Bonaparte. Thinks him a great liberator! I almost lost patience with him.'

'That's unlike you,' said Lady Helen.

In the end, everybody came. 'For two pins, I'd be nervous.' Cristabel had found Martha alone for the moment, surveying the crowded rooms.

'Oh, no, you would not. It's not in your character.' Martha smiled at her. 'Forget the crowd; sing for Herr Wengel. He's the one who matters.'

'But is he here?'

'Not yet, but neither is Bonaparte, and it is his arrival that is your cue to sing. How glad I am that it is Monsieur Talleyrand arranging all this, not I.' She turned to receive the compliments of one of her devoted suitors, turned back to Cristabel: 'When the time comes, remind yourself that you never looked better. No need to think about your voice; we know about that.' The two girls had gone to a dressmaker recommended by Lady Helen's old friend, Madame Recamier, and the results had more than justified the expense. Cristabel was in clinging high-waisted white with a deep blue sash, that matched the blue of Martha's dress. The cut of this, combined with the newest thing in Paris corsets, had made Martha laugh, surveying herself in the glass. 'I look positively elegant.

I hope I do not find myself believing my wooers when they speak of my charms.' But her thoughts now were all for Cristabel. 'Don't think about Wengel,' she was inspired to say. 'Think you are singing for that poor Prince Max. I like the sound of him.' And, turning quickly at a stir among the crowd, 'He's here, Bonaparte. And Wengel, too,' she added, seeing that young man in the little crowd around the First Consul. 'Best get ready, love. You know you can do it.'

'Thank you. Oh, Martha,' the unexpected endearment had touched her. 'I do thank you . . .'

'Not now!' She took her arm and led her through the curious crowd to the ball-room where Talleyrand had had a small platform built. He had offered to obtain any selection of musicians to accompany her that Cristabel had wished, but she had refused, with thanks, preferring the familiar figure of Signor Arioso at the fortepiano.

As he settled himself at it, Bonaparte came briskly in to seat himself in the front row of the gilded chairs and the rest of the party followed, talking and laughing, many still holding glasses of champagne, a volatile, unpredictable audience.

Cristabel turned from the piano, where she had been talking to Arioso, moved quietly across to the centre of the little stage, stood for a moment, looking beyond the audience, then swept a low, slow curtsy to where Bonaparte sat with Talleyrand beside him. It got her a round of applause, which she silenced with a gesture. 'I am going to sing you an English song,' she said, and gave them 'Greensleeves'.

4

Three days later, they were still receiving the congratulations of their friends. Everyone had called except Franz Wengel. Their rooms were so full of flowers that they had started sending them to Madame Campan's school for girls, since its formidable headmistress was another of Lady Helen's old friends. They had become fond of two of her pupils, Henriette and Stephanie de Beauharnais, motherless nieces of Josephine, who were being educated there, thanks to Bonaparte. Since they were too young to attend Talleyrand's party, Cristabel was consoling them with a personal recital in her music-room when Herr Wengel finally called and found Martha alone in the salon.

'Hush!' Instead of greeting her, he raised a brusque hand for silence. 'Just what I needed! A chance to hear her in peace, when she's relaxed.' He moved closer to the door and listened with all his attention as Cristabel finished 'Greensleeves' and plunged straight into the next thing she had sung, an aria from Gluck's *Alceste*. 'Just as I thought,' he said when this was over. 'Amazing that Arioso has not noticed, but I suppose being always with her, and the voice – the range – so extraordinary as it is. Is she going to sing the whole programme over again?' he went on impatiently. 'I must speak to her.' He made to open the door.

'No, Herr Wengel.' Martha's patience snapped. 'She is singing to two young friends. You will not interrupt her. Your affairs must be pressing indeed, if it has not been possible for you to call before this to congratulate Lady Cristabel on her performance. I know she has been wanting to hear what you thought. I trust you managed to get yourself to Monsieur Talleyrand's house for the necessary visit? If not, I must remember to apologise to him on your behalf, since you were invited there as our guest.'

He was hardly listening to her. 'Congratulate? No time for

that. I have to return to Lissenberg sooner than I expected. If I am to get her breathing right we must lose no time in going to work.'

'Her breathing right? What do you mean? Everyone says –'

'Everyone is a fool. Listen! Can't you hear the tension in it? The natural voice God gave her ruined by over-training? First she will lose her top notes, then, if she goes on like this, her voice will be gone by the time she's thirty. Amazing Arioso has not noticed. One can only assume it's his fault. But I can rectify it; no need to look so anxious.'

'I'm not looking anxious, Herr Wengel, I'm looking furious. What right have you to come bursting in here, as if you owned the place, criticising, finding fault –'

'What right? That of a fellow musician. She will recognise it, see if she does not.' And he pushed open the door and went in as Cristabel finished her Handel aria. After a few moments of confusion, he was established at the piano in Arioso's place while Arioso and Cristabel listened intently to what he had to say.

'We had better leave them to it, I think.' Martha shepherded the two girls into the other room and closed the door behind her with an angry click. 'No room there for amateurs. What can I give you young ladies to drink? Minette? Stephanie?'

They asked, greatly daring, for ratafia and she indulged them with a thimbleful each, letting them chatter on about life at school and how delightful it was after the country convent where they had been immured until Bonaparte heard of their plight.

'Just think, he made Father give us up to him,' said Minette.

'Well, Father had never done anything about us. It was the English lady who paid our bills. Dreary old convent,' said Stephanie.

'All that praying.' Minette made a face. 'Too old-fashioned for words. Tell me, Miss Peabody, what did you wear for Monsieur Talleyrand's party? If we could but have gone to that! Is Madame Grond really such an old fright as they say? Poor man, only think of Uncle Bonaparte trying to make him marry her! Our uncle can do anything, I believe. He's promised to find us charming husbands, just as soon as we are old enough, hasn't he, Stephanie?'

45

'I'd rather find my own,' Stephanie shrugged an elegant shoulder.

For once, Martha was glad to see them go. Their cheerful chatter usually entertained her, and was improving her French by leaps and bounds, but today she longed to know what was going on in the next room. Could there really be something wrong with the way Cristabel sang? Might she be in danger of losing the voice on which they counted for their future? Appalling thought. But how could she think of anything else? What would they do? Impossible for Lady Helen and Cristabel to return to England and Sarum House. She was responsible for them, and, for the first time, realised just what she had taken on.

When they emerged from the music-room at last, Cristabel was white, Arioso drawn and pale, Wengel self-confident as always. 'Do what I say, and you have nothing to fear.' He took Cristabel's hand in farewell. 'Relaxation. Calm. Half an hour's practice a day, as I have shown you. Not a note else. Not if Bonaparte himself should ask it. I shall come every day, to make sure you are getting it right.'

'Thank you.' Cristabel looked up at him, her eyes full of unshed tears. 'I do thank you, Herr Wengel.'

'No need.' Smiling down at her. 'I have a stake in this too. You are to sing in my opera, remember.'

'When it is written,' said Martha, unexpectedly tart. 'What time shall we expect you tomorrow, Herr Wengel?'

'That I am afraid I cannot say. I have a mass of business on my hands. But you may count on my coming, Lady Cristabel.'

'A fine thing!' Martha exploded after he had left. 'And you are to stay home all day awaiting his coming! Who does he think he is? Why are you laughing, Lady Helen?'

'At you, I am afraid, my dear. I thought you were the American democrat; believed in the aristocracy of the intellect. And there you go, just like the rest of us, expecting young Herr Wengel to bow and scrape to Cristabel just because she is a duke's daughter.'

'Dear me.' Martha thought about it. Then: 'No, Lady Helen. Because she is a singer, a fellow musician, and a woman. Surely we are entitled to a little consideration on that score?'

'Our frailty? It's a dangerous argument. And while we are

arguing, I wish you would stop calling me "Lady Helen". It makes me feel a thousand years old.'

For a week, the household revolved around Wengel's daily visits. By common, if tacit, consent they had suspended their arrangements for the move to Venice, but did not discuss what they would do if Wengel's verdict, at the end of the trial period, was discouraging. Cristabel was pale and withdrawn, and Lady Helen unusually quiet. As for Martha, she turned down a couple of proposals from eligible young Frenchmen so sharply that they went away vowing never to call again. Only Wengel remained his usual confident self, and Martha had to admit that she was grateful to him. He turned up at the most impossible moments, entirely regardless of the household routine, always cheerful, always ready for a few minutes' talk before he and Cristabel retired to the music-room. Every day he had a new possible subject for the opera he was to write for her. 'Joan of Arc' perhaps? 'Dido and Aeneas'? Or a subject from Shakespeare? *Romeo and Juliet*; *Antony and Cleopatra*?

'He does us good,' Martha said to Lady Helen after he and Cristabel had retired to begin work, with Arioso, as always, in attendance.

'He most certainly does. A remarkable young man, if not entirely a likeable one.'

'You don't find him so?'

Lady Helen laughed. 'I never pretended to be anything but an old-fashioned aristocrat, my dear. I find his manners, or lack of them, deplorable.'

'Not his fault, I suppose.' Martha was surprised to find herself defending Wengel.

'Nor mine, that I don't enjoy seeing how cavalierly he treats you and Cristabel. Besides, have you not noticed? It is not that he is ignorant of how to behave. It's something quite different. He's caught the French infection, I think; believes that Jack is as good as his master.'

'That's what we Americans think.' Martha changed sides suddenly.

'All very well in your United States. Herr Wengel had better apply himself to learning more conduct if he hopes to succeed as an operatic composer at home in Lissenberg, or anywhere else in the German Principalities. He'll need an aristocratic

47

patron if he is to get on, and you cannot treat a patron as Wengel does us.'

'To bow and scrape and wear livery,' said Martha. 'Disgusting. At home in America it all goes by talent.'

'Does it go well?'

'Not yet, but it will.' She sounded more confident than she felt. 'But do you really think it will damage his chances, that he cannot curry favour?'

'That he does not behave with ordinary courtesy, you mean? Yes, I do.'

'Then someone should tell him so.'

'I don't advise it, my dear, not if you wish to keep him for your friend. I never knew a young man yet who enjoyed being lectured by a young woman. Not even for his own good. Or maybe I should say particularly not when it is for his own good. Ah, the lesson is over.' A triumphant arpeggio had sounded from the next room and now Cristabel appeared, flushed and smiling, with Arioso and Wengel behind her.

'He says the worst is over!' For Cristabel, just now, there was only one 'he'. 'It is only to keep practising, when we get to Venice, as I have been doing. And, Martha, Aunt Helen, he thinks I shall be ready for the stage sooner than we thought. Two years from now!'

'So soon? That's wonderful news. Do you agree, Signor Arioso?' Martha had felt both sorry for Arioso during their anxious week, and impressed by the dignity with which he had accepted his suddenly changed position.

'Heartily,' he said now. 'The change in her breathing is actually extending Lady Cristabel's already amazing range. Herr Wengel does indeed speak of a début two years from now. He has even suggested where it might take place.'

'Wonderful!' There was a new sparkle to Cristabel. 'In Lissenberg, of all places, where I began. They are celebrating the twenty-fifth year of Prince Gustav's reign in two years' time. A new opera is to be performed, singers engaged from all over the world, no expense spared. Well, we all know about Prince Gustav. It is bound to be a tremendous occasion. Everyone who matters will be there. What could be better?'

'And the opera?' asked Martha.

'It's early days,' Wengel interrupted Cristabel. 'But I have great hopes that there will be an open competition for the most

48

suitable one. I know this is what Prince Maximilian would like; the question is whether he can convince his father. I leave for Lissenberg tomorrow. I shall do what I can to see that Prince Maximilian gets his way.'

'And what can you do, Herr Wengel?' Lady Helen's voice was cool, interested.

'More than you think!' He turned to her, more brusque than usual. 'I may seem a nobody to you, but at home in Lissenberg my name is respected among the people who matter. Musicians . . . men of letters . . . Besides, my opera will be the best one submitted.' It was said with complete self-confidence and absolutely no sense of boasting.

'I really believe I agree with you,' said Lady Helen.

'I know I do,' said Cristabel eagerly. 'And it will be written for me, for my voice. I've been so afraid all week, now I know I can do it. I do thank you, Herr Wengel.'

'It's been a great pleasure.' He turned to Martha. 'How soon can you leave for Venice? It's time she went to work.'

Martha lost her temper. 'We have a saying, where I come from, that "she" is the cat's mother. It means, in case you do not understand, that it is uncivil to refer to a lady as you do to Lady Cristabel. You boast about your lack of manners, I wonder if you understand what harm you do yourself.' Out of the corner of her eye she saw that Lady Helen had contrived to draw Cristabel and Arioso to the other side of the room, giving her a clear field. 'Just because we have borne with your rudeness, your total lack of consideration, all this week, don't expect that the rest of the world will do so, because it won't. The manners of the *sans culottes* won't do in nineteenth-century society, Herr Wengel, and the sooner you learn this, the better it will be for you and for all of us who are associated with you.' She raised a quelling hand. 'Don't interrupt me, as you usually do. I have started; let me finish. We have a stake in your future. I think this opera you speak of could be the ideal début for Lady Cristabel. So, I want you to succeed. And you won't if you go home and behave to Prince Gustav as you have to us.'

'Have you quite finished?' His colour was high, his voice icy, as he made her a sweeping mockery of a servile bow. 'Is that better? Should I rub my hands and fawn on you, because you are rich and the two other ladies have titles that mean

49

nothing? Because they are dukes' daughters? Have you learned nothing from the sight of Bonaparte, that great man? Who came from nowhere. I thought better of you, an American lady. But let me tell you, Miss Peabody, about our Prince Gustav, to whom you wish me to creep and grovel. He's got a pedigree back to Adam. Oh yes! And he's rotten with disease; there is no way the new little prince will ever live to succeed him, poor baby. He is bankrupting our country for his vulgar pleasures –'

'Of which your opera is to be one.' This time she interrupted him, and was surprised at doing so.

'One of the more respectable!' He acknowledged the hit with an out-thrown hand, like a duellist, and suddenly laughed, a short, angry bark of a laugh. 'I wish you could meet my grandmother, Miss Peabody.'

'Your –'

'Grandmother. You thought me a child of the gutter? I'm not, you know. I come from a long line of Lissenberg artisans; the backbone of the country. My father led the protests when Prince Gustav bought the title, back in seventy-nine. If only there had been more like him! Nothing violent; democratic protest in the best tradition of the enlightenment. Gustav did nothing either; just ruined my father. He died when I was a baby. Left nothing. My mother would have been out in the streets if it had not been for Grandma. She had a tiny pension; we lived on that. Bread, and small beer, and the wolf never far from the door, but not the gutter. When I reached my teens, I found that Grandma had been scrimping and saving all that time, so there would be funds for my education. Looking back, I'm afraid she and my mother may have gone short. I never did. Grandma never will again. I shall see to that. Why in the world am I telling you this?'

'You said you'd like me to meet her. Your grandmother. What happened to your mother?'

'She died when I was young. Pined for my father, Grandma says. And I imagine being hungry didn't help. You can see why I don't much love Prince Gustav. Why should I ape his manners, those of the aristocrats? That's what I tell Grandma, but she won't see it. She says good manners oil the wheels of society.'

'And so they do.' Martha had never liked him so well. Then

50

she spoiled it. 'Lady Helen says you'll never get a patron if you don't temper your conduct a little.'

'Lady Helen can go to the devil. Good day, Miss Peabody.'

'I am so sorry. I truly meant it for the best.' Martha was trying to explain to Cristabel why Franz Wengel had stormed out of the house.

'For the best! I'd like to see your worst. And he left without giving me a chance to thank him properly. What business of yours are his manners, anyway?'

'None,' said Martha. 'I am truly sorry, Cristabel. Forgive me? Please? I do so badly want him to succeed.'

'And so do I!' They exchanged a long, thoughtful look. 'He leaves for Lissenberg next week. That was his goodbye. But he'll write me my opera; I'm sure of it. Martha, how soon can we start for Venice?'

It was raining in Venice. The gondoliers who brought them over from Mestre, on the mainland, demanded extortionate fees and the landlord of the Scudo di Francia Inn received them with churlish surprise. When Martha told him she had written to reserve apartments, he shrugged his shoulders and said something *sotto voce* about the Austrians and censorship. But he gradually became more civil as he recognised the obvious affluence of the damp little party that had come dripping in from his landing-stage.

'But I don't like him much,' said Cristabel. 'Nor his inn, though it's not quite so bad when one gets upstairs.'

'No,' Martha agreed. 'That ground floor was horrible was it not? Damp as a fishmarket.'

'And smells like one. Mr. Kelly made it sound such a romantic city.'

'I expect it is when the sun shines,' said Lady Helen. 'But just now one can understand why British tourists don't come here much.'

'It must have been quite different when it was still an independent republic, the *Serenissima*, the mistress of the seas.' Martha was fighting bitter disappointment. 'I suppose I should have realised that Mr. Kelly was talking about an era that has passed.'

'You don't think we should move on to Naples after all?'

Lady Helen had urged Naples all along, as another centre of musical excellence, but Martha and Signor Arioso, as well as Michael Kelly, had opposed her because of the precarious political situation there. 'No, I'm sorry,' she went on now. 'I didn't mean to raise that again. And after all, we have come here to work, not for pleasure. What are you and I going to do, Martha, while Cristabel studies?'

'I'm going to learn all the languages I can,' said Martha. 'But first, Signor Arioso and I are going to find us a house of our own.'

Salomon Rothschild, calling for his letter next day, undertook to do this. Easy enough, he told her, since many of the old noble families of Venice's Golden Book had retired to their country estates to sit out the Austrian occupation, which they were convinced could not last long.

A week later the sun came out and they moved to two floors of a medium-sized palazzo on the Grand Canal, west of St. Mark's and convenient for the San Moise Opera House and the ten-year-old Fenice Theatre. There, too, it had been easy to secure boxes for the forthcoming season, though Arioso shook his head over the plans for it.

'Things are even worse than I had feared,' he told Martha. 'When I think that Venice once had thirteen opera houses! Now all the four conservatories of music are closed, the singers scattered God knows where. But to look on the cheerful side of things, I have found teachers in every aspect of opera. Singing, languages, stagecraft – there are masters here in them all. And, another good thing, our stay here should be free from public notice.'

'So that Lady Cristabel's début will have all the more éclat when it happens?'

'Just so. I think we will do very well here.'

'I'm sure we will. But I wish my books would come.' Martha had sent off an order to Hookham's Library from Paris, just as soon as their plans for Venice were settled. She and Cristabel had discovered a shared wish to study the history of Central Europe. If both of them had secretly hoped that Wengel would call again before he left Paris for Lissenberg, both had been disappointed and neither had said a word about it. But it made obvious sense to learn something about the country where Cristabel hoped to make her début.

She was soon hard at work, setting off in their private gondola for her lesson every morning, returning for a light luncheon, and siesta, before they set off to explore the city they were beginning to love. Their gondolier, known as 'Momolo' for no reason they ever understood, soon became a good friend, and Lady Helen was happy to let them go off alone with him when the variable weather was suddenly too hot for her. They were well and truly launched into Venetian society now, but not finding it much to their taste. Inevitably, Lady Helen had had introductions to many of the remaining noble families, and they were soon on visiting terms with ladies like the Countesses Albrizzi and Cigognera. 'All the old noble families have been allowed to take the title of "count" by the Austrians,' explained Lady Helen.

'It doesn't make their receptions any more interesting,' grumbled Martha. 'Two rows of chairs like country-dance lines leading up to the sofa where your hostess sits, and not one with a word to say for herself. All dying for the moment when the card playing begins and their *cavaliere servente* can come out from behind their chair and partner them.'

'Are we going to set ourselves up with them?' asked Cristabel.

'Cicisbeos? Attendant knights? What do you think, Lady Helen?'

'I have no doubt they will offer themselves, and, really, it seems a harmless enough custom. You know, when in Rome . . . Besides, for some of your sightseeing, I think I'd feel happier if you had gentlemen with you. For the long excursions, Murano and Torcello, I hardly think our dear Momolo would be protection enough.'

'I told Countess Benzoni we thought of going to Torcello,' said Martha. 'She looked as shocked as if we meant to fly to the moon. Do you know how she spends her days?'

'No, did she tell you?'

'I asked her. She gets up about twelve o'clock and goes off to Mass, with her *cavaliere servente* in attendance, of course. Then she takes a turn or two in the Piazza San Marco, pays visits or receives them until dinner time – between three and four. Then she undresses and goes to bed! About eight o'clock she's up again for her evening toilette and so to the theatre and then the casino until three or four in the morning. In summer, I believe, she spends the time in the cafés on the Piazza.'

'Where the ladies pay their own shot!' put in Cristabel. 'An odd custom.'

'One I like,' said Martha. 'Do tell me, how are we going to accommodate ourselves to this programme?'

'With difficulty,' agreed Cristabel. 'Wild horses wouldn't get me to go to bed in the daytime, and I must start work betimes in the morning. But do we really need to go to the casino after the theatre? It doesn't open until midnight, I believe, when the opera is over. If we come home then . . .'

'We'll save daylight and money. I quite agree. So, all we need is a pair of adaptable cicisbeos. It's a pity one cannot advertise for them.'

'I think you will find they present themselves,' said Lady Helen.

A few days later she returned from her afternoon round of visits looking so white and shaken that both girls jumped to their feet. 'What is it, Aunt Helen?' asked Cristabel. 'What's the matter?'

'Thank you, child.' She accepted the smelling salts Martha offered her, and sank on to a chair. 'My dears, I've had such a shock . . . Such an unpleasant surprise. I don't know how to tell you. And as for my poor brother . . . How in the world am I going to break it to him?'

'My father?' asked Cristabel. 'What has he to do with anything?' They had heard nothing from the Duke since they had left England.

'Madame Benzoni told me,' Lady Helen accepted a glass of cordial from Martha and took a grateful sip, 'Just casually, in passing. I couldn't believe my ears, didn't want to show my surprise for my poor brother's sake. The scandal will be appalling. I must write to him at once. It shows how cut off they are in Venice, that Madame Benzoni obviously did not know of his remarriage. It will be a nine days' wonder when the news gets out!'

'But what news, Aunt Helen?'

'It's your mother, child.'

'My mother? But she's dead!'

'So we all thought. She never took the allowance Sarum sent her. He must have had enquiries made. But she was here

54

all the time, living in a quiet way in the Giudecca. Madame Benzoni seemed to think it was amusing for some reason. I didn't dare ask why.'

'Mother's alive – here in Venice! But, Aunt Helen, I don't understand. Don't go, Martha!' She had made to leave them. 'You are part of the family now! Father would never speak about my mother. Just said she was dead. What happened to her? What did he do to her?'

'She was a singer, here in Venice, a 'seconda donna', I believe, at the San Benedetto Theatre. He was on his grand tour, fell in love, and married her out of hand. Well, of course it was a disaster. When he got her home to England he saw that soon enough, and so did our father. You were born a year later and they paid her off, sent her back here with a pension on the understanding that she would keep quiet. I was a child still,' she anticipated Cristabel's question. 'I only met her a few times. She seemed a very brilliant lady to me.'

'And nobody ever troubled to find out what happened to her?' Cristabel was outraged. 'Or tell me.' She thought about it. 'A singer! How delightful. We shall have so much to talk about.' And then, with an angry little laugh. 'No wonder Father hated my singing. Signor Arioso must have known!'

'Of course he knew. He was her teacher. Your father must have made him promise not to speak of her, as he did the rest of us.'

'How like Father! And what a judgment that this has happened to him. But how could it?'

'She went back to her maiden name, apparently. Lucia Aldini. I suppose, when he had enquiries made, they were for the Duchess of Sarum. No one had heard of her. It's not really very funny, Cristabel.'

'I'm sorry! But it's so like Father. Of course, I'm dreadfully sorry for my poor stepmother. *Not* my stepmother! Goodness, what do they do to dukes who commit bigamy?'

'Give them a quick divorce in the House of Lords, I imagine,' said Helen. 'I shall write to my brother today. I owe it to him, though I dread doing it. And until we hear from him I am sure you will understand that it is better for you not to visit your mother.'

5

Cristabel slept badly that night. Waking unrefreshed, but at her normal hour, she went off as usual to her music lesson and returned to find Martha alone. 'Where's Aunt Helen?'

'Gone to pay an early call on Countess Benzoni. I suspect she is having trouble writing that letter to your father.'

'I should just about think she is,' said Cristabel. 'Martha, I'm going to visit my mother. I don't care what Aunt Helen says, Mother must have heard I am here; you know how talk travels around the lagoon. How can I not call on her? I'd like it very much if you would come with me, but I can see you may not wish to, granted what Aunt Helen said.'

'Of course I'll come! I was hoping you'd decide to go. None of my business, but why in the world should you – or your aunt, come to that – take a moment's notice of your father's feelings in this? When shall we go?'

'Now? It would save discussion with Aunt Helen. And I'm sure Momolo will be able to find out where Mother lives on the Giudecca. Do you think it will be very miserable, Martha?'

Martha had been thinking about this, during a wakeful night of her own. 'I'm afraid it may be, Belle. From what your aunt said, it does not sound as if your mother went back on the stage when she returned here, does it? If she had, surely she would have been found when your father made his enquiries. Poor man, one does have to feel sorry for him.'

'Not very. But, Martha,' she hesitated: 'I'm ashamed to have to ask it of you. Only, you know how I am placed . . . If we should find Mama in very distressed circumstances . . .'

'We will help her. Naturally. And you will not give it a second thought, since we have already agreed that you are going to pay everything back once you are established as Prima Donna, at Lissenberg or anywhere else.'

'Oh, Martha, I do bless the day we met! Lord, how you have changed my life!'

'It's a great responsibility. I was thinking of that in the night.'

'You slept badly too?'

'Yes. Let us go now and visit your mother. However she is placed, it will be better to know. Besides, I long to meet her.'

'And so do I!'

'The Signora Aldini?' Momolo did not seem surprised. 'But naturally, Principessa, I had wondered when you would wish to visit her.'

'You mean, you knew?'

'Everyone knows, Principessa. Here in Venice, everyone has always known everything. Most especially we gondoliers. It is our business. The other young lady goes too? That's good.' He settled them with his usual care for their comfort and pushed off across the Grand Canal.

'Your mother must live on the south side of the island,' Martha said as the gondola headed for the narrow channel between St. George's and the Giudecca. 'I do hope it is not going to be too sad for you, Cristabel.'

'But I'm right to come?' It was half a question.

'Of course you are.'

They were silent for a while, both wondering what they were going to find. Then, 'We must be almost there,' exclaimed Cristabel as the gondola turned into the mouth of a narrow canal that ran north across the Giudecca. 'Goodness!' Momolo had swooped across the canal to bring his craft to a halt at a well-kept quay with a black and gold striped mooring-post. High walls of rose-red brick were pierced by ornamental iron gates, so closely wrought that they allowed only glimpses of an evergreen garden behind. 'Can this be the place?' Momolo had jumped ashore, moored the gondola with the usual expert fling of the rope, and rung a peal at the ornamental bell beside the gate.

'It must be.' Martha stood up, shaking out muslin skirts.

The gates opened slowly. There was a quick exchange in the incomprehensible Venetian lingo, then Momolo returned to the gondola. 'The Signora is at home,' he told Cristabel. 'She will receive you. I will be here again in two hours.' He helped them ashore.

'Two hours?' Martha had noticed with amusement that Momolo always directed his first attention to Cristabel. Now she thought she was beginning to understand. He had known that her friend was half Italian as well as being, in his terms, a princess.

'Look!' said Cristabel. The bowing, black-clad servant had led them through the evergreen hedge that masked the gates into a fantastic garden. More evergreen hedges, lawns, small, frivolous baroque statues.

'A garden in Venice?' she said in Italian to the servant.

'Ah, Signora,' the old man smiled at her. 'In Venice, there are gardens, but one must be of the elect to find them.'

The elect? They had reached the house, where another servant stood bowing at a welcoming open door. Inside was the usual cool, shadowy vault, part entry, part storeroom, from which marble steps took them up to the living-quarters. As carved doors opened before them they stopped, dazzled by light. The high, square room looked south on to the garden, and crimson velvet curtains had been drawn well back to admit the afternoon sun. Its rays made a Titian aureole for the woman who sat there, enthroned on the kind of sofa Madame Recamier had made fashionable in Paris. Since her back was to the light, she was a half-defined figure except for the flaming statement of her hair. Deep blue draperies, brilliant against the crimson of the sofa, suggested a figure of some grandeur.

'Cristabel.' She held out a plump white hand. 'My darling child. Come, kiss your idle old mother, who stirs herself for no one, not even a long-lost daughter.' She aimed the remark directly at Cristabel, with merely a civil side glance for Martha.

Cristabel bent into a cloud of exquisite, unidentifiable perfume, kissed a soft, delicious cheek, stood, looking down, still holding the hand. 'Mama?'

Her mother patted her hand. 'I wonder which of us is the more surprised, I to acquire a full grown daughter, or you to find a mother you had not looked for.'

'I thought you dead.'

If there was a hint of reproach in her tone, her mother chose to ignore it. 'Poor Sarum,' she laughed musically. 'When I stopped taking that pittance he allowed me, he jumped to the most hopeful conclusion, decided I was dead. Well, you see he was gravely mistaken. I'm very much alive.'

She was. Now that they had got used to the light, they could see that she was enormous, a Rubens Venus miraculously without the jowled, sullen look that often goes with such proportions.

'I'm glad you are!' Cristabel bent impulsively to kiss her again. 'So very glad!' She looked around the room, noticing as Martha already had the huge Canaletto on the wall facing them, the evidence, everywhere, of great wealth. 'And glad to find you –' She hesitated.

'Dear child.' Her mother laughed again. 'You had thought to find me living in a slum, taking in washing, destitute. You were coming to my rescue? You and your friend – introduce your friend, of whom I have heard so much.' She turned her ravishing smile full on Martha. 'I owe this happy surprise to you, do I not, Miss Peabody? I cannot tell you how grateful I am.'

'Happy indeed.' Martha shook the plump hand in her firm American way. 'But hardly a surprise, Signora Aldini?'

'Ah ha!' It was a little crow of pleasure. 'They told me you were no fool, Miss Peabody. You are quite right, of course. I am well served, here on my quiet island. Yes, I did know you were coming. Such a touching scene deserved a proper setting. Do you not agree with me?' She clapped white hands. 'And now we are going to dine. No need to fret about your aunt, my dear. I've sent her a message to say you will dine with me. That way, the worst of her surprise will be over by the time you get back to her. She's turned out quite a formidable creature, they tell me. I'd never have thought it of her. Such a timid little thing as I remember her. Ah,' with obvious satisfaction, 'here comes our dinner. I do love my food. You will find it one of our more lasting pleasures.' She turned the conversation to ask about Cristabel's singing lessons, as a troop of servants wheeled a table close to her sofa and set out a lavish selection of antipasto and a huge, savoury-smelling, silver tureen. When their green-gold Venetian glass goblets had been filled with chianti, she dismissed the servants. 'We will wait on ourselves. Or rather you will wait on me. My own information system is good enough, so I know better than to talk before even my faithful servants. Not that we intend to talk secrets today.' She helped herself liberally to antipasto, raised her glass. 'I drink to you both. Now tell me, Cristabel,

59

what is puzzling you? You have the look of one who is doing sums in her head.'

'Exactly!' Cristabel was surprised into frankness. 'Mama – may I call you mama? – Aunt Helen, what you said about her . . . and I remember something she said about you. You cannot possibly be older than Aunt Helen?'

'Oh yes I can. I enjoy life, you see. It makes a great difference. And I enjoy my food.' Having disposed of six anchovies, a handful of olives and a large slice of prosciutto as she talked, she now reached over to take the lid off the tureen. 'Ah, lasagne today. I often think it is my favourite kind of pasta. Will you help us all, my dear? Poor Helen, has she aged so much? And what did she say about me, pray?'

'She remembers you as brilliant.'

'Ah.' Purring a little. 'You must bring her to see me. Perhaps we could make life a little more interesting for her.'

'She has written to my father,' said Cristabel.

'Well, of course. Poor man, what a shock for him. But I am sure, with his influence, and mine, there should be no problem about a divorce – or maybe even an annulment. So much simpler.'

'But where would that leave me?' asked Cristabel, and was greeted by another peal of delicious laughter.

'In limbo? Never mind, we'll make sure you continue to exist, one way or another. I've a friend who will look after it for me.' She looked at the gold clock. 'He'll be here soon, so I'd best tell you about him. Are you going to be very badly shocked?'

'If we are,' Martha had already come to her own conclusions, 'we promise to hide it gallantly.'

'Ah! I am going to like you, Miss Peabody! No, on second thoughts, I think I shall begin as I mean to go on and call you Martha.'

'That will please me very much.'

'That's settled then. So – to my good friend, Count Gabriel Tafur, whose palace this is. He was waiting for me, when I got back from England, full of reproaches that I had not waited for him. He had been a younger son, you see, penniless, powerless. By the time I came back, he had inherited the Tafur riches. He had this palace ready for me. His own is on the Grand Canal, you must have seen it, the one with the lions, near the Ca' d'Oro; this was just something that had come into the family by marriage, been left to fall into ruins. He had had it entirely refitted, as you see it now. His gondola was waiting for me at Mestre, with a note. I have been here ever since. Ah, here he is! My dear, may I present my daughter Cristabel, and her friend Miss Peabody.'

'Enchanted.' He came forward, slim and erect in old-fashioned elegant black. 'Lady Cristabel,' he bent over her hand. 'Welcome to Venice! And, Miss Peabody,' he turned to her. 'We thank you for bringing her.' His English was as fluent as the Signora's. He looked very much older than her, but there was nothing elderly about the sparkling black eyes which were busy summing them both up. Doing a little summing of her own, Martha decided they were a couple to be reckoned with. 'You are going to let us help you, I hope, in this gallant enterprise of yours,' the Count went on, confirming this. 'A bold plan indeed, three unaccompanied ladies to conquer at once the social and the musical world. You have my congratulations on your success so far.'

'In which you have, in fact, helped us?' Martha smiled at him. 'I believe we should be thanking you already, Count.'

He smiled and shrugged, spreading expressive, capable hands. 'You are quick, Miss Peabody. Yes, a word here, a word there. Even in today's deplorable society we Tafurs are not entirely without influence. And everyone in the world of music loves your mother.' He turned to Cristabel. 'Since she retired, that is, and stopped being a threat to them.'

'Which is a long time!' The Signora smiled and stretched out a lazy hand to him.

'And a most happy one.' He kissed it and Martha and Cristabel, watching, both realised that perhaps for the first time in their lives they were seeing a truly happy marriage. Except that it was no such thing.

'Why –' began Cristabel, went crimson and stopped.

'You're quick, too.' The Count smiled at her very kindly. 'You want to know why I didn't ask my friend the Pope to annul your mother's marriage, and marry her myself? Well, at first she refused – said one marriage was enough for a lifetime – and by the time I had managed to make her see the situation a little differently, it hardly seemed worth the trouble – and the talk.'

'We are very well as we are,' said the Signora. 'I have no wish to go out – except to the theatre of course – and everyone I care about comes to me. And, really, we find our two establishments very comfortable, do we not, Gabriel?'

'Your mother is a brilliantly idle woman who likes her own way in everything,' the Count told Cristabel. 'This way, as you can see, she gets it.'

'Lady Helen is going to be a problem,' said Martha.

'I'm afraid so.' The Count smiled ruefully, and she found herself liking him more and more. 'We are counting on you to deal with her,' he went on. 'After all, you persuaded her into this bold scheme in the first place.'

'No,' Martha told him. 'In fact, she volunteered.'

'Better and better.' He turned to a servant who had appeared in the doorway. 'Your gondola is here, Lady Cristabel, will you ask Lady Helen if I may call on her tomorrow?'

'You mean, tell her you are going to?' Cristabel's smile took any sting out of the words.

He laughed and threw out a hand. 'What a pair of Amazons! I wonder if I dare volunteer my next suggestion.'

'I expect you will.'

'Of course I shall. May I bring a couple of gentlemen to call on you two ladies? If you are going to honour our scandalous ménage with your friendship, you need, I think, to be extra punctilious in other social respects. A pair of reliable cicisbeos will help to establish your position.'

'You guarantee them reliable?' asked Martha, amused.

'They'll be terrified of you.'

'As well as of you? Yes, do bring them, Count. We had been thinking it was time we set ourselves up with a couple of cavaliers.'

'I long to see Torcello,' said Cristabel.

'That certainly settles it. I will look forward to calling on you tomorrow.'

'When will I see you again, Mama?' Cristabel bent to kiss her mother's fragrant cheek.

'Just as soon as we have squared Lady Helen. It will not do for you to be quarrelling with her. You owe her a great deal for cutting loose and coming with you, as I am sure you are aware. But just persuade her I am wicked but harmless, and I see my friends on Thursdays.'

'Not wicked,' said Cristabel. 'How strange it all is.'

'And hardly harmless either,' said Martha and got another delighted laugh.

When Lady Helen agreed to receive Count Tafur, the two girls thought the battle as good as won, and turned their attention to the young men he had brought with him, their prospective adorers. Surprisingly, neither of them was Venetian. Or was it so surprising? Barham Lodge was American, tall and gangling, and over in Europe on what he called a voyage of exploration. His friend Dominic Playfair was intensely English, the fair-haired, fine-boned, younger son of a north-country family. 'I slipped the leash,' he told them. 'M'mother wants me to go into the Church, m'father wants me to go into the army. I said I must have time to think it over, came away as soon as the peace was confirmed, met Barham in Paris, decided to join forces.'

'A grand day for me,' confirmed Barham Lodge. 'Dominic has been able to show me how to go on in Society; I'd be nowhere without him. Wonderful to be born knowing how to behave. And now you ladies are going to be our guides here in Venice.'

'Hardly that,' objected Cristabel. 'We've been here no time ourselves.'

'Ah, but with such connections!' Lodge laughed. 'Now I am learning about connections. Your mother is the most amazing woman, Lady Cristabel. To see her sitting on that sofa of hers, like a queen, ruling her soirées . . . Not a word out of place, not a look; my Aunt Priscilla would be happy there . . . And she talk's the best in Venice. Everyone says so.'

'And for once, everyone is right,' Dominic Playfair told Martha. 'I hope we are to have the pleasure of escorting you here tomorrow evening.'

'So do I.' Martha wondered just how much he knew about their situation.

'The Count's a remarkable man too,' he said. 'I'll bet you a pair of Venetian gloves he and Lady Helen emerge from their conference the best of friends.'

'I'm not a betting woman, Mr. Playfair, but I certainly hope you are right.'

'Bound to be,' he said cheerfully. 'Lady Helen's a woman

of the world; must be, stands to reason. And everyone knows that Society here in Venice has its own rules, goes on quite otherwise than anywhere else in the civilised world.'

'I know this used to be true,' she said doubtfully. 'But even now, under the Austrians . . .'

'More than ever now, don't you see? The old families hanging together. Oh, on the surface it's all conformity and curtsies, but have you thought, Miss Peabody, about what is seething underneath?'

'Why, no, not really. You make me ashamed. We've been so busy, you see, getting ourselves settled, trying to find our way around, arranging for Lady Cristabel's studies . . .'

'I long to hear her voice. Is it really so extraordinary?'

'We think so.' Who was the 'we', she wondered, herself and Franz Wengel, perhaps? 'But this seething you speak of . . . You mean there is really a spirit of revolt here in Venice? I thought they gave in so easily, crumbled so completely before Bonaparte . . . That it was all over with them.'

'With the old régime, yes indeed, and good riddance. A régime of black tyranny and wicked secrecy. You have only to see the lions' heads in the streets, where the informers dropped their evil messages, or those horrible torture chambers under the Doge's Palace, to recognise that the *Serenissima* was doomed. It was ripe and ready to fall, half the population, more, were ready to receive the French with open arms. Trees of liberty sprouting of their own accord . . . The authorities were between the devil of Bonaparte, and the deep blue sea of their own revolutionaries. No wonder they yielded to the devil they thought they knew and ferried his soldiers across the lagoon to save themselves from the excesses of their own people. But not even they could reckon on his duplicity. To hand them over to Austria as he did –' He broke off. 'I do apologise, Miss Peabody. I am lecturing you like a public meeting.'

'I like it, Mr. Playfair. It's what my father used to do.'

'Thank you.' He was looking beyond her. 'I think you get your gloves, Miss Peabody.'

Lady Helen and the Count had just emerged from the music room, talking with the ease of old friends.

As she got to know them better, Martha was increasingly sure that Lodge and Playfair were involved in some kind of plotting against the Austrian authorities. Convinced that they were rather playing at it than serious, she decided not to mention her suspicion to Lady Helen, or Cristabel, who was so totally immersed in her music that she only noticed politics when Signor Carpani, the Director and Censor of the Theatres, committed some particularly ridiculous act of censorship.

'He's a poet himself. And a librettist,' she fumed. 'How can he do it?'

'To curry favour with his Austrian masters, I am afraid. I'm glad you never thought of making your début here, Belle.'

'I should just about think not! But, oh, Martha, do you think I ever will? Sometimes I think it is all cloud-cuckoo-land and I shall be a charge on you for ever.'

'And a great pleasure it would be. But don't think it for a minute. Signor Arioso was saying just the other day what wonderful progress you have made this winter. You must be aware of it yourself.'

'Oh, the singing, yes. Since Herr Wengel sorted my breathing for me, I do know how I have come on. I wish we would hear from him, or about him. The thing is, Martha, I need to get on to a stage. You know as well as I do that it's not just singing that makes an opera. It must be acted, too. And there's a limit to the amount that one can study by oneself. But there's another reason why I long to hear from Herr Wengel. This Congress sitting at Rastatt. I hadn't realised, but Mr. Lodge said something the other day about how many small German principalities are going to vanish without trace. Martha, it's horribly selfish of me, but I couldn't help thinking of Lissenberg. Suppose it gets swallowed up by one of its neighbours, Baden or Württemberg?'

'From everything I've heard, it would serve Prince Gustav richly right.'

'That's no comfort to me,' said Cristabel.

'Never mind.' Martha was disconcerted to realise how much her friend had been counting on Franz Wengel's casual proposal. 'If the peace just holds I am sure you can do better than the small tyrannical court at Lissenberg. Why not La Scala? Or the San Carlo? I confess I sometimes find myself wishing we had gone to Naples as Helen suggested.'

'Oh, no,' said Cristabel. 'Then I wouldn't have met Mama.'

*   *   *

65

Salomon Rothschild paid Martha one of his rare visits a few days later. As always he contrived to find her alone, and she was more and more convinced that he actually owned the house where they had their apartments, and probably the servants too. It was odd how little she minded, and another of the things she had not mentioned to Cristabel or Helen.

She greeted him now like the business friend she felt him to be. As usual, he refused her offer of refreshment and came straight to the point. 'I have a piece of news that I think will please you, Miss Peabody.' He sat on the edge of his chair, neat and inconspicuous in his habitual black, a bulging brief-case under his arm. 'You know, I am sure, about the Congress at Rastatt?'

'Yes?' She liked him for the assumption.

'You will be pleased to hear that they have decided to leave Lissenberg out of their discussions. Prince Gustav will be able to celebrate his twenty-fifth anniversary after all.'

'That's good news,' she said, 'but surprising. I thought Lissenberg just the kind of small principality that was bound to be lost.'

'Quite true. But it also serves a very useful financial purpose just as it is. So – by some curious chance its name got left out of the original draft for discussion.'

'And nobody noticed?'

'Nobody mentioned it.' He picked up his brief-case, then rose. 'You don't plan to leave Venice, I hope, when war breaks out.'

'It's going to?' Startled.

'Quite soon, I think. And my advice, if you will allow me to give it, is that your party stay here. Don't think of trying to get home to England. I am leaving for Vienna in the morning. Can I count on finding you here when I return?'

'The news is as bad as the weather.' Dominic Playfair shook March raindrops out of his hair. 'I'm afraid it begins to look very much like war, Miss Peabody. I'm told on the very best authority that Bonaparte has made one of his scenes with Whitworth, the British Ambassador. Deliberately provocative. We British will never take it lying down. But there must be a little time before it actually comes to blows. I came to you at once, in case you and the other ladies thought you should make haste for home.'

'Do you think we should?'

'I would hesitate to counsel so wise a young lady, but, just the same . . . Venice is a volcano, Miss Peabody, which might erupt any day.'

'You really think so?'

'Miss Peabody, I know it. The Austrian occupiers keep the lid screwed down tight, but underneath there is a seething mess ready to boil over. If Austria throws in her lot with us against France, the Venetians may well think their moment has come. There is hot blood stirring. I would not wish you ladies to be here when the day of vengeance comes. Though of course I should be desolated to see you go.' With a languishing glance.

She laughed and shook her head at him. 'What a waste of a pretty speech, Mr. Playfair. Save it, please, for when we are in company. Did you notice the man in the snuff-coloured suit at the opera last night, by the way? I thought he was keeping a very close eye on you.'

'On all of us.' He did not attempt to deny it. 'But I did hope you had not noticed. Did Lady Cristabel?'

'I doubt it. She was totally absorbed in the performance, as usual. I certainly hope not. She has enough on her mind as it is, without being troubled with your conspiracies. I rather wish I knew how far her mother is involved. Is it with her knowledge – and the Count's – that you use her house as your meeting-place? No,' she threw out a hand, 'don't tell me. On second thoughts, I believe I would rather not know. And besides,' she paused, thinking about it, 'it is obvious that what I have noticed, the Signora and the Count will have noticed too. My only concern is to keep Lady Cristabel out of it. Why are you laughing?'

'With admiration, Miss Peabody, for your singleness of mind. Venice can rot in chains, so far as you are concerned, as long as your friend becomes a prima donna?'

'The chains don't seem so dreadful to me. And richly earned! Frankly, I think the Venetians need to learn how to use liberty before they are entitled to demand it. Maybe a few years of bondage will make for a more humane society in the end. I have had it on my mind to suggest to you that you were taking great risks – for yourself and other people – for a cause you do not sufficiently understand.'

'The cause of freedom? How can you say so, Miss Peabody?' He laughed ruefully. 'But I am sorry to have been so transparent. Our snuff-coloured friend was a warning to me as well as to you – I'm just sorry you noticed him too. If I promise to be more careful in future, will you allow me to remain your devoted servant?'

'Oh, I think so. In other respects, you suit me very well. It would be tedious to have to replace you. And might be a little awkward for you to be seen to be replaced.'

'Extremely so! Miss Peabody, what a conspirator you would make. If only you would join us! Now you are laughing at me!'

'Not really. I was only thinking how pleasant it is to be asked to join a madcap plot, instead of having marriage proposed to me.'

'You make me want to do that too!'

'Nonsense.' She turned as Cristabel and Lodge joined them from the music-room. 'Just in time! Mr. Playfair was threatening to propose marriage!'

'An admirable idea,' said Barham Lodge. 'A joint wedding? St. Mark's perhaps? Gondolas for four down the Grand Canal –'

'*Così Fan' Tutte* –' Cristabel interrupted him. 'And if we are not to miss the overture, it is time we were going.'

'Music first, last and all the time.' Lodge helped her into the voluminous black cape worn by ladies in the evening.

Cristabel had made it clear, from her first appearance in a Venetian theatre, that she went for the music, not to entertain her friends, and now, no one disturbed them while the opera was being performed. But when tumultuous applause greeted the sweep of velvet curtains, and the audience relaxed for the afterpiece, she and Martha prepared to hold court in their box, while the two young men went off to make some calls of their own. They returned sooner than usual, ushering a tall, dark-haired stranger.

'Lady Cristabel, Miss Peabody,' Playfair was at his most formal, 'may I present –'

Cristabel's gilt chair overturned as she rose, dropping gloves and opera glasses. 'Max –' She held out both hands, stopped, coloured, curtsied. 'I mean –'

'You mean Max.' He took her hands, kissed them one after the other, held them for a moment, looking at her. 'It never struck me you would be beautiful,' he said at last. 'It's better than I dreamed.'

'Better? But I'm forgetting my manners. May I present you to my dear friend, Miss Peabody. Prince Maximilian of Lissenberg, Martha. My childhood friend.'

'Highness.' Curtsying.

'No, no. I am not here at all as a prince. I am simply my father's musical emissary, and very happy to be so.' He turned back to Cristabel. 'Prince Gustav took one of his dislikes to his German Opera Company this winter. He has sent the lot of them packing, I'm sorry to say – some of them were my good friends – but there is no arguing with my father, as I am sure you will remember. And at least it means that I have the happy task of finding him Italian replacements for next season.'

'A whole new company?'

'Precisely. I thought I would begin here in Venice because here I shall have the benefit of your advice. But the orchestra is tuning up. I must get back to my place. May I call on you tomorrow, Lady Cristabel, and talk about old times and my new project?'

'We will look forward to it. And I promise to smother you in good advice.'

That night, Martha was surprised by a long, highly-coloured and alarmingly erotic dream of Franz Wengel. She woke angry with herself and baffled at what had put him into her mind.

Cristabel had talked about possible singers for Lissenberg all the way home, and now returned from her music lesson full of it. 'Arioso is going to make me a list of singers,' she told Martha and Helen over coffee and rolls. 'What do you think Max meant about my being beautiful and it's better than he dreamed?'

'You had better ask the Prince when he calls,' said Lady Helen. 'And, Cristabel, I do think you should cure yourself, at once, of this habit of calling him Max. It really will not do, now that you are grown up.'

'No! Of course not. But, you see, he hasn't changed a bit. I feel just as if I had known him always. Do you think he will tell us, today, about the plans for the twenty-fifth anniversary of his father's arrival in Lissenberg?'

'Purchase of it?' asked Martha. 'I suppose if there is really to be a specially commissioned opera for it next autumn, they will need to get a company built up quickly.'

'I should just about think they will,' Cristabel smiled to herself, 'I wonder if Prince Maximilian knows about Franz Wengel? We must ask him when he comes.'

'I doubt it,' said Martha. 'Wengel comes from the wrong end of the country, remember.'

'But the country is tiny. About the size of Wales, I'd think, and just as mountainous. There didn't seem to be a great deal of communication between the capital and Brundt where the mines are, except when it came to taxes, of course.'

'But Wengel spoke as if he had influence, knew people in Lissenberg. I don't suppose there's much music, or much influence, at Brundt.'

'Oh, I don't know,' said Cristabel. 'They all seem to be musical in Lissenberg. It's going to be a terrible slap in the face to have an Italian opera company thrust upon them. I wonder how the little prince is,' she went on thoughtfully. 'Herr Wengel never seemed to think he had much chance of surviving, but if Prince Maximilian is here as his father's musical representative . . .'

'The baby must be thriving.'

Prince Maximilian confirmed this when he called early, by arrangement. 'Yes, he's beginning to outgrow the ailments of his infancy, I'm glad to say, our little Prince Gustav the Second. I cannot begin to tell you what a liberation it has been for me, Lady Cristabel.' Smiling at her. 'How I wish I could call you Bella, as I used to, but it won't do, and we must resign ourselves.'

'Just what my aunt was saying. But I shall always remember my friend Max who gave me my chance as a singer.'

'And I, how you took it. I long to hear you sing. There has been talk about you even in remote Lissenberg and that is something else I want to tell you about.' And he plunged into a description of his father's plans for his twenty-fifth anniversary. 'The little prince will be five next year, over the worst of the hazards of childhood. We will be celebrating that too.'

'You really don't mind?'

'Mind? I should think not. I cannot think of anyone less suitable than I am to rule Lissenberg, and not many people who want to less. My ambition is quite other, nearer to yours. I want to write opera. Not just the music, the words too. Imagine if Mozart could have written his own libretti!'

'You don't want to sing?' asked Cristabel.

'I've hardly done so, since my voice broke. One of my father's many prohibitions. Or at least, only in private, but I let myself think that if I go in for the competition for the festival opera, next year, under an alias, of course, and win, he will find it in his heart to forgive me. Success has always appealed to Prince Gustav. I think part of why he was so angry all those years ago, was because it was you, not I, who held the audience in the palm of your hand. And you can still do it, I hear. So – when am I to hear you sing?'

'Now?' suggested Martha. 'I'd be happy to play for you, Cristabel.'

'Get it over with? Why not.' They moved into the music-room. 'What shall I sing for you?'

'Orpheus, please. I remember it so well, have never heard it sung better.'

'I'm afraid you've glamorised me in my absence,' she said. 'I'll never live up to it.'

They were beginning to talk, already, like old friends, Martha noticed. She sat down at the piano. 'The first lament?' she asked.

'Yes, please. And then I'll go straight on to 'Che farò', and you will not say a word, Prince Maximilian, until I finish.'

'Your obedient servant.'

Most unusually, Cristabel was nervous. It showed at first, and Martha understood why she had wanted no break between the two laments. It was only with the opening words of 'Che farò' that she began to sing as Martha knew she could.

'Yes,' Prince Maximilian said at last, 'Most absolutely, yes. So, what is the opera to be? And are you to sing hero, or heroine, Lady Cristabel?'

'You ask us?' Martha was amazed.

'Why not? To tell you the truth, I have had to revise all my ideas since I reached Venice. Don't be angry with me, Lady Cristabel, but for some reason I had remembered you as a plain child. I had been thinking of subjects where character would outweigh looks. And now I find you a great beauty, I have to start my thinking all over again.'

'That's what you meant last night.' Cristabel laughed. 'I do apologise for inconveniencing you. But what had you in mind for me?'

'I had thought of Cassandra, perhaps, the unlucky prophetess, and the triumph of the Greeks. There will have to be some element of royal triumph in our theme, or what hope of winning the competition?'

'I can see that,' said Martha. 'But, surely Agamemnon is not the happiest subject? He came to a bad enough end, poor man, murdered by his wife when he returned home.'

'You think I might be putting ideas into my stepmother's head?' He looked at her with new respect. 'Dear Miss Peabody, do, I beg you, think of a better subject for me?'

'You intend a classical one?'

'I think so. Something along the lines of Mozart's *Clemenza di Tito*, a great favourite of mine – and of my father's.'

'But *Idomeneo*, perhaps, a more interesting model?'

'Dear me, no. A more interesting opera, yes, of course. But you are forgetting, Miss Peabody, that in *Idomeneo* the young heirs take over the country. It would hardly be considered tactful.'

She laughed. 'Stupid of me. Would *Il Re Pastore* be more the thing?'

'Very much so. I'm sure my father would like to see himself as Alexander the Great. But not an interesting subject.' He was on his feet, riffling through the manuscript music that lay on the fortepiano. 'A king who sacrifices himself for his people? The king who must die? No, my father would not like that at all. Self-sacrifice was never his line.'

'*Persephone*?' suggested Martha. 'A delicate tribute to your stepmother?'

'And who would I sing?' asked Cristabel. 'Persephone herself, or Pluto who carries her off, or Hermes who rescues her?'

'None of them, I think,' said Maximilian. 'There's not enough to it, and, besides, I believe Paisiello is at work on the theme at this very moment. *Alceste*, maybe?'

'The king doesn't come out very well in that either,' said Martha.

'Interesting about kings, is it not? They do tend not to come out very well. Sacrificing their daughters, letting their wives sacrifice themselves for them. It's quite enough to put a man off the whole business.'

'Oh, Max,' said Cristabel impulsively. 'It is so good to see you again! But, tell me, truly, what did you think of my singing?'

'I thought you very nervous, and was flattered. And what is this trouble you have been having with your breathing?'

'You noticed?' Delighted. 'Oh, such a story, such a drama. Do you know Herr Franz Wengel? He comes from Lissenberg.'

'I've heard the name. A man active both in music and in politics?'

'That's the one. He came to see us in Paris. I should warn you, he means to write an opera for the competition too, and it will be a good one. And – God bless him – the first time he heard me, he told me I'd lose my voice if I didn't change my breathing. And taught me how. It's the strangest thing; I've been breath-perfect ever since, until I sang for you today. You heard?'

'Of course I heard. And heard the difference when you got it under control. A clever man, this Wengel, I must look out for him when I get back to Lissenberg. He's going in for the competition, too, you say? What's his subject?'

'He's like you, finding it hard to choose one.'

6

May, and the canals were beginning to smell. 'High time we moved to the country,' said Signora Aldini. 'You'll stay with me, of course.'

'All three of us?' asked Cristabel.

'Naturally. And Signor Arioso, too, so you can continue your studies while you wait to hear from Prince Maximilian. It is all of the highest respectability,' turning to Martha, 'Count Tafur and I have adjacent villas on the Brenta. And, frankly, I think it would be best for you two to get out of town, and leave your hot-headed young cavaliers behind.'

'You expect trouble?'

'They hope for it. I am getting old and lazy.' She reached out to refill their glasses. 'I'm sure the immortal garland, freedom, is worth fighting for, but I don't much want to be there when it starts. Besides, and entirely between ourselves – as usual, they were eating without benefit of servants, 'I think they are miscalculating. The Austrians will not be as distracted by the outbreak of war as they hope.'

'They seem frighteningly competent to me,' said Martha.

'That's why we are going to the country. I'm not so sure now that it was a good idea to attach those two young firebrands to you. Frankly, I'll be delighted when Prince Maximilian returns and I can see you off to safe little Lissenberg.'

Salomon Rothschild, calling on Martha next day, said very much the same thing. 'You've not heard from the Prince? I think you should perhaps write to him – or get Lady Cristabel to do so – saying how eager you are to get to Lissenberg. It is bound to be read by the authorities and should help to dispel their suspicions of you. The beginning of a war is always a dangerous time, Miss Peabody. The authorities are nervous, suspect everyone, act rashly, as Bonaparte has.'

'I've been meaning to thank you for your good advice about not travelling back through France. This arrest of

British citizens, caught there by the war, is a monstrous thing.'

'If that's just the worst of it . . . I hope you are going to accept Signora Aldini's invitation.'

'Oh, I think so.' She was not in the least surprised that he knew about it.

'Good. And, do, pray, let me know as soon as you arrange to go to Lissenberg. I should like to give you an introduction to a friend of mine there.'

'If he is half as helpful to us as you have been, I shall be happy to have it. I do hope you find it worth your while, Mr. Rothschild.'

'Never trouble yourself about that. We Rothschilds are not known for unlucky investments.'

She smiled at him. 'The interesting thing about you Rothschilds is how little you are known at all.'

Life at the Palladian villa on the Brenta went with the smooth luxury of a summer daydream. Only Cristabel was restless. Singing lessons were no longer enough for her, and it had been easy to persuade her to write to Prince Maximilian, last heard of in Naples, and ask him when she could hope to get to Lissenberg and to work. He answered the letter in person, arriving at the villa one hot August evening, tired and dusty from a hard day's travel.

'I am summoned home.' He had found the two girls sitting on the terrace that overlooked the Brenta. 'I wish I knew why. And I hope I can persuade you ladies to let me be your escort.'

'At once?' asked Martha.

'As soon as possible. It was an urgent summons. Characteristic of my father not to explain.'

'I long to meet him,' said Martha.

They left two days later, sped lovingly on their way by Lucia Aldini. 'I never thought I should be so fortunate as to find myself with two daughters.' She kissed them both impartially. 'Never forget, either of you, that there is always a home for you with me.'

'With us.' Tafur turned to Lady Helen. 'And for you too, Lady Helen, if you would honour us by asking for it. Who knows, you might even find us a respectable old married couple.'

'As if I would care for that.' She surprised everyone, including herself, by a quick shine of tears. 'I've never been so happy in my life as this last year.'

They crossed Lake Constance on a brilliant September day and found carriages awaiting them on the Lissenberg quay. 'I can't believe it!' Cristabel's spirits had risen with every stage of the journey. 'To find myself actually here again. Oh, Max, do you remember the day we rode down to meet your new stepmother?'

'And got here before my father! I do indeed, Lady Cristabel.' And then, as she blushed at the warning use of her title, he hurried on. 'I just hope it is not bad news about the little prince that has caused my summons home.'

'So do I, but for the most selfish of reasons. What will become of your Italian company if you have to go back to being Crown Prince?'

'You'll do very well I am sure. I pray it will not come to that, but I have taken the precaution of securing the services of an admirable second-in-command who is hard at work already – or so I devoutly hope – with the rest of the company. I rather expect some kind of performance of welcome, something to give me an idea of how they are shaping up.'

'So soon?'

'Yes, but nothing formal.' He had received letters at the quay and been glancing quickly through them as the little cortège set forward up the mountain road. 'Franzosi writes to say he hopes to entertain us tomorrow night. And – something else – I do hope you will not mind, Lady Cristabel . . . I asked him to arrange for you ladies to be lodged in the performers' quarters, rather than at the Palace, as your rank demands. Lady Helen,' he leaned across from the backward-facing seat he shared with Martha, 'I hope you will understand . . .'

'I'm delighted,' she said. 'I have had it in mind to ask you whether you had heard at all how your father feels about Cristabel's coming.'

'He has said nothing. He keeps his counsel, my father.' The little party was silent for a while, until the increasing steepness of the hill suggested that they get out and walk to spare the horses. 'It's such a beautiful day,' Cristabel urged. She was soon walking ahead with Prince Maximilian while Martha accommodated herself to Lady Helen's slower pace. 'You have still no idea why your father wants you home so suddenly?' she went on.

'Not the least in the world. Franzosi does not mention anything amiss, but then he says nothing about the Palace at all.'

'Wise man. I can't tell you how relieved I am that we are to be lodged with the other artists. Your father frightens me a little, but I long to meet your stepmother again.'

'You will find her very much changed, poor lady, but as kind as ever.'

'How strange it seems to be coming back. And how right. Have you hit on the subject for my opera yet?'

'No, I'm quite in despair. But that's for the future. I told Franzosi that you would make your first appearance as Orpheus. It seemed fitting.'

'Bold,' she said. 'I do pray I justify your confidence in me.'

'Oh, you will. But you have walked far enough.' They had reached a bend in the mountain road and could see that the stretch ahead was less steep. 'We had best wait here for the others.'

'Must we?'

'I think so. We are in Lissenberg now, Lady Cristabel.'

'We are indeed!' A little toss of her head as she walked away from him to look at the view back to Lake Constance, deep blue in the waning light.

It was already dusk when they reached the castle gates and all three ladies were weary enough to be relieved that there was no sign of a reception for them. The driver had paused to light the lanterns for the difficult road down to the Opera House and the gate-keeper came hurrying out to speak to Prince Maximilian in an unintelligible Liss.

'I am so very sorry,' Max turned to them as the door was opened and the steps let down, 'my father wants me urgently. I dislike letting you finish the journey unescorted . . .'

'Nonsense,' said Martha robustly, 'Signor Franzosi will have a welcome for us. Prince Gustav is our employer, and yours, I suppose.' Smiling at Max, 'I am sure he will have made every arrangement for our comfort. And you should not be keeping him waiting. He is your father after all.'

'For what that is worth.' But he said it almost in a whisper, into the carriage, so that only the three of them could hear. Martha felt a little shiver run down her spine. If Prince Gustav frightened his own son . . . For the first time, she wondered if they had been wise to come.

The doors slammed shut; the carriage rolled forward. 'Things will seem more cheerful in the morning,' said Lady Helen.

'I do hope so,' said Cristabel.

They woke next morning to sunshine and more cheerful thoughts. Their apartments were comfortable to the point of luxury, and the other members of the little company seemed friendly. 'A great relief,' said Cristabel, 'they might so easily have resented me. But I wish there would be a word from the Palace.'

'They are coming to the performance tonight.' Martha had more than half expected that Lady Helen and Cristabel would be invited to dine at the Palace, and found the total silence disturbing.

'Clever of Signor Franzosi to think of Pergolesi's *La Serva Padrona*,' Cristabel was determinedly optimistic. 'Short, with only two singers; it's just right for an occasion like this. And I'm glad we are to dine with the rest of the company. Anything else would have been fatal.'

'I'm glad you see it that way.'

Lady Helen laughed. 'What a fortunate thing we are women,' she said, 'otherwise I have the strongest feeling Prince Gustav would have expected us to wear his livery . . . But I do think, my dears, that we must recognise that he is making a point of a kind.'

'A sound one,' said Cristabel, 'I do not wish to be treated differently from the rest of the company, Aunt, so long as you don't mind.'

'I think it is going to be enormously entertaining.' Lady Helen had breathed a silent sigh of relief at finding the other singers such agreeable people, and privately thought that Prince Maximilian must have had a hard hunt for them.

The performance was to begin at nine o'clock and Franzosi begged them to be ready in good time, explaining that Prince Gustav was a martinet for punctuality. The small audience

78

must be already seated, and the company drawn up in the foyer of the Opera House to receive their patron. Lady Helen and Martha presented a problem which Lady Helen solved by announcing that they would join the rest of the company, 'as chaperone and manager to the leading lady'. She smiled at Martha, who bobbed her a little curtsy. They were all very much in their formal best and Martha was unhappily aware of a jealous glance or two from the less elegantly garbed ladies of the company. But Cristabel's manner with them was perfect, with its hint of shyness, its tacit admission that she was the tyro, with much to learn from them.

A fanfare of trumpets outside. 'The Prince moves in style,' whispered Martha and got a look of reproach from Franzosi, who was rigid with nerves.

The doors of the foyer swung wide, massed candles flickered in their wind as the royal party advanced along the lines of bowing and curtsying singers. Prince Gustav had not changed much, Cristabel thought, but she would not have recognised his wife. They had reached her now. The Prince inclined his head ever so slightly, 'You are welcome to Lissenberg, Lady Cristabel.' He was passing straight on, but his wife paused for a moment to put out a shaking, tentative hand and mutter, 'So glad,' then turned, stumbling a little in her hurry to catch up with her husband. But Cristabel was looking the other way, at Maximilian, following his father, and the brilliantly dressed girl on his arm.

'Minette.' She moved forward impulsively. 'What a delightful surprise! And Stephanie, is she here too?' She leaned forward to kiss Minette de Beauharnais on both cheeks. Then stood back, aware of tension in Maximilian. 'But I should not be keeping you. Later!'

Being practically servants, the singers were lucky to have inconspicuous seats at the very back of the gallery, but they could still see that Prince Gustav was not enjoying himself. His applause for the soprano's bravura singing was merely a token gesture; inevitably, the rest of the audience followed his lead. At one point, Cristabel, carried away by her own enthusiasm, would have gone on clapping had Martha not put a warning hand on hers. It was the same when the singers took their final bows, but by now they knew what to expect and made them as short and formal as possible. Just as well. Prince Gustav was rising already and there was an undignified scramble at the back of the house as the rest of the company got back into line to see the royal party on its way. Franzosi was bone-white. Cristabel put a hand on his shoulder. 'It was brilliant,' she said. 'Don't mind – Here they come!'

Martha had assumed there would be some mingling at this point, that the Prince would wish to greet his new company of artists, and that there would be a chance of general talk. Nothing of the kind. He walked through the singers as if they were not there, ignoring bows and curtsies alike. The Princess, beside him, looked miserably straight ahead. Only Minette de Beauharnais caught Cristabel's eye and mouthed, 'Tomorrow,' then turned back to Prince Maximilian, who was almost as white as Franzosi.

There should have been a celebration afterwards. 'Celebrate?' Franzosi said bitterly. 'Celebrate what, pray?'

'What do we do?' asked Cristabel next morning.

'Wait and see. What else can we do?' Martha had seldom felt so discouraged.

'But the road out could be closed any day now,' Cristabel reminded her.

'Then it is up to Prince Gustav to make his wishes clear before it happens. And I have no doubt he will,' Martha went on. 'He hardly hides his feelings, that man. I don't know when I have taken such an instant dislike to anyone. But what in the world is Minette de Beauharnais doing here?' She turned to a less painful subject.

'I've been thinking about that.' Lady Helen poured coffee. 'I'd clean forgotten, but I believe there was some kind of remote relationship between those girls' mother and Princess Amelia.'

'So it's just a family visit?' Did Cristabel sound relieved?

'I wonder how long she has been here,' said Martha.

'And whether she is planning to let herself be caught here by winter.' Lady Helen rose and moved over to the window. 'There's a carriage coming down from the Palace now so we should know soon enough.'

'Unless it's our notice to quit.' Martha had been up early that morning, writing a quick, careful note to Salomon

Rothschild's Lissenberg friend. If they found themselves having to leave suddenly, she would be in urgent need of funds.

Minette de Beauharnais was announced a few minutes later, and Martha thought it a bad sign that she had come alone. Had Prince Maximilian been forbidden to visit them?

'Such a to-do at the Palace! Such a carry-on!' Minette kissed both girls impulsively. 'I couldn't wait a moment longer to come and tell you all about it. Prince Gustav is neither to hold nor to bind. Lord what a tartar! More like an Eastern despot than a Christian prince. It does rather make one wonder . . . My poor Cousin Amelia looks like death and one can't get a word out of Prince Max. So I just put on my bonnet and pelisse and called a carriage to come to you. They haven't forbidden that yet!'

'What do you mean?' asked Martha.

'Well, I rather think poor Prince Max is confined to the Palace. He's in such disgrace!' She giggled. 'And all because of little me.'

'Of you?' asked Cristabel, amazed. But Martha thought she was beginning to understand.

'I thought you wouldn't have heard.' Minette was enjoying herself. 'That's why it seemed the act of a friend to come quickly, and tell you.'

'Tell us what, child?' Lady Helen took control of the conversation. 'But, first, sit down, compose yourself. A cup of coffee perhaps?'

'Delicious!' Accepting the Sèvres cup she cast sharp glances round the room. 'You're very snug here! The best of everything, I'm glad to see. Prince Max's doing, I have no doubt. Such a charming man, so considerate . . .' Another giggle. 'And so obstinate! It really is too, too unflattering, but he will come round, you see if he doesn't. He's not stupid, that one; he'll see where his interest lies. And then I hope after all you will be able to stay, dear, dearest Cristabel, maybe sing at the wedding, even? Think what delightful times we shall all have together, you and I and dear Martha, when the snow comes down and the roads are blocked and we are all snug together here in Lissenberg.'

'Take us with you, child,' said Lady Helen. 'What wedding is this you speak of?'

'Why, mine and Max's! Did you not guess that is why I am

here? Uncle Bonaparte's idea, of course. I always told you he would marry us well in the end, Stephanie and I. Mind you, I was not best pleased at first. Such a tiny country, and miles from everywhere, and then there is that poor ailing little boy, but Uncle's doctors say he hasn't a chance. And anyway, my Max is the older. Uncle will manage all that for us. There seems to be something about Lissenberg that makes it important to him. And then my darling Max will see how lucky he is! Such a dear, dear man.' She turned impulsively to Cristabel. 'You must stay! I'll see to it. You and I will have so much to talk about. I knew, the minute I saw my Max, that I had been right to give way to Uncle Bonaparte and come. I can't wait for Stephanie to meet Max. Her nose will be quite out of joint. He will have to come to Paris for the wedding, of course; Notre Dame, and Uncle Bonaparte giving me away. Lord, how delightful life is!'

'Aside from the little difficulty of Prince Maximilian's refusing the handsome offer?' Lady Helen was at her driest.

'Oh that! Poor boy, I don't blame him a bit. The way his father put it to him was enough to get anyone's gall up. And my Max has his pride; we will all have to make it as easy as possible for him to make his peace with his father. That's partly why I am here, to ask your help, dearest Cristabel, as his childhood friend. I know I can count on you to talk some sense into the poor sweet. For everybody's sake. Naturally, in your position the cancellation of your contract won't mean a thing. La Scala, or the San Carlo, will toss you the handkerchief at once, no doubt, when they hear you are so suddenly available. But what about the rest of Max's new troupe? What will happen to them? It will be out, neck and crop, if Max don't give in to his father, for the lot of you. Not the least doubt about that. My future pa-in-law is not a reasonable man, no good pretending otherwise. So, dear, darling Cristabel, if I get leave for poor Max to come and see you, will you talk to him like a wise old friend?' She laughed and tossed her head. 'My Uncle Bonaparte is not the easiest of men either. He has his reasons, no doubt, for marrying me to Max. It would not be wise to cross him.' She rose, pulling on elegant Parisian gloves. 'Shall I send Max to you, Bella?'

A small, hard silence: Cristabel had turned very white, Martha was biting her lips. In the end, Lady Helen spoke: 'I am sure Lady Cristabel will be happy to see the Prince if he can get leave to come to her. There are all kinds of things to discuss about the forthcoming season.'

'What season?' asked Minette, vulgarly direct. 'There won't be a season if Max don't see sense. More like a season of war, with Uncle Bonaparte's armies walking over little Lissenberg. Don't ask me why, but he does seem to want to be sure of an alliance here. Your English friends know by now what happens to people who cross him.'

'Illegal arrest,' said Martha. 'Yes, we are aware of how your uncle behaves, but we thank you for the reminder, Mademoiselle de Beauharnais. You have given us a great deal to think about.' She looked at the clock. 'It is time for Lady Cristabel to go to the Opera House. May I suggest that you use your great influence on Prince Gustav to arrange for Prince Maximilian to visit us tomorrow? I am sure we will have good advice to give him then.' She had risen. 'May I show you out? You see, we treat you quite like an old friend.'

She took Minette down two flights of stairs to the front door and parted from her with a cool curtsy. Returning, she was waylaid by a servant with the information that a gentleman was waiting to see her. 'A Jewish gentleman.' A slight sneer suggested that the man thought it a contradiction in terms.

'In that case he is most certainly a friend of mine. I'll see him at once.'

Salomon Rothschild's friend was called Ishmael Brodski. He was tall, dark haired, beak-nosed, immensely handsome. 'Miss Peabody,' he surprised her by kissing her hand, 'by sheer good fortune your letter found me here in town. In what way can I serve you? You spoke of funds for a journey?'

'I think I am even more in need of advice,' she said.

'Ah,' he smiled at her, 'that is much harder than money, and comes more expensive. But for a friend of my friend, Salomon Rothschild, I will do my absolute best.'

'I am sure of it, thank you. And I propose to trust you, Mr. Brodski.' She quickly outlined the situation in which they found themselves. 'What should we do?' she asked finally.

'Interesting,' he said, 'most interesting. I knew, of course, of Mademoiselle de Beauharnais's coming. And rumour had guessed at the reason for it. Bonaparte is setting himself up, already, in the dynastic line. It would not be a wise moment to cross him, I think. It was Bonaparte, Miss Peabody, who saw to it that Lissenberg was "forgotten" when the Treaty of Rastatt was drawn up. I think you should remind your friend how easily he could have it remembered, even at this late stage.'

'And Lissenberg would cease to exist?'

'Just so. Which would be –' he paused, 'unfortunate, for all kinds of reasons which I would rather not go into. Do, please, persuade your friend to urge the young man to give way. I think she can honestly tell him it is a sacrifice he must make for Lissenberg.'

7

The engagement was announced a few days later and was celebrated by an 'impromptu' performance of Mozart's *La Clemenza di Tito* with Cristabel singing the part of Sextus. There had been no word from Max, and Martha wondered what threats had been used. Cristabel said nothing, but threw herself passionately into rehearsing her new part. Max, dancing attendance on his fiancée, had kept away, and so, to Martha's great relief, had Minette, who was to leave the day after the performance for Paris, and preparations for a spring wedding.

'A great deal can happen between now and spring,' said Martha.

'Please don't think like that.' Cristabel gave her a very straight look. 'Or rather, yes, indeed it can. Between now and spring I intend to become a prima donna, someone to whom La Scala, or the San Carlo, really will throw the handkerchief.'

'I'm delighted to hear it. Or La Fenice perhaps? Do you know who came to see me this morning, while you were rehearsing? Lodge and Playfair.'

'Our Venetian cicisbeos? What in the world are they doing here?'

'Languishing after us, if you choose to believe them. But in fact they make no bones about it – they had made Venice too hot to hold them. The Austrians are not to be so easily expelled as they and their friends imagined.'

'They mean to spend the winter here?'

'So they say. I wish I quite knew why. They have secured seats for the performance tonight and asked me to tell you how passionately they look forward to it.'

'So I am sure of two pairs of applauding hands.'

'Oh, I think you will find everything quite different tonight.'

She was right. This time the royal party arrived in the blandest of spirits. Prince Gustav paused for a friendly word with Franzosi, then moved on to greet Lady Helen as if for the first time. 'Welcome to Lissenberg! I hope you will all dine with us tomorrow, so that Lady Cristabel can receive the congratulations I am sure she will earn tonight.'

Behind him, Minette was radiant, Max grey with misery beside her. Martha was glad Cristabel was not there to see.

In the intervals of frantic, last-minute, rehearsal, Cristabel had told Martha about the problems of her part, written for a castrato. She was to play the hero/villain who tries to kill the Emperor Titus for a woman's sake, and goes on adoring her through disgrace and the threat of death. When the curtain rose to reveal her, kneeling at the soprano's feet, the audience burst into applause and Martha could not help a gasp of surprise. It was Cristabel there on stage, of course, but it was also a young, elegant, tunicked Roman. From then on, she had the audience with her, every inch of the way. Tonight, Martha thought, it would not have been possible for Prince Gustav to quell the applause, but tonight he led it.

At the end, when the Emperor Titus had forgiven everyone, and the singers came forward to take their bows, the stage was strewn with flowers and Prince Gustav was standing to applaud, like everyone else.

'A better début than Orpheus would have been,' said Lady Helen as they made their way to the lobby.

'Certainly more tactful.' Martha had never heard Mozart's opera before and was amazed at its glorification of the merciful sovereign.

The royal party was leaving. There was some colour in Max's cheeks now, and Minette looked slightly subdued. Was she remembering that cruel remark she had made about Cristabel's being able to count on offers from the great opera houses? Martha rather hoped so.

Minette paused for a moment beside Lady Helen. 'You will convey my congratulations to your niece, I beg. I am sorry not to be able to give them in person, but I leave in the morning for Paris. There are a million things to do before my darling Max and I can marry, and every moment's delay is an anguish to us, is it not, my dear?' He was not listening, and Martha thought she saw Minette pinch his arm.

'Oh, yes, indeed,' he said. 'Forgive me, Lady Helen, I was thinking of Lady Cristabel's triumph. Tell her, from me, that the world is at her feet, but that I do hope she will stay with us, here in Lissenberg.'

'She'll have to, won't she,' said Minette. 'Unless she decides to come out with me tomorrow, which I do not recommend.'

'He did come to hear me!' Cristabel exclaimed a few days later, 'Franz Wengel! He's written –' her colour was high. 'Praise, from him! . . .' She read on eagerly. 'He sends you his regards, Martha, and to you, Aunt Helen. He was in the gallery, of course, with the other Lissenbergers. Didn't feel he could venture to make himself known to you.' Her face fell. 'And now he's back in Brundt, writing what he calls my opera.'

'Does he tell you the subject.' Martha controlled her disappointment.

'No. Too soon, he says.'

'I wonder if Prince Max has hit on a theme.'

'Or whether he'll give it up,' said Cristabel. 'I cannot imagine that his future Uncle Bonaparte would approve. Do you realise that he has not been near us since Minette left?'

'I had noticed,' said Martha drily. 'Understandable enough, surely.'

'Busy with royal duties? I hope he doesn't mean to wash his hands of the Opera House entirely. Signor Franzosi is well enough as a substitute but I doubt he's got the character to make a real company of us. Some of the chorus work in *Clemenza* was deplorable, and did you hear how flat Annius was in her big aria?'

'Poor girl,' said Martha, 'you have to see it was hard on her to know what a fright she looked in her tunic, when you were so admirable in yours. Does Herr Wengel say whether your part in his opera is male or female?'

'No, nothing, wretched man . . . I have it! Next time Franzosi decides to rest us for a day or so, shall we go sightseeing? Go to Brundt and beard the lion in his den? It's crazy only to have made that one short visit to Lissenberg town, not to see a little more of the country before the valley roads get bad. Aunt Helen, do let us go! You know how hard I have been working!'

'It would mean spending at least a night away,' said Lady Helen doubtfully, 'and we could hardly go unescorted.'

'Lodge and Playfair would be happy to do that,' said Martha. 'They were saying yesterday that they wanted to see more of the country, especially Brundt, and the mines there.'

'Not planning to stir up trouble, I hope,' said Lady Helen. 'Frankly, I wonder if we might not be better without their escort,' and then hastily, 'which does not mean I think it a good plan at all, Cristabel. If you really want to talk to Herr Wengel about his opera, I think you should ask him to call on you here.'

'But he won't come.'

'Well, then . . .'

Cristabel returned from rehearsing *Orpheus* a few days later gleaming with pleasure. 'I've news for you, Aunt,' she announced. 'Signor Franzosi has accepted an invitation from the citizens of Brundt. We are to perform for them in their Town Hall, just before Christmas. Will that be respectable enough for you?'

'Prince Gustav does not object?'

'Why should he? And Prince Max is actually going to give us the benefit of his company. I rather think it is intended as some sort of a sop to the good people of Brundt, who pay their taxes and don't see much return for their money. We shall have to stay a week at least, getting things set up in the Town Hall. It will be a real holiday.'

'A working one,' said Martha.

'The best kind. It's just what we need as a company, a challenge to overcome together.'

'What are you going to put on?'

'Ah, that's the question! Franzosi suggested *Clemenza*, but Prince Max seems to be against it.'

'The citizens of Brundt maybe not quite so devoted to their Prince as the courtiers of Lissenberg?' suggested Martha. 'I do look forward to going there.'

In the end, they settled on the *Orpheus* that was already in rehearsal and the whole company set out in the highest spirits, half-way through November. The only disappointment was that, at the last moment, Prince Gustav intervened to prevent Max from accompanying them. 'He's afraid he might make himself too well liked in Brundt,' said Cristabel shrewdly.

'I wouldn't say that even to Lodge or Playfair,' Martha warned her.

Cristabel made a face, 'Lissenberg is turning us all into politicians.'

'Better a live politician than a dead innocent,' said Martha, and then regretted it.

Brundt was a dour, dark, mining town, a striking contrast to Lissenberg's cheerful mix of timbered houses, vineyards and farms. They were lodged comfortably enough in the town's main inn, which had been entirely taken over for them, and stood on the same side of the town square as the hall where they were to perform.

'The people don't like us much, do they?' Cristabel had just returned from the first meeting of the whole troupe in the Town Hall. 'From the sour looks we are getting, I am beginning to wonder whether we will even have an audience. I've never felt myself so disliked before. It's not pleasant.'

'No.' Martha had felt it too when she and Lady Helen had gone out to explore the dark and crowded little town. 'What's that phrase in the Bible, about drawing aside the hem of one's garment? They manage it without actually doing anything. I smiled at a child in the street. Her mother pulled her away as if I were the devil incarnate.'

'Imagining things,' said Lady Helen. 'And better not, don't you think?'

'Imagining?' said Cristabel. 'It wasn't imagination that nothing was ready for us in the Town Hall, as it was supposed to be. The way things are going, it looks as if we are going to have to do everything ourselves. Poor Franzosi is at his wits' end. I can't think why they invited us in the first place.'

'I wonder just who did,' said Martha thoughtfully.

Ishmael Brodski called that afternoon and she greeted him with enthusiasm. 'I can't tell you how glad I am to see you.' Lady Helen had gone with Cristabel to the Town Hall. As moral support? 'I don't much like the feel of things here,' Martha went on. 'Do you think there is any chance that there might be some kind of demonstration against the opera? It would be a complete disaster for Lady Cristabel. She's not experienced enough to face it yet. It could mean the end of her career. What can we do, Herr Brodski? And why did they ask us if they don't want us?'

'No one has told you? I thought probably not.'

'Told us what?'

'Of the swingeing new taxes Prince Gustav has just announced, to pay for his son's wedding. As always, they hit harder here in Brundt than they will in Lissenberg. And will be levied with less mercy. Citizens of Lissenberg can sometimes appeal to Princess Amelia with some hope of success. Here, they have no hope at all. If Prince Gustav thought the opera would sweeten the pill he was far out in his calculations, as he often is when it comes to things here in Brundt. At least he had the wits not to let Prince Maximilian come. That really would have been a disaster.'

'It's bad enough as it is,' said Martha. 'What should we do?'

'What can you do! The singers are in Prince Gustav's pay. They can hardly refuse to perform. The road out is closed, remember. You're all here till spring.'

'Yes.' She shivered. 'And Prince Gustav would stop their pay?'

'Of course, and throw them out of their lodgings.'

'Into the snow?'

'Into the snow. I always believe in facing facts, Miss Peabody. I only wish I could be more help to you, but frankly, I am unpopular enough myself just now. We Jews are always blamed when there is trouble. I just hope I have not made your position worse by coming to see you.' He rose. 'And I should not stay longer. Believe me, Miss Peabody, any help I can give, you can count on.'

'Thank you.' After he left, she moved restlessly to the window, wondering what to do next. As usual, the square was crowded with dark-clad, grim-faced people going dourly about their business, but there seemed to be some kind of disturbance outside the inn. She heard shouts, saw a thickening turbulence in the crowd. Now she watched Brodski try to push his way through a mob that was not yet openly hostile, but might turn so any minute. She held her breath. No way she could intervene; the windows were already double-sealed for winter. Probably as well. She would do more harm than good.

A rare carriage was approaching from the far side of the square. She saw its window go down and a white head emerge.

A woman's head? A black-sleeved arm demanded silence, and, amazingly, got it. The woman uttered a short, sharp sentence, inaudible through the double windows. The crowd was beginning to disperse already; Brodski bowed to the woman in the carriage, received a nod in return, and went on his way, head high, as the carriage rumbled forward and disappeared out of sight through the archway into the inn-yard.

A caller? They were the inn's only occupants. Martha gave a quick look round the room and recognised, for the first time, that it had a slightly neglected look. There was a faint blur of dust on furniture and mirrors, a plant, in a pot, drooping for lack of water. How could she not have noticed? She was moving to fetch water from her bedroom when the door swung open and a scared-looking servant-girl announced 'Frau Schmidt,' bobbed a curtsy, and was about to withdraw, when the white-haired woman behind her said something short and sharp in Liss.

Another, deeper curtsy and the girl scuttled away. 'Forgive me, Fraülein Peabody,' Frau Schmidt smiled and held out her hand. 'You have been ill served here, I am afraid. I took the liberty of speaking to the girl about it. It will not happen again.' She was immensely tall and formidably upright, a valkyrie of fifty-five or so. 'My grandson asked me to call on you,' she went on in her surprisingly fluent English, 'Franz Wengel. He deeply regrets not being here to greet you and your friends.'

Martha's heart sank. 'He is out of the country?'

'Oh, no. He always tries to be home for the winter, my Franz. No, he felt it his duty to go to Lissenberg, to try and make the Prince see reason about these new taxes, about which, I have no doubt, Herr Brodski was telling you.'

'Yes,' said Martha. 'Lucky for him you came along.'

'You saw? I'm afraid there are strong feelings here in Brundt, focused on all the wrong targets as usual. Franz will be furious when he gets back and finds the way you and your companions have been treated. I've told the ringleaders so; I think you will find things go better now.'

'You seem to have a good deal of influence yourself. That was a very ugly situation down there in the square. I do hope there is not going to be trouble at the performance, Frau Schmidt.'

'There won't be,' she said with absolute confidence. 'I've sent for Franz; he'll be back tomorrow to talk some sense into them. But in the meantime I am come to you, Miss Peabody, with a suggestion.'

'Yes?'

'What's needed is a gesture of some kind. You know what public opinion is like, swaying with every breeze. Well, the day before your performance is the festival of Brundt's patron saint. I don't suppose you know about him.'

'I'm afraid not. I'm ashamed to tell you how little I know about Lissenberg altogether. I had rather counted on your grandson . . .'

'Oh, yes, Franz would tell you all right, if he would take the time, but you might as well count on a wave of the sea, Miss Peabody. I don't suppose you even know that Brundt is the old capital of Lissenberg. It's named after St. Brandt who is buried in the cathedral-church here and used to work all kinds of miracles until this age of enlightenment they talk of put him out of commission. Franz could tell you about him, but what you need to know now is that there is always a sung service in his honour on his day. A procession first, of course. They take him through the town and then bring him home with a triumphal mass. If Lady Cristabel would agree to sing in that I think you would find it did the trick.'

'But, Frau Schmidt . . .' Hesitating, 'I'm only an ignorant Protestant, but I thought women couldn't sing in your churches.'

'You really don't know anything about Lissenberg, do you? Well, why should you? I don't pretend to know much about your United States. We're a very independent lot, we Lissenbergers. Women and men have always been treated as equals here. Until Prince Gustav bought us.' For the first time her tone was bitter. 'He would have none of that "nonsense". We women have been back in our "place", as he calls it, since he took over. It hasn't made him much loved. But he hasn't tried to interfere in the Church. We have always had women in our choirs, always will I hope. Just as we have always refused to have castrati. So, if Lady Cristabel will sing at our sacred occasion, I think she can be sure of her audience at the profane one.'

'I'm sure she would want to anyway, but, Frau Schmidt, Prince Gustav . . . ? Herr Brodski was pointing out to me how totally we are in his power.'

'Useful to remember. But he has never tampered with the Church. I do not see what objection he could possibly make, though it would doubtless be wise to make a formal request for his permission.' She rose. 'Franz told me I would like you, Miss Peabody, and he was right as usual. You smile?'

'He told me he would like me to meet you. Now I think I understand why. But, Frau Schmidt, I have given you nothing, no wine, no cake . . .'

'I told the girl not to interrupt us. You may entertain me another day, Miss Peabody, when there is less to do.'

'Now you sound like your grandson.'

'I should be happy to think he resembled me in some ways.'

'Of course I'll sing for them,' Cristabel greeted the suggestion with enthusiasm. 'And Herr Wengel will be back tomorrow? That's good. He'll tell me how to go on. It will make the rehearsal schedule quite tight, mind you, but luckily we had *Orpheus* as good as ready, and now we are getting some co-operation in the Town Hall it should all go well enough. Frau Schmidt must be a powerful old lady, I long to meet her.'

'I long to know more about her,' said Martha.

Her wish was granted when Lodge and Playfair called that afternoon. They had come to Brundt for the opera and had already heard that Cristabel was also to sing in the cathedral-church.

'News travels fast in Lissenberg,' said Lodge. 'I hear you have met the formidable Frau Schmidt, Miss Peabody, the uncrowned queen of Brundt. You did not know she was called that?'

'No, but I can well believe it. A formidable lady indeed. But "uncrowned queen", Mr. Lodge?'

'She belongs to the family that ruled Lissenberg before Prince Gustav bought his way in. It had dwindled into females only, you understand, and a great many of them, so there was no specific claim. Gustav's first wife was another of them, with no better, and not much worse, a claim than hers. So, with a vast deal of money passed in bribes to the Emperor, and some fine talk of the Salic law, and women not succeeding, Gustav had it. A bad day for Lissenberg, but for God's sake don't tell anyone I said so, Miss Peabody.'

8

'Of course I wrote it.' Franz Wengel looked older, Martha thought, the mouth showing firmer than ever under the luxuriant beard, the eyes heavily shadowed. 'I've written the Brandt Oratorio every year since I came home from Heidelberg. I'm glad you like it, Lady Cristabel.'

'Like it! It's tremendous. I'm proud to have the chance to sing in it.' She had been practising in her room when he was announced and had hurried in to greet him like an old friend. 'And my opera?' she asked now, 'am I to see it at last, Herr Wengel?'

'Not yet, I am afraid. Prince Gustav has decided that he must see the libretti first. Give them his preliminary approval.'

'But that's outrageous,' protested Martha.

He turned to her smiling. 'Just old-fashioned. He fancies himself as another Sun King. Louis XIV always saw his man Lully's texts,' he explained. 'And changed them too, when he felt like it. And Lully took it like the state servant he was. It may be partly why we don't find his operas very interesting today.'

'They do stick to safe subjects,' agreed Cristabel. 'But yours, Herr Wengel, will Prince Gustav approve of yours?'

'I'm doing a little rewriting, just to be on the safe side. But my subject is unexceptionable enough.'

'What is your subject?' Cristabel was in tremendous looks today, Martha thought.

'It's one of the early adventures of our patron saint, Brandt, whose oratorio you are to sing, Lady Cristabel. There is a whole mythology attached to him, absolutely fascinating. Modern scholars think he probably was an illegitimate son of Charlemagne, as is claimed for him, but he picked up all kinds of other legends on his way to sainthood.'

'A saint! I'm not to sing him, I do hope.'

'You do not see yourself as a saint? No, Brandt is a tenor

rôle. You are to be his wife, the Princess Algisa, who followed her husband on his crusade, disguised as a page. Unfortunately her disguise was too successful. He never recognised her, so when he got home and found she had been absent, he accused her of unfaithfulness. She went through the ordeal of red-hot ploughshares and triumphantly proved her innocence. It's all there, carved on their tomb, in the cathedral-church. You've not been to see it?'

'Not yet,' said Martha. 'Frankly, the atmosphere here has not been conducive to sightseeing. Not till your splendid grandmother came to our rescue. What did St. Brandt get canonised for, Herr Wengel? Going on the crusade?'

'Among other things. His wife was canonised too, so I'm afraid you are to be a saint after all, Lady Cristabel. But not a martyr,' he added, as if in extenuation.

'That's something.' Smiling at him. 'So the part is half breeches, half petticoat, is it?'

'Yes. The second act takes place outside the walls of Jerusalem, with the devoted page, Algisa, saving her husband's life, which she naturally did several times.'

'Brandt is one of Charlemagne's twelve peers, is he?' asked Martha.

'You know the story?' He turned to her eagerly. 'Yes, I thought I'd stretch a point and make him one. He must be a gallant knight as well as a saint, or I doubt Prince Gustav would approve.'

'Was he?' she asked.

'Who knows?' Shrugging. 'It's all myth, really, but he must have done something outstanding, simply to be remembered.'

'I suppose so.' Why did she feel he was not quite answering her? 'How soon will your text be ready for Prince Gustav?'

'That's a problem. The friend I had counted on to fair copy it for me is ill and I am at my wits' end to find a substitute. It must be perfect, or Prince Gustav won't even look at it, and we aren't much in the calligraphic line here in Brundt.'

'I could do it for you,' said Martha, then laughed at his expression of polite doubt. 'My father was a stickler for good handwriting,' she told him. 'He had me taught by an expert and watched my progress week by week. No fair copy, no pin-money. There is nothing like the economic argument after all.'

'I can tell that you haven't seen Miss Peabody's handwriting.' Lady Helen was getting a little anxious about the way Cristabel hung on the young man's words. 'If I were you, Herr Wengel, I would accept her offer with the enthusiasm it deserves. Look,' she delved in her pocket book to produce a sheet of paper, 'it's a favourite of mine among Mr. Cowper's poems. I asked Miss Peabody to copy it for me the other day.'

He took one look, turned eagerly to Martha. 'I ask you a thousand pardons. But, could you really spare the time? It is no light task, I am afraid, and my own handwriting is nothing to boast about.'

'I shall enjoy it. Lady Helen is an expert decipherer of crossed letters; she will help me if I am at a stand. To tell you the truth, I am finding that time here in Brundt hangs a little heavy on my hands. Maddening to be without occupation while Lady Cristabel is working so hard.'

'Lucky for me.' He rose. 'I'll go home and fetch the first act at once. I have not found it necessary to make any changes in it, but unfortunately my friend was waiting to fair copy it as a whole.'

'Then I had certainly better get started,' said Martha. 'There is a date to be met?'

'Before Christmas. Do you think . . .'

'Of course.'

Martha was not surprised to find Franz Wengel and Frau Schmidt in the little group of dignitaries who greeted their party when they arrived at the cathedral for the Brundt Oratorio. If she was disappointed to find herself sitting next to the grandmother, not the grandson, she still found the old lady a lively companion. They were deep in an amicable difference about the works of Madame de Staël when the first notes of the organ hushed the great church.

'But it's –' When it was over, she turned to her companion, hesitated, then said, 'It's a work of genius!'

'I think so,' Frau Schmidt smiled at her very kindly. 'If he would only take more trouble, more time. There were imperfections, you must have noticed them; Lady Cristabel most certainly will have. If you can contrive to persuade him to throw his whole heart into this opera of his, you will be doing me a kindness – and him too.'

'Can one persuade Herr Wengel of anything?'

'Absolutely not.' The bright eyes snapped with pleasure. 'You have seen that so soon, Miss Peabody? I'm glad. Have you been inspired to mention the discovery to your friend?'

'Lady Cristabel?' But the congregation had risen and there was no more chance for talk. Passing along the crowded aisle, Martha was aware, as she had been all day, of a total change in the atmosphere. Two days ago, she had felt herself an object almost of hatred, now, following Frau Schmidt, she knew that the wave of affection, the friendly bobs and curtsies, were for Lady Helen and herself, as well as for the splendid old lady.

Cristabel was waiting for them in the great carved porch of the church with Franz at her side. She glowed with pleasure as she received the congratulations that could not be expressed in applause. Wengel, too, looked almost relaxed, almost happy. The first time she had seen him so, Martha thought, and it suited him. The lines that usually made him seem older than he was, had smoothed from his face; he was suddenly human, laughing, shaking hands with friends, presenting them to Cristabel, insisting that all the credit was hers.

'Just wait till you hear her as Orpheus tomorrow,' he told his grandmother, who had swept up to kiss him on both cheeks.

'Herr Gluck's great music,' she said. 'A great man who devoted his life to his work.'

'A very fortunate man.' He turned to Martha. 'We should all be thanking you, Miss Peabody, for recognising our prima donna when you heard her, for making today possible.'

'Why, thank you.' How strange to find herself so close to tears.

'And how does the copying go?' His next question brought her back to herself with a jerk.

'Slowly! You told me your writing was not good, Herr Wengel, you did not tell me it was a mad mousetrack! But we are doing our best, Lady Helen and I. You will have your fair copy in time.' But he had already had to turn away to greet a new wave of enthusiasts.

For Martha, Gluck's *Orpheus* came almost as an anti-climax after the passion of the oratorio. Could she really prefer Wengel's music to Gluck's? She had wanted to suggest to

98

Frau Schmidt that what she criticised as imperfections in her grandson's work were, in fact, rather innovations, a little in the style of that fierce, young, modern composer, Ludwig van Beethoven, whose difficult work she had occasionally heard in Venice.

It was Cristabel's evening. From the moment when the curtain rose to reveal her kneeling by her lost love's grave, she held her audience spellbound, and at the end she accepted their ovation with the calm dignity of one who knew she had earned it. Afterwards, moving among the dignitaries of Brundt, she had exactly the right touch with everyone.

'She will go far,' Playfair told Martha, watching her.

'A pity there is no one here from the outside world but us,' said Lodge. 'Do you realise, Miss Peabody, that no one will even hear about her amazing début until the roads are open again in the spring?'

'Good gracious! I never thought. There is absolutely no communication?'

'Nothing. I believe that when Prince Gustav first took over, he tried to install some simple kind of telegraph system: signals from hill to hill; you must have something of the kind in England?'

'Yes. But we don't have such mountains.'

'Exactly. It was no good. You had best write a full description of this brilliant evening in your diary, Miss Peabody, for use in the spring.'

'It would be more to the point if you were to do so, Mr. Lodge. As an independent witness, what you say will carry much more weight.'

'But I don't keep a diary, and if you do, Miss Peabody, I hope you are a little careful about what you write in it.'

Here was another disconcerting thought, made more so by her suspicion that he had deliberately led the conversation to where he could deliver the casual-seeming warning. 'I'm too busy with Herr Wengel's libretto to write anything else at the moment,' she told him.

'The Gest of Saint Brandt? A very clever choice, they are backing him heavily in the town.'

'Well, they would, wouldn't they,' said Playfair. 'Besides, where's the competition, now the roads are closed?'

*　　*　　*

99

Martha was less confident about Wengel's opera. He had brought her the revised second half that afternoon and she had read it through as quickly as the appalling handwriting had allowed, so as to ask him about any sticking-points before she left. Reaching the end, she was aware of a feeling of disappointment. Something was lacking; hard to tell what. Algisa's part struck her as immensely promising but Brandt himself remained a shadowy figure, with not quite enough to do aside from being unreasonably jealous of his wife, an unendearing trait in a future saint, who should, she felt, have known better. But, of course, it was absurd to criticise words without music. And, besides, she knew she had been put off by the laudatory prologue which drew a parallel between St. Brandt, saviour of his country, and Prince Gustav. 'You won't like it,' Wengel had told her, 'but believe me, it's essential.'

'Do you think Prince Max will manage one?' She was talking to Lady Helen and Cristabel later.

'I imagine he will have to,' said Lady Helen.

'I doubt it will carry conviction.'

'Then he won't win the contest.'

'I don't know,' said Martha. 'Didn't it strike you the other night, Cristabel, that Herr Wengel's music was quite daring? Quite innovative? Do we know who the judges are to be?'

'Prince Gustav for one,' Cristabel made a wry face, 'and Paisiello and Salieri are his favourite composers.'

It was raining when they left Brundt next morning and only a few well-wishers turned out to see them go. Franz Wengel was not among them and Martha, concealing her own disappointment, could only sympathise with Cristabel's.

'Uncivil,' said Lady Helen forthrightly. 'I would have thought his grandmother would have taught him better manners.'

It rained steadily all the way, casting a further gloom on the rather quiet little party, and when the road began to rise towards Lissenberg town, Lodge, who was riding beside the coach tapped on the window. 'It looks like snow ahead. A fortunate thing we made an early start.'

Princess Amelia came to see them the day after they got back. 'The last time I'll be able to come in the carriage, I'm afraid.' She had shed snow-dappled furs in the ante-room. 'To tell the truth, I never much liked the tunnel, though goodness knows how we'd manage without it! Not so bad when it's illuminated for the Prince's formal progress to the theatre, but I don't much like it on my own with only a torch-bearer. Will you be very kind, Lady Helen, and come to me when the road is blocked?'

'Of course I shall.' Lady Helen had grown very fond of the quiet, badgered Princess. 'You should have sent for me today.'

'Oh, no. I enjoy the drive! It's quite a treat for me, to get away from the Palace.' And then, hurriedly, aware of having said too much. 'Where are your charming young ladies today?'

'Lady Cristabel is rehearsing next week's opera, and I believe Miss Peabody went to advise her about something.'

'That's a formidable young lady.'

'She should have been a man. I worry about her sometimes . . .' She too felt she had said more than she intended and changed the subject. 'I was sorry not to see you in Brundt.'

'Oh, we never go to Brundt. The castle there has been let fall to ruins – not a castle, really, just a big house. The Prince has always disliked the place.' She always called her husband 'the Prince'. 'I did try to persuade him that it's time the people there saw little Gustav. Now he is stronger, he should be going about more, but the Prince won't have it. I'm afraid he still thinks he is backward because he does not take easily to riding and sport. Time enough to go to Brundt, the Prince said, when he could ride there on his own pony. And I did so long to hear your niece sing in the Brandt Oratorio. I hear it was quite outstanding this year, and long to meet that young Franz Wengel. He sounds a most unusual young man. He is putting in an entry for the opera competition, I understand.'

'Yes. We have quite a stake in it,' said Lady Helen, 'since Miss Peabody has undertaken to copy it for him. Have there been many libretti submitted?' She had hoped for the chance to ask the question.

'Two or three, I think, before the roads were closed. I know the Prince was disappointed, and angry, that there were not more.' She smiled and Lady Helen thought what a charming girl she must have been. 'It's a great state secret, but my stepson is busy writing a libretto for anonymous submission. I think the Prince may be glad to have it, just to swell the numbers.'

'He knows about it?'

'Lady Helen, you should always assume that the Prince knows everything that goes on in Lissenberg.'

'Never forget that.' Lady Helen was telling the two girls about the Princess's visit.

'No.' Cristabel, who had come in glowing from a successful rehearsal, now looked quenched, subdued. 'Poor Max, so his father knows about it . . . What does that make his chance worth?'

'I don't know,' said Martha, thoughtfully. 'If the Prince really wants Prince Max out of the way, might this not be a means of downclassing him a little?'

'Oh, no.' Cristabel was firm. 'The Emperor Leopold used to write opera, remember.'

'A Holy Roman Emperor can do almost anything he pleases. And I doubt he ever won a competition. Something just a little vulgar about that, don't you think? Is there to be a prize, by the way?'

'Just production of the opera, I believe. How are you getting on with your copying, Martha, and when may I read *Crusader Prince*?'

'I think I shall finish tomorrow. In fact, I must, as I've sent a message to Herr Wengel to tell him so. But, Cristabel, he did say no one was to see it.'

'He can't have meant me!'

'I promised him. I'm sorry; I should have asked about you, but you know what his visits are like; he's come and gone before you know what's happening.'

'But I'm to sing in it!'

'If it wins. Cristabel, it may be one of the terms of the competition, that no one is to see it before the Prince does.'

'Max would let me see his!' Cristabel was angry now, her colour high. 'He knows that my advice might be useful. I do know something about opera after all.'

'Of course you do! That may be why Herr Wengel is nervous. It's quite an undertaking to write both libretto and music. He may be unsure of himself, not ready yet for criticism.'

'Herr Wengel, unsure of himself! Don't be ridiculous.'

'When he comes for the fair copy, I promise I'll ask if you may see the original.'

'I'll see to it that I'm here to ask him myself,' said Cristabel.

But it was Ishmael Brodski who arrived to collect the fair copy. 'I have business with Prince Gustav,' he told Martha. 'And undertook the commission for Herr Wengel. He asks me to thank you a thousand times, and begs you to forgive him for not coming in person.'

'We might have known he would not.' Cristabel was angry, and Martha could hardly blame her.

The snow came early that year. It fell quietly, persistently, all through December, piling up in great drifts on either side of the narrow track that was kept open, with difficulty, down to the town of Lissenberg. Supplies for the Palace were brought up by cart as far as the opera buildings, then transferred laboriously to huge baskets for cartage up the tunnel to the castle.

'It's women who carry the baskets!' Martha and Lady Helen were watching the loading from the window.

'Yes, the Princess told me. She doesn't much like it, but they have always been the burden-bearers here in Lissenberg. It's not thought fit work for men, and, she says, women are only too glad to get the extra winter wage it brings in.'

'It can't be good for them. Look, there's one with a child at her skirts. And they all look starved and cold. Do they live up here, do you know?'

'No, they come up on the first cart of the morning; work all day; go home at night. Only two days a week, mind you. The tunnel is kept clear for the Prince and his guests the rest of the time.'

'It must be a long day. I wonder what they get to eat.'

Martha had not penetrated into the rear quadrangle of the opera complex where the servants lived and worked, having felt at first that she was very far from welcome there. But things had changed since their visit to Brundt. Maids encountered in passages now smiled shyly as they curtsied; there was a friendly informality about the menservants' bobs. Emboldened by this, she went down now to the ground floor and pushed her way through the heavy swinging-door that divided masters' from servants' quarters.

The air struck chill. The change was extraordinary. Bare

walls gleamed damp in the light of flares, stuck in sockets on the wall. No daylight. Of course, she worked it out, the whole complex had been built into the side of the hill. The gentry quarters were on the lower side, with daylight, servants worked without windows.

More light ahead and the sound of women's voices. Walking carefully over the roughly flagged floor, she came to an archway opening on to a room below. Stone steps led down, but she paused for a moment in the entrance. It was noon and the women basket-bearers, who had started at first light, were eating their mid-day meal huddled around a huge fire that burned in the centre of the room, its smoke, or at least some of it, escaping through a hole in the ceiling. The air was heavy with this smoke and the smell of damp clothing, but something was missing. There was no smell of food. Used now to the half-light, she could see that the women were eating individually, out of little bundles they had brought with them. Some had no bundles and were sitting listlessly, gazing into the fire, if they had been so lucky as to get near it. Where Martha stood, it was ice cold, and damp.

'Fräulein Peabody, what are you doing here?' One of the maids had appeared from a doorway further down the corridor and was looking at her in amazement. 'Did you get lost?'

'Not precisely. But, tell me, are they given nothing hot, these poor women?'

'They are given nothing, Fräulein. Lucky to get the work! My mother is down there, with my little brother. Promise not to tell on me, Fräulein, I was bringing her this.' Martha now saw that she was carrying a steaming flagon wrapped in a cloth. 'The trouble is to get it to her without the others noticing.'

'She'd get mobbed? I'll help you. I'll go down first, ask some silly questions. You come quietly after.'

'Thank you, Fräulein. It's her first year, you see, since my father died. She's not used to it.'

'Nor should she be! It's wicked. But we must lose no time.' Martha moved forward and down the slippery flight of stone steps. 'What in the world is going on here?' she asked, in her American-German.

'We're eating our lunch, Fräulein.' A woman came towards her from close to the fire. 'And not much time to do it in.' She spoke with the flat civility of exhaustion. 'The bell will ring any minute now.' She had packed up her diminished bundle, now tucked it into a capacious pocket of her ragged dress.

'Take this.' Martha reached into her own pocket for her purse, wishing there was more in it. 'Share it among you. Something for tomorrow. I'm sorry it's so little. May I come again?'

'And with a blessing.' The woman seized the purse. A bell clanged and frantic activity broke out. Children cried as their mothers formed hurriedly into line. 'First come, first basket and first to go home.' The woman gave Martha a ghost of a smile and moved away to take her place in the line.

'Thank you Fräulein, they had it all.' The maid was waiting for Martha by the steps.

'So quickly? But it's monstrous. They should all have hot soup. They shouldn't be doing this work at all.'

'Someone has to.'

What could she say? 'I must think about this. Come to me this evening – it's Anna, isn't it?'

'Fancy your knowing,' said the girl.

'Yes, I agree it is entirely monstrous,' Lady Helen had listened to Martha's explosive report of what she had found. 'But you must be careful what you do, my dear. This isn't your United States of America, you know.'

'I should just about think it isn't,' said Martha angrily. And then, more soberly. 'But you're right, of course. No use going at it like a bat at a brick wall, as my father would say. Lady Helen, may I come with you next time you call on the Princess?'

9

The Princess received them alone and listened in grey silence to Martha's story. Then she sighed, and said, 'I know. It's wretched. I was as shocked as you when I first came here and heard about those poor women. But I had no idea their conditions were as frightful as you say. I'm ashamed not to have found out.' She looked from Martha to Lady Helen. 'No need to tell you how little influence I have now.'

'You are the mother of the heir,' said forthright Martha, shocking Lady Helen.

'I'm not even sure about that any more. This engagement of Prince Max's may change everything. I've never been told what the terms of the agreement with Bonaparte are, but sometimes I see the Prince looking at little Gustav as if . . . as if he disliked him. It's not the child's fault he's afraid of his father. The Prince has always been so rough with him.' She was crying now, suddenly pouring out her troubles. 'I thought everything would be better after he was born, but it's not, it's worse. Before, I had only myself to worry about, now, there's little Gustav.' She looked from one of them to the other. 'I've put my life in your hands.'

'Hardly that, surely.' Lady Helen was shocked all over again.

'You don't know, nor do I. I can't have another child: the Prince hasn't been near me since the doctors told him that. Once or twice I saw him looking at Minette de Beauharnais as if he was thinking, wondering . . . Why am I telling you this?'

'Because you need to,' Lady Helen told her, 'and because you know it is entirely safe with us. You have no one here in the Palace that you can trust?'

'Not since the Prince sent my ladies back to Baden. Long ago. Oh – I trust Max entirely. But he's a man. And the Lissenbergers don't like me, and I hardly blame them. I've been so useless, so inadequate. I sometimes wish the Prince would get rid of me; send Gustav and me home to Baden.'

'Don't think like that.' Lady Helen frowned at her. 'Defeatist thinking. You have your son's future to think of, Highness.' Did she use the title on purpose? 'And your duty to your family and to both your countries, Lissenberg and Baden. A public rift between you and the Prince might so easily mean trouble between the two states . . . Just the kind of thing Bonaparte wants. We all know how swift he is to take advantage. I'm talking too much!' She rose. 'Forgive me. Our attendants will be waiting to light us down the tunnel. You may count on our absolute discretion, Highness.'

'I am sure of it.' Was there a shine of tears in the Princess's tired blue eyes? 'And come again next week?'

'If you wish me to.'

'Both of you. Please. I am so very sorry about those poor women, Miss Peabody, but you do understand, don't you?'

'Of course I do.' Warmly. 'I'm only sorry I brought it up, to distress you. If there was ever anything I could do –' She had been angered by Lady Helen's reproof, the hint of a drawing aside of skirts. For the first time, she felt herself and the Princess as the younger generation, together against the disapproving old.

'Thank you.' As Martha began her unpractised curtsy, the Princess surprised her with a quick, shy kiss. 'I'll remember that.'

They went down the long tunnel in silence. With torch-bearers in front and behind, the need for discretion was absolute, but Martha did not much want to talk.

'Will you do something for me, Cristabel?' There had been a hint of coolness between the two girls since Martha had refused to let Cristabel read *Crusader Prince*.

'If I can.' Cristabel was trying on the scarlet tunic she was to wear for the Christmas performance of Mozart's *Il Re Pastore*.

'Those poor women. I can't get them out of my mind. The Princess says it would be of no use her speaking to her husband, and I believe her. But if you were to say something, when he congratulates you on your performance as the shepherd-king – he's bound to be feeling pleased, the flattery in that opera is laid on with a trowel – could you say something then about your crazy friend who wants to pay for a soup-kitchen for the women porters? I truly think he might listen to you.'

'You don't think speaking to Prince Max would be better?'

'What use would that be? Besides, we see him so seldom.'

'He's been coming to rehearsals again.' (Was Cristabel blushing?) 'He says he wants the Christmas performance to be a tremendous success. He's got us all working like maniacs, and as for the orchestra, he says they are as important as us singers in this one!'

'What does Franzosi think about all this?'

'Oh, such a good man! He's delighted; says he had no idea that early opera of Mozart's could be made so interesting; thinks Prince Gustav is bound to be impressed. And I'm sure he will give all the credit to Prince Max – I could ask him to approach his father then.'

'You don't want to do it yourself,' Martha went to the heart of the matter.

'Martha, you have to understand. It's a difficult part for me – it's always hard taking on the ones written for castrati – and Mozart is something special. I have to think about nothing else; I can't get involved in your politics.'

'Politics? Some poor, cold, hungry women?' And then, seeing she had hurt her friend. 'I'm sorry, Belle, forget I said it. You concentrate on your music! I'm a fine one to suggest anything else, am I not? I'll find some other way.'

The conversation left her with a good deal to think about. Prince Max was coming to rehearsals again and Cristabel had not thought fit to mention it. Enormously tempted to drop in on a rehearsal herself, she did not do so and was glad to be at home when an unexpected caller was announced.

'I thought I'd come to see you before the snow got any deeper,' Frau Schmidt greeted her like an old friend. 'That bad grandson of mine has been urging me to do so. He sends his regards and his thanks all over again for your great kindness. I'm afraid you must have thought him very uncivil not to come himself and collect his manuscript. It's the Palace he keeps away from, you know. He has a very profound detestation for protocol, poor boy. Frankly, I'm always terrified he'll lose his temper, say something he shouldn't, so I do urge him to keep away.'

'He has a temper, Herr Wengel?'

'Be glad you haven't encountered it. There were times, when he was a boy, that I was frightened for him. Bullying at school, the kind of casual cruelties you see every day in the street, he would fly out, say anything, do anything. Many's the time I've had to talk him out of trouble.'

'I know how he feels,' said Martha. 'You're just the person I need to talk to, Frau Schmidt.' She poured out the story of the women porters. 'I so badly want to help them,' she concluded, 'but, like your grandson, I have learned to control myself a little. I do see that I can't do anything for them without the Prince's permission, but how do I set about getting it?'

'The Christmas gift,' said the old lady at once, 'I'm surprised the Princess didn't suggest it, but she has troubles of her own, poor lady.'

'The Christmas gift?'

'You've not heard of it, why should you? It's an old Lissenberg custom, going back long before Prince Gustav bought us. After the Christmas performance, the Prince holds court for his subjects. It used to happen up at the castle. In the old days, everyone was welcome up there, the tunnel was open to all, and the theatre was within the castle wall. Tiny, of course, only room for the royal circle, but when the performance was over they all went outside and the Prince mounted a covered dais and held court. It was the time for petitions, things people didn't dare ask in the ordinary way, and traditionally, he granted one unusual request: the Christmas gift. Lives have been saved that way, unlikely marriages made, taxes forgiven. So far as I know, there's nothing of great significance likely to come up this year. I think you might have a very good chance, if you made your request then. He'd be having it both ways, wouldn't he? Being good to a foreigner, and getting his workers fed for nothing. And naturally it would be very popular in town.' She rose. 'I must be down the hill before dark. I think if I put the word around you will be safe from competition. I'll get my cousin Anna to explain the routine to you. She thinks the world of you, Miss Peabody.'

'Anna's your cousin?'

'We're all cousins, here in Lissenberg.'

'Except Prince Gustav?'

'Acute of you.'

'And Prince Max? Don't tell me his mother was a cousin of yours too?'

'Naturally. Goodbye, Miss Peabody. And God bless you.'

Prince Gustav did not approve of open-air ceremonies in mid-winter. After the curtain had fallen for the last time on *Il Re Pastore* and the roar of applause had died away, flunkeys hurried to clear the stage and set up what Martha thought a rather theatrical-looking throne. As the royal party moved up to take its places, the gilded chairs they had sat on were hurriedly removed from the auditorium to make room for a silent crowd of Lissenbergers who had not found room in the gallery, and had been waiting outside all through the performance.

'Poor things, they look frozen. No wonder they choose a short opera for this occasion,' said Martha as a flunkey ushered her and Lady Helen forward to the few remaining chairs at the front of the house.

Lodge and Playfair came to sit beside them. 'I wouldn't have missed this for the world,' said Lodge. 'Quite aside from Lady Cristabel's singing, which is more brilliant every time I hear her, I understand this is the one time in the year that the Prince actually meets his "devoted" subjects.'

He was speaking in English, but Martha flashed him a warning look, more for his tone than his words. 'A fine old Lissenberg tradition, I believe.'

'Quite so. Ah, here comes Lady Cristabel.' He held a chair for her. 'I cannot begin to congratulate you.'

'Thank you.' She was always exhausted after a performance, but today she looked drained, blanched.

'Hard work holding an audience like that?' Lodge recognised this and turned back to Martha. 'Tell me about this Lissenberg tradition, Miss Peabody.'

'Later!' The small orchestra had struck up the Lissenberg national song and those of the audience who had chairs had risen to their feet to sing it. Martha hoped that she was the only person who noticed that Cristabel did not join in.

The long ceremony unrolled as Anna had described it. Oaths of allegiance, Max looking white and tense, little Gustav looking terrified, the rest of the court concealing boredom under sycophancy. Then Prince Gustav's loving speech to his people, all rolling periods and empty phrases. He told them of Prince Maximilian's forthcoming alliance with the niece of the great liberator Bonaparte, and got something between a gasp and a sigh from his audience. Martha, rigid with tension herself, felt Cristabel beginning to shake beside her and put a steadying hand on hers. Something was terribly wrong.

Prince Gustav had finished. Trumpets sounded a fanfare. The Court Chamberlain stepped forward to announce that the time had come for the Christmas gift. Anna had warned Martha that the actual announcement would be in Liss, but the gist of it was that anyone who had a boon to beg must now come forward. She stood up, took a step forward and was aware that nobody else had moved.

'A stranger asks the gift, Highness.' The Chamberlain turned to Prince Gustav and spoke in German.

'Let the stranger come forward, since it seems our beloved Lissenbergers are content with their lot.' Anna had told her that Prince Gustav did not speak Liss, so she would be able to understand him. The audience did too; she felt a kind of frisson when he spoke of their contentment and wondered whether he was aware of it. But she was being helped up the improvised steps to the stage by another flunkey. She had never felt plainer, dumpier, less sure of herself. 'Breathe deeply,' Cristabel had said, their rôles reversed for once. 'Take your time. Speak slowly. No fear of losing your audience.'

She breathed, curtsied to the Prince, who had stood to receive her, saw Prince Max's anxious face behind his father's shoulder, and spoke her piece. As she made her offer of a hot meal for the women porters every day they worked, she realised, for the first time, just what an affront the Prince might feel it to be. She was telling an absolute monarch how absolutely he had failed his subjects. Where are the dungeons in Lissenberg, she thought wildly, bringing her short, well-prepared speech to a close? There were doors here and there off the tunnel. Torch-bearers hurried past them. Dungeons there, in the cold, and dark, and damp? And no news to the outside world till spring.

She had finished. The Prince was looking at her coldly, thoughtfully. Behind him, Prince Max made an infinitesimal move. The crowd in the theatre began to sing, in a whisper, the Lissenberg national song again.

Prince Gustav relaxed into a smile. 'My loving subjects have spoken for me, Miss Peabody. We accept your generous offer and are only sad that it has been necessary for you, a stranger in our midst, to tell us about the plight of these poor women. This must be looked into.' A glance for the Chamberlain. 'Now,' he held out his hand. 'It is my privilege to take you to supper, Miss Peabody, as winner of the gift.'

Anna had warned her about this too. 'If he decides to treat you as a commoner,' she had explained, 'you will be given supper by the Chamberlain. It's hard to tell . . .'

Martha had known exactly what she meant, but had bet with herself that her money would put her above the salt. She had dressed for the possible occasion, and had been proved right. The diamonds had, in fact, been Salomon Rothschild's suggestion. A Venetian lady had had to sell them to fund her retreat from the city and he had got them for Martha at a price he described as 'making everyone happy'. 'They will act both as your passport in Lissenberg Society and your insurance policy if you should need to leave in a hurry.'

'Like the poor Venetian lady?'

'Precisely.'

Today, she felt comfortably invisible behind their glitter and was able to return Prince Gustav's polite nothings in the detached spirit in which they were offered. They would get through the rest of the evening well enough, and she was happy to have won her point. Tomorrow she would arrange a trip to Brundt to buy kitchen equipment. Should she ask Franz Wengel to help her?

The Prince had turned to his other neighbour and she was free for Prince Max who had been quiet beside her. Beyond him Cristabel was pushing food about her silver plate. Musicians were playing in the gallery above.

She had not seen Max for some time, and now realised with a stab of surprise that he looked even worse than Cristabel. There had always been a kind of glow about Max, the burnished look of one who may have known anxiety but has never known discomfort. Now he was sallow with fatigue and – something else? Despair?

She racked her brains for a safe subject. 'When are we to hear if the libretti have been approved?'

'Some time in the New Year, I believe. The Prince has been

very much occupied with affairs of state.' Like his stepmother, Prince Max now always referred to his father as 'the Prince'. 'You picked a lucky day for your request.' He did not explain why, plunging instead into a series of extremely knowledgeable questions about her plans for her soup-kitchen. 'You'll need to go to Brundt for the equipment, of course. Be sure you wait until the roads are hard-frozen and you can do it by sledge. You will find it an interesting experience, I am sure, if you dress warmly enough. Will Lady Cristabel go with you?'

'I most certainly shall.' Cristabel had stopped pretending to eat. She had turned a shoulder to her other neighbour and was unashamedly listening. 'Can we hope for your escort, Prince?' She used the title, Martha thought, as if it had been his Christian name.

'Ah, if I only could. But, should you, Lady Cristabel? Your voice . . . It will be ferociously cold.'

'Oh, my voice! That's all I am to any of you! A voice.' She turned ostentatiously back to the neighbour she had been neglecting.

'What in the world is the matter with everyone?' asked Lady Helen next day. 'The poor Princess looked like death last night, and so did Prince Max. And Cristabel has gone off to rehearsal without eating any breakfast.'

'Oh, dear, has she?' For once Martha had slept late, after a night spent dreaming of dungeons. 'Yes, I did think Prince Max looked wretched. I'm afraid I didn't notice Princess Amelia. One does tend not to. But the Prince himself seemed in good enough spirits.'

'Not necessarily a good sign,' said Lady Helen. 'Tell me, Martha, do you sometimes wonder if we were wise to come here?'

Martha moved to the door and made sure it was shut. 'Frankly, yes. I was afraid last night. I'm ashamed to tell you, but I was actually afraid of what might happen when I made my request.'

'And in fact, the Prince seemed pleased,' said Lady Helen thoughtfully.

'Prince Max said I had picked a lucky day for my petition. I wonder what he meant.'

'It's frightening to know so absolutely nothing about what

is really going on,' said Lady Helen. 'Whatever we do, Martha, let's not plan to spend another winter cut off here in Lissenberg.'

'No, indeed. I wish I knew what was the matter with Cristabel.'

10

Prince Gustav did not give orders for another opera during the Christmas festivities, and neither did he invite the three ladies up to the castle for any of the merrymaking there. Instead, the company were to give a New Year's Day performance for the citizens of Lissenberg. Signor Franzosi had written *The Bride Confused* for the occasion.

'The rascally lover is a marvellous part for me,' said Cristabel. 'But it's sad enough stuff otherwise. Just as well the royal party do not mean to honour us with their presence.'

'Not even Prince Max?' asked Martha.

'Especially not Prince Max.' Something in her tone drew a quick look from Martha.

'Cristabel, what's the matter?'

'Nothing! Everything. Oh, Martha, sometimes I wish I was dead.'

'That's wicked.'

'I know. I can't help it. What am I going to do? I love him! And I can't help that either. Not his fault. He didn't mean it to happen. Or want it to! He only touched me on the shoulder; he was showing me how to move; when we were rehearsing.' It came out in a series of hiccups. 'It was like catching fire, Martha. No, like freezing. I don't know what it was like . . . The end of the world . . . Well, the end of me.'

'Cristabel! But . . . what about him?'

'I doubt he even noticed. It was the last rehearsal for *Il Re Pastore*. You remember what it was like, up at the castle, afterwards. He talked to you mostly.'

'He's engaged to be married, Cristabel.'

'Of course he is! To Minette de Beauharnais who always knew her uncle would make a good match for her. Not an idea in her head save clothes and class. I don't think I can bear it, Martha.'

'Oh, Belle, I am so sorry! I thought . . . I hoped you had

got over it – whatever there was of it. A childhood thing, one of those stories one tells oneself. I thought . . . I believed . . .' She was actually blushing. '. . . I truly thought it was Franz Wengel.'

'Herr Wengel? Martha, you must be joking! Oh, he's well enough, and his music is extraordinary, but, Martha –' she was almost laughing, 'imagine me as Frau Wengel! Keeping my kitchen among the good people of Brundt, with Frau Schmidt for my granddame!' She paused, savouring the humour of it.

'I'd rather have Frau Schmidt for a grandmother than Lady Helen for an aunt.' Martha was surprised at herself.

'Good gracious me!' Cristabel forgot her own affairs for a moment to gaze in astonishment at her friend. 'What in the world has got into you, Martha Peabody? What can poor innocent Aunt Helen have done to offend you?'

'Nothing! Not really. Only, sometimes Cristabel I just cannot understand you aristocrats. Your rules aren't my rules, something like that.'

'No, I suppose not,' said Cristabel thoughtfully. 'Well, Martha dear, they're not going to be mine either from now on. I wonder . . .' She paused for a minute. 'Did I really decide to be a prima donna in the hope of meeting Max again? If I did, I've paid for it, have I not? I've met him with a vengeance. Max, the affianced young man. I'll make him sorry! When he has five fat little sons by Minette and is wondering who their fathers really are, I shall be prima donna at La Scala, fêted, courted, adored. Why are you laughing?'

'I was thinking you sound just as bad as poor Minette.'

'Oh, Martha, I do thank God for you.' She threw her arms round her and burst into tears. 'I shall understand my tragic parts better now,' she said, much later. 'Do you think Franzosi would put on *Dido and Aeneas* for me?'

'Don't ask him, Cristabel. At least, not until Prince Max is safely married.'

'Safely? Not the word I'd choose! Poor Max . . . Oh, Martha, let's do something wild! I know! Let's go to the masked ball tonight. Shall we? No one's seen me in my breeches as Glarus in *The Confused Wife*, and they wear dominoes for New Year's here. Let me be your escort.' She rose, swept a professional bow. 'Do . . . do . . . do say yes!' And then as

Martha battled with her wiser self. 'I need it, Martha, believe me, I need it.'

Martha knew how she felt. With snow piling up outside, life was more and more a matter of dour routine. No wonder the Lissenbergers anticipated the licence of carnival time. Much later, as Cristabel handed her into the crowded Opera House where the New Year's ball was held, she thought she must have taken leave of her senses. But it was true that Cristabel looked every inch a young blood in the costume she was to wear in Franzosi's modern comedy. 'I'd not have known you myself,' she comforted herself by saying it, and by observing that Cristabel had got her young man's stride to perfection.

'A useful rehearsal for me,' Cristabel adjusted her mask for the plunge into the crowded theatre, where the revelry was already at its height. A fine, bright night had eased the way up from town and the theatre was so crowded that only a pretence of dancing was being made near the stage, where the orchestra was playing. Martha had stipulated for just one dance, a look at the decorations and the jovial crowd, and then a strategic retreat, pointing out that though Cristabel might pass for a German, there was no chance that she herself could. 'We'll speak French,' said Cristabel. 'They all speak it so badly here, there is no chance of their spotting us.'

It had seemed sensible enough, back in the safety of their rooms, now it struck Martha as pure madness. No one had entered or left Lissenberg for more than six weeks. Inevitably, any foreigners had to be well-known.

She was about to make a last protest; turn and flee. Too late. Cristabel had seen an opening in the crowd and handed her solicitously through towards where one could hear the music. 'Our dance, Madame.'

Bow and curtsy. A minuet had just ended, now, to Martha's relief, the orchestra struck up one of the modern Polonaises, made fashionable by the light-hearted court of Dresden. All one had to do was parade, two and two, in time to the music. They fell in step behind a couple dressed as clowns in baggy, identical costumes.

The man turned and saw them. 'You're wearing dominoes!' He spoke French. 'Both of you! A forfeit. You don't know it's against the rules? Never mind.' Taking Martha's hand. 'Singly you'll do well enough.'

Lodge. He had tried to disguise his voice but the English accent, with its slight transatlantic twang, was unmistakable to anyone who knew him. Well, it could have been much worse. Impossible to exchange a glance with Cristabel, masked as they were, but she had obviously already started playing along and was bowing over the female clown's hand. Playfair of course. Both sexes can play at dressing-up, and he was both shorter and more slender than his friend.

As the two of them fell in behind, Lodge bent to kiss Martha's hand. Then: 'Who are you?' Sharply, a total change of note.

'M'sieur forgets, this is a masquerade.' She tried to pitch her voice into the unintelligible squeak used on such occasions, but knew she had failed.

'God Almighty! Miss Peabody!' They were moving forward now, bound by the rule of the dance. 'And your companion?' He remembered to speak French. 'Of course! This is madness, Mademoiselle; you must leave at once.'

'Nothing I'd like better.' Tartly. 'We had agreed it was just to be for one dance. Now you have separated us!'

It was true. Other people had now pushed in between the two couples. 'Damnation,' he said. And then, 'Forgive me. Of all the unhappy chances!'

'Dominoes aren't really forbidden,' she worked it out. 'Just rare. And you had an assignation with two of them.' What secret plot were Lodge and Playfair hatching now? Not a very sensible one, she thought. 'Look! Those must be your friends.' Across the room a pair of dominoes were moving the other way in the great circle of dance. Who could they be? Who would be mad enough to involve himself with these two incompetent conspirators?

'Do you know them?'

'No. This was the meeting place. What should we do'. Distracted. 'We'd better go there to sort things out.'

'I don't like it!'

'No more do I, but we must do something. Where must we go?' A sense of urgency was growing in her as he havered.

'The refreshment room, but only as a last resort; in an emergency.'

'If this isn't an emergency, I don't know what is. Look!' She saw Cristabel and her partner move out of line, 'the others are going.'

'Maybe we can catch them.' But the crowd was too thick and too good-humoured for anything but the slowest of progresses, if one did not want to be unduly conspicuous.

Refreshments were to be served in the artists' green room, behind the stage, and Cristabel understood her companion's reluctance when she realised what a cul-de-sac it was. Like the artists' lodgings, the Opera House was built into the slope of the mountain. To reach the green room they had to cross the stage, getting venomous looks from the orchestra. The rest of the revellers would not come up here until the supper interval, when the orchestra had its break.

In the green room, servants were busy setting out a lavish cold collation, and here too they got angry looks as they crossed the room to join the four people who were there already, deep in agitated talk. Cristabel and her clown, and the two other dominoes.

'Thank God!' Cristabel saw her. 'Let's go.'

'A promise first,' the male of the two unknown dominoes spoke falsetto, but Martha's heart lurched. 'Not a word of this contretemps, if you value all our lives.'

'What in the world –?' Cristabel had forgotten to disguise her voice.

'Best not to ask,' said Martha. 'Yes, you have our promise sir. Time to go,' she turned to Cristabel.

Too late. There was a stir among the servants at the entrance from the stage: a ringing curse, the crash of breaking glass, and six soldiers of the Prince's Guard pushed their way through the servants, one of them angrily mopping syllabub off his jerkin. Behind them came the Prince's Chamberlain, also looking ruffled. 'You're under arrest! All four of you!'

Four? Concentrating on him, Martha had not noticed that the two other dominoes had disappeared.

'There were six, Excellency.' One of the soldiers had noticed too.

'Six? Nonsense. Two clowns and two dominoes, conspiracy against the State. Take them out the back way; cells for the night; they'll be glad to talk in the morning.'

'Sir, I protest!' Lodge whipped off his mask. 'I'm a foreigner, an American! Is this the way you treat your guests, here in Lissenberg?'

'It's the way we treat plotters against the State. Complain

to the presiding-judge in the morning, Herr Lodge. I must return to my duties as the Prince's representative.'

'But the ladies!' Playfair was trying to silence Lodge, but he went on with his protest.

'Ladies? I see no ladies. Just a nest of criminals, providentially exposed. A night in our cells will make you more amenable to reason. Sleep well!' He replaced his own mask and turned to go.

'This way.' One of the soldiers opened a door concealed in the panelling at the back of the green room. 'Quick now. We're armed; you're not. Don't make things worse for yourselves.'

The door gaped black and narrow. Passing through it one at a time they felt the icy damp beyond. 'My voice!' Cristabel put a hand to her throat. 'You can't!' No pretence of manhood now.

'Gawd! It's the Prince's nightingale.' A soldier pulled off her mask and held his torch to her face. 'What's to do, friends? He won't half be angry if we spoil his prima donna's voice for her. You know what the cells are like.'

'What can we do?' said the leader. 'We've our orders, from the Prince's man. You know what happens to them as don't obey orders.' He gestured a sliced throat. 'Pity about your voice, Fraülein, you should have thought about it before you got involved in this little plot.'

'But we're not involved,' protested Martha. The two other dominoes must be clear away by now, she thought. 'It's all a total mistake. We only came to the ball, Lady Cristabel and I, to practise her in her role as a man in *The Bride Confused*. Which is to be performed tomorrow night,' she pointed out. 'And there is no understudy. You won't be very popular with your fellow citizens if you keep her in the freezing cold all night, and she can't sing. And Prince Maximilian will be furious!'

'So will my mum,' said another of the soldiers surprisingly. 'You're Fraülein Peabody, ain't you Miss, the one that spoke up for Mum and the other women to the Prince. Hot soup and the fire kept up all day,' he turned to his fellows. 'We can't put her in a cold cell for the night. Mum would never let me hear the end of it, nor my cousin Anna.'

'We can't let them go.' The leader stuck to his point.

'Course we can't. Much as our lives are worth. But why

can't they spend the night by the watch-room fire with the rest of us? So long as you promise to look cold and miserable in the morning, Miss.' He turned to Martha.

'Of course! But they'll be worried to death about us at the hostel. Is there any way you can get a message to let them know what's happened? Nobody even knows we came to the ball!'

'Playing truant was you?' Rough sympathy in the man's tone. 'And fell into a pack of trouble, you didn't reckon on. Sure we can get a message through by the back stairs. Though likely enough they'll have heard frontways about this. News travels fast here in Lissenberg. But what are we going to do with the other two?'

'Put them in the cells.' The leader spoke with absolute decision. 'Someone's got to look proper cold in the morning. Besides . . . What was that you said, Hans, about there being six masks?'

'Six? I never! What made you think that? Ask me, it's all one of the Chamberlain's mare's-nests. Let's not look more foolish in the morning than we have to. Arresting masks at New Year's! Two ladies and two foreigners!'

'Who are keeping pretty quiet,' said the leader. 'What have you to say for yourselves, gentlemen?'

'We'll say it to the judge in the morning.' Playfair took the lead. 'No use blaming you men for this bit of idiocy. It's a bad sign of a country's state when the authorities imagine conspiracies that don't exist, and so I shall tell the examining judge. In the meantime, so long as you are so good as to keep the ladies warm, my companion and I will be happy enough in your cold cell, though we may complain to our governments about our treatment afterwards. But not about you. We promise you that, do we not, Lodge?'

'Naturally.' But Martha thought Lodge sounded very much less sure of himself than his companion. Was he beginning to realise just how serious his situation might be? She had always been sure that the two odd companions were fellow conspirators in some kind of international revolutionary plot, but all the evidence so far had suggested that they were not very capable ones. So what in the world was Franz Wengel doing getting involved with them? And should she be angry or relieved that he and his companion had quietly melted away, leaving the four of them to face arrest. Relieved, she thought. And, besides, what reason had he to suspect her and Cristabel's identity? Of his own, she was in no doubt. She was beginning to think that she would recognise him, by instinct, if they were to be tied, blindfold at the opposite ends of one of the cold cells the Chamberlain had threatened. And where was that going to get her? Nowhere, she told herself, and settled obediently by the guard-room fire to try to sleep.

Morning brought Baron Hals, the Chamberlain, abjectly apologetic, and visibly relieved when Cristabel decided to reveal that they had not, in fact, spent the night in the cells. The two of them had had no moment alone, and Martha was glad that Cristabel followed her lead in denying all knowledge of any other dominoes. 'I trust you will see to it that Mr. Lodge and Mr. Playfair are released forthwith.' Cristabel was suddenly the great lady.

'I shall have to consult my master about that, but you ladies are free to go.'

For a moment, Martha was tempted to refuse to leave until the other two were also released, but Cristabel needed to rest before the evening performance. Lodge and Playfair would have to fend for themselves. After all, they undoubtedly had been conspiring against the State, or trying to. Perhaps the near disaster would teach them to be more careful in future. As for her, she could not decide whether to be amused or irritated by the assumption that, as women, they were automatically free from suspicion. 'They don't seem to have heard of Charlotte Corday here in Lissenberg,' she remarked to Cristabel, as they crossed the square from the prison entrance to that of their hostel. It was very early still, but she saw a little crowd outside the hostel entrance. 'Be ready for an audience,' she warned Cristabel who was still wondering what Charlotte Corday had to do with anything.

Someone in the crowd turned, saw them coming and raised a cheer. 'Huzza!' The others caught it up.

'Your public.' She took Cristabel's arm and felt her stiffen into her rôle as cavalier.

'And yours, I think.' Cristabel had noticed how many of the crowd were women.

The cheering continued. Nothing was said, but friendly

hands reached out to touch them as they passed, and the hostel door swung open to reveal Lady Helen awaiting them.

'Now for our scolding.' Cristabel braced herself.

The evening performance was a brilliant success before it even started. Signor Franzosi, who had begun by being furious at the escapade, was their humble servant again by the end of the evening. Cristabel's first entrance was greeted by a cheer that stopped the performance, and, at the end, even the orchestra rose to join in the ovation. 'You won't believe how cross they were with us last night.' Martha had described their adventures to Lady Helen without any mention of the two vanished dominoes. 'I suppose they are doing their best to make amends.'

She had an expected caller the next day. Frau Schmidt came early and found her alone, since Cristabel liked to sleep late after a performance. 'I have come to thank you,' she said after the first greetings.

'No need. But on the other hand . . .' Martha had been hoping for just this opportunity, 'There is something I would like to say. The two gentlemen who were arrested with us last night, our charming cicisbeos who cooled their heels in the Prince's dungeons, I devoutly hope it will have taught them some sense, but, Frau Schmidt, I feel honour-bound to tell you – and anyone else whom it may concern – that sense is a commodity with which they are not richly endowed. They play at conspiracy, I think, as other young men play at love, or war. It makes them infinitely dangerous to anyone with whom they chance to associate. I only wish that they could be ordered out of the country as a result of last night's work, but as that is impossible, they should be avoided like the plague. I have been considering what would have happened if Lady Cristabel and I had not chanced to go to the masquerade last night, costumed as we were.'

'So have I. All four of them would have been arrested, not a doubt of it. The musicians did their best to impede the arresting party, and so did the servants, but their best would not have been good enough if it had not been for your delaying presence, and the confusion it caused. The assignation had been blown, of course, by someone's carelessness.'

'Lodge's, probably, but Playfair is not much better. Shall I suggest to them that they keep out of politics – at least Lissenberg ones – until spring? And that they take their leave as soon as the pass is open?'

'We'd be most grateful.' The old lady rose. 'Pray give my regards and congratulations to Lady Cristabel. And to Lady Helen, of course.' Unspoken between them, like so much else, was the fact that Lady Helen looked on Frau Schmidt as quite below her touch, and did not trouble herself to appear when she called.

Martha rather enjoyed the interview with Lodge and Playfair who had been kept under lock and key for several days, awaiting Prince Gustav's pleasure. They were both sorry for themselves, and thoroughly frightened. And a good thing too! They had seen the dark underside of life in Lissenberg and it had shaken them. 'Those cells, Miss Peabody,' Lodge shuddered, 'I'm happier than I can say that you and Lady Cristabel were spared them. We wouldn't keep a dog in such conditions, in our United States of America.'

'Of course we wouldn't.' It was part of his general unconcern with her that he tended to forget she was as American as he. 'But I hope it has been a useful warning to you both, and that you are planning to leave Lissenberg just as soon as the pass is open.'

'We most certainly are,' Playfair told her. 'Spring can't come soon enough for me. No need for your warnings, Miss Peabody, I'd not raise a finger to help these Lissenbergers after the way they let us down the other night. They just melted away at the first sign of danger, left the four of us to bear the brunt of it. I wish I knew who they were and how they got away. Have you any idea, Miss Peabody?'

'Not the least in the world.' Martha breathed a secret sigh of relief. 'And if I were you, Mr. Playfair, I'd neither ask, nor wish to know. Ignorance is sometimes safety.'

Lodge laughed nervously. 'I was never more glad of ignorance than when the Prince was questioning us. Able to say we had brought fraternal greetings, but had no idea to whom.'

'None at all? But how did you get in touch?'

'Oh, no problem about that. Letters through a safe house, don't you see. Only, in the end, before we came through with the funds, we had to see someone face-to-face.'

'Should you be telling me this?'

'I can't see why not,' said Playfair wearily. 'We told the Prince.'

'Hard on the safe house.' Martha was wondering where the funds would have come from.

'Not a bit of it. Perfectly respectable address. *Poste restante* with that banker fellow – I've seen him calling on you. Nothing against the Jews, myself, but they can look after themselves, that's one thing certain. Lord, I never thought of that. Could it have been – One of the dominoes spoke, do you remember, Miss Peabody? Asked for a promise. Could it have been that Brodski?'

'Good gracious no!' She was able to answer with complete conviction.

'You sound very sure, Miss Peabody,' said Playfair. 'I wonder why, since you say you didn't recognise the man.'

'Man?' she said. 'Are you sure it was a man?'

11

'Lodge and Playfair are gone at last.' Ishmael Brodski had called to tell Martha that the passes were clear. 'They were in the first carriage that got through. I'm afraid they may paint quite a highly coloured picture of life here in Lissenberg.'

'Dungeons and torture?' said Martha. 'I suppose so. Not that torture was in the least necessary. I'm so glad their revelations did you no harm, Herr Brodski.'

'Well, not much, thanks to your warning.' Smiling. 'I didn't perish in the dungeons, nor do I have to leave in the first carriage, but it has all been, shall we say, inconvenient? And expensive. But it would have been much worse without your warning. I am indebted to you, I won't forget.'

'Thank you. But, tell me . . .' Eagerly. 'If the pass is open, there must be news in. What has happened in the world outside, while we have been shut up here?'

'Shut up? You feel it, even though you have done so much to keep us sane, with Lady Cristabel's brilliant performances. That was an inspiration of Prince Maximilian's. She gets better every time I hear her. Deeper . . . That Dido last week. Miss Peabody, I'm a hardened businessman, I cried!'

'Do tell her! She'd be so pleased. But, you're putting me off, Herr Brodski. The news?'

'Terrible. Bonaparte seems to have taken leave of his senses. The liberator has turned bloody tyrant. You'll not believe it, Miss Peabody. He sent his soldiers across the border into neutral Baden. They arrested the young Duc d'Enghien, took him back to Paris, killed him.'

'Killed?'

'A mock trial in the night, shot in the morning. Murder.'

'The heir to the Condés, isn't he? But, why?'

'There's talk of a conspiracy. Pichegru . . . Moreau . . . And d'Enghien was living just across the French border. Said to hold the threads . . . Nonsense of course. Everyone knows he was

living in Baden to be with the woman he loved, Madame de
Rohan-Rochefort. Some say he was even married to her. He's
the soul of honour that young man. Was the soul of honour.'

'He's really dead?'

'He's dead all right. Judicial murder. Not just a crime of
Bonaparte's. A folly.'

'Doesn't Princess Amelia come from Baden?'

'Yes. And her sister, the Tsarina of Russia.'

'What will Prince Gustav do, do you think?'

'If I knew that, Miss Peabody, I'd be a rich man.'

'I thought you were already.'

'Richer then.'

Outraged, Prince Gustav put his whole court into mourning
for the murdered duke. Shops in Lissenberg ran out of black
crêpe, and all performances at the Opera House were cancelled.

'Prince Max came himself to tell us,' Cristabel reported.
'Closed until further notice, he said. Some of the company talk
of asking for leave of absence, going to get a breath of outside
air.'

'Will they be allowed to go, do you think?' Martha got up
and prowled over to the window. 'Blue sky! Shall we ask leave,
Cristabel? Go and visit your mother? Venice in spring! It
would do us all good. Your aunt has been looking tired for
weeks, and I wouldn't mind a change of scene. And you have
most certainly earned a holiday. Herr Brodski was singing
your praises the other day. Your Dido made him cry, he says.'

'You have the oddest friends. No, we can't possibly go,
Martha. Prince Gustav is going to announce the result of the
opera competition.'

'At last!'

'Signor Franzosi thinks he must have been waiting till the
road was open. Hoping against hope for a late entry. Which
doesn't speak too highly for the ones he has received.'

'Or for his taste. And what an insult to the local competitors
if that is really what he is doing. Did Prince Max submit one
in the end, do you know?'

'Nobody knows anything about anything. Extraordinary in
so small a country.'

'Not in Lissenberg. Do you know, when I got to Brundt,

back in February, they didn't even know of Lodge and Play-fair's arrest.'

'Your Frau Schmidt did.'

'My Frau Schmidt, as you choose to call her, is a very discreet old lady.' Too discreet to volunteer any news of her grandson. And Martha too proud to ask. Altogether it had been a frustrating visit. 'Cristabel, do let's go and see your mother! A change of air would be wonderful. Maybe a permanent change. A few appearances at the Fenice – I'm sure Count Tafur could arrange that for you – and you should be well-launched into the Italian circuit. You could laugh at Prince Gustav and his opera competition.'

'But I don't want to,' said Cristabel. 'Not yet. I intend to sing in the anniversary opera. It's going to be a great occasion, just the kind of start I need. I want the world at my feet, Martha.'

'What to do with it?'

'Kick it away? Enjoy it? Find happiness, perhaps? Do you believe in happiness, Martha?'

'I don't know.' Slowly. 'Yes, in a way. I've been happy this winter, getting my kitchen going. The way you are in your singing, Belle. A little. I like making things work. And then, suddenly, it doesn't seem quite enough. Cristabel,' she had been meaning to ask this. 'Have you thought at all how Bonaparte's dastardly murder of the Duc d'Enghien may affect Prince Max?'

'You mean, will Prince Gustav change his orders? Make him break off his engagement? Well – if he does, no doubt Prince Max will submit as tamely as he did before. It's no affair of mine, Martha. Don't ever think it is. I've fought my battle this winter. Won it, thank God. I'm a singer now, first last, always.'

Martha volunteered to join Lady Helen on her weekly visit to the Palace the next day. It was a long time since she had been up there, and she felt guilty about it. But sometimes she found Lady Helen's preaching of aristocratic duty to the poor beleaguered Princess hard to bear. And, besides, setting up her soup-kitchen had proved harder work than she had expected. She had soon seen that everyone meant to swindle her right and left, both for services and supplies, and this wa something that, as her father's daughter, she would not allow. It had taken a great deal of time and effort, and some very plain speaking, both in Lissenberg and on her trip to Brundt, before her willing helpers understood that she meant to have value for her money. She had shocked Lady Helen and even Cristabel, she knew, by her insistence that she get a Lissmark's worth for every Lissmark, but she had finally got it recognised, and now felt able to leave the day-to-day running of affairs to a group of women, organised by Anna, who had proved a staunch ally throughout.

The road was clear at last up to the Palace. She was ashamed of it, but since the night of the New Year's masquerade, she had found the walk up through the tunnel almost unbearable. Now she did not just suspect, she knew, that those sinister doors into the mountain led to a cold network of dungeons. Who else might be languishing there, in the cold cells that had frightened Lodge and Playfair into flight?

But today they rode up in the carriage, windows down to let in the sun and a hint of spring in the breeze. They found Princess Amelia in deep mourning and the whole atmosphere of the Palace subdued. 'I've never seen the Prince so angry,' she told them. 'It's lucky Maximilian's heart wasn't in that engagement.'

'Has the Prince said anything?'

'Not yet. We're all treading on egg-shells. The Prince has shut himself up in his rooms; he says he is making up his mind about the choice of opera for the celebrations this autumn, but I am sure he is also deciding what to do about Bonaparte. I wish I'd hear from my sister the Tsarina, but, of course, the news will have taken for ever to reach Petersburg.' She shuddered. 'It was cold murder. A prince of the blood!'

'The true blood,' said Lady Helen. 'Not Bonaparte's. Tell me, Highness, your stepson, does he correspond with Mademoiselle de Beauharnais?' And then. 'No, how stupid of me. The roads have been closed since she left. It's hard to get used to.'

'I never shall,' said Princess Amelia. 'I'm always racked by fear, when the roads open at last, of bad news from my family. You must have found it just the same, shut up here for the first time. Your brother – Lady Cristabel's father – I trust he is well?'

'My brother is always well.' Lady Helen evaded the question, as well she might, since the Duke had never answered the letter warning him that he was an unconscious bigamist.

'I was so sorry not to hear your niece sing Dido,' Princess Amelia went on now. 'Everyone said she exceeded even her own brilliant standards. A new depth to the characterisation, someone told me.'

'She made me cry,' said Martha, 'which I don't do easily.'

'I'm sure of that.' The Princess smiled at her. 'I hear great things of you, Miss Peabody. I understand you have been quite a surprise to our Lissenbergers, who thought you a fowl for their plucking. I'm glad you came today, to give me a chance to congratulate you – and, forgive me – to warn you that you may have made yourself some enemies, some of whom have the Prince's ear. He is not a great believer in female enterprise. I understand that one of the operas submitted in the competition earned his disapproval on that count. The hero took second place to the heroine, he thought. Understandable enough, I suppose, when we all know the operas are being written for Lady Cristabel. Everyone knows the tenor can't hold a candle to her, poor man.'

'He seems to take it very well,' said Lady Helen. 'When can we hope to hear the Prince's decision, Highness?'

'I wish I knew. About everything. It's hard on my poor stepson, who looks wretched, and no wonder. God knows, he entered into that engagement reluctantly enough, but just because he did so, I am very much afraid he may feel honour-bound to stick to it. After all, it is not the poor girl's fault that her uncle has turned despot.'

'Not her uncle,' said Lady Helen. 'I don't know whether it makes it better or worse, but the fact is that Minette de Beauharnais is merely his wife's niece by marriage, no blood kin of hers, even let alone his. And if he is getting these dynastic ideas into his head, may he not arrive at the logical conclusion of a divorce from the wife who has failed to give him an heir?'

'But he adores her.' This was clearly a new and unpleasant idea to the Princess.

'Despite the slanderous rumours?' Lady Helen made it just a question. Martha, listening to this extraordinary exchange, thought the two older women had forgotten her presence, deep in a discussion that went much further than the words. 'If he is setting up to be a Caesar, he may begin to think of the old saying about Caesar's wife.'

'And then the Beauharnais girls would be back to the nothing from which they came.'

'Just so.' Lady Helen rose, and Martha had a curious sense of a mission accomplished. Her mind was thick with questions as they drove back down the hill, but she waited until they were alone in their sitting-room to ask them.

'The opera the Prince doesn't like,' she began when they were alone, 'the one with too strong a heroine . . . I wish you had asked more about it –'

'Princess Amelia would not have told me. I hope you took her warning to heart, my dear. Have you really been stirring things up among the Lissenbergers? I had no idea. I wish I had known.'

'I've just been insisting on value for money, Lady Helen.' When had she finally found it impossible to address her friend by anything but her title?

'And trodden on some toes in the process. There are times, dear child, when other things are more important than money.'

'But it's the principle of the thing . . . Father always said –'

'What your father said, he said in your United States of America, where, by all reports, things go on in a most unusual way. I do not think you should take his word for law here in Lissenberg. Patronage is important here, as you must have realised.'

'All too well! And you think I should set up as a patron.'

'But you have. What else are you to Cristabel and me?'

'A friend, I thought.'

'That too, of course.' Lady Helen surprised her with a kiss, which she felt herself accept ungraciously. 'But as our patron, I can understand your anxiety about the choice of opera. Personally, and for what it is worth, I suspect that the one of which the Prince has chosen to disapprove is the anonymous one by his son, which he will certainly have known about. I'm afraid poor Prince Maximilian is about to be disappointed in art as well as in love. If it is a disappointment.'

This gave Martha the opening for her other question: 'Will Princess Amelia tell the Prince what you said to her?'

'Undoubtedly. I think those two work much more closely

together than appears on the surface. That is why I beg you to take the Princess's warning with the greatest seriousness.'

'I see.' What she would do about it was another matter.

The trumpeters were out in the streets of Lissenberg a few days later, to summon the Prince's loyal subjects to the theatre for the result of the opera competition.

'Will they come?' asked Martha.

'Will there be room for them all?' said Lady Helen. 'You don't yet seem to understand, dear child, the power of an absolute monarch.'

'Besides,' said Cristabel, 'there is great interest both in the opera and the general plans for the celebration this autumn. I've heard some wild talk among the staff at the Opera House. They seem to think that the Prince will celebrate his twenty-fifth anniversary with some kind of liberalisation of the law here in Lissenberg.'

'A gesture towards the democratic principle?' asked Martha. 'It doesn't seem very likely to me.'

'No, I was amazed how seriously it seemed to be expected.'

'What a disappointment it will be if it doesn't happen,' said Martha thoughtfully. 'Are there any rumours at the theatre about the winning opera?'

'Not a word. That really is going to be a complete surprise. We're all to be on stage to hear the announcement, along with the composers of the various operas. But there has been no list of their names even.'

'I wonder if Prince Gustav is going to enter a dark horse. Imagine if after all the local excitement, he has commissioned a work from outside, maybe by that wild young man, Beethoven.'

'If he has, he must be regretting it now,' said Cristabel. 'Someone told me that Beethoven is a devoted worshipper of Bonaparte, and has been working on a symphony in his honour this winter, to be dedicated to the "world's great man". If Prince Gustav is really going to announce a complete break with Bonaparte tomorrow night, which is another of the rumours, he would hardly produce the work of one of his devotees. A pity. I would dearly like to sing in a work of Herr van Beethoven.'

'Maybe we could arrange it.' But Martha was thinking about something else. If the composers of the operas were to be lined up on stage for the announcement, Franz Wengel must be there. Even he could hardly ignore a direct order from his Prince. 'Do you know where your aunt and I are to be placed?' she asked.

'On stage with the rest of us. I asked Signor Franzosi to make a point of it. You are our Maecenas, after all, dear Martha.'

'You don't need me any more.' As she said it, she knew it was true, and minded. She had lost both her occupations. Now that the roads were open and the tunnel no longer in use, her friends, the porter-women, had gone back to their homes, mainly in Brundt, and she was surprised how much she missed them, and the day-to-day occupation with their affairs.

The long-awaited day came at last. Theatre and stage were packed with people and so was the square outside, where the announcement would be relayed by the Lissenberg town-crier. Only the dais for the royal party was still empty, and, Martha craned to look, one of the seats reserved for the competitors. Now, as she watched, there was a little stirring on the crowded stage, and the unmistakable, erect figure of Frau Schmidt moved forward to take the vacant seat beside Prince Maximilian. Martha watched with interest as she dropped him a token bob of a curtsy, received a respectful nod in return, and bent forward to talk to him. What possible excuse could she be making for her grandson?

The orchestra struck up the Lissenberg national song and Martha rose to her feet wondering if by any amazing chance Herr Haydn, who had written it on Prince Gustav's orders, might have been persuaded to enter an opera in the competition? But he was in his seventies now, living in honourable retirement in Vienna. It did not seem likely.

The royal party was arriving now, and for the first time Martha thought how odd it was that Prince Max was down among the competitors. The young Prince had grown since she last saw him, turned into a little boy with flaxen curls and a pale, sullen-looking face. As he settled on a stool at his mother's feet he saw his half-brother down on the stage, and made to get up to join him. His father's hand on his shoulder held him back. She saw him bite his lips in pain, the colour ebbing from his face as he subsided on to the stool.

The trumpets sounded. Prince Gustav rose to his feet. 'Loyal and beloved subjects,' he began.

12

'I must speak to you.' The speech over, Prince Maximilian pushed his way through the excited crowd to where Cristabel stood. And then, to Franzosi, beside her: 'Where can we talk, Signor? By what my father said, Herr Wengel's winning opera is going to be very much of a challenge. The sooner we begin to plan for it, the better. The Prince is no mean judge of music; if he says it is modern and unusual, we must believe him, and I cannot help wondering if Signor Carlucci will be up to the part of St. Brandt. If we are going to need a replacement tenor, there is not a moment to be lost. I have the score here.'

'At last!' said Cristabel. 'I am finally to be allowed to see this opera that is supposed to have been written for me! A pity Herr Wengel did not have the courtesy to come himself. I'm surprised the Prince was so tolerant about that.'

'So am I,' agreed Maximilian. 'But Frau Schmidt says Wengel is a very sick man. We must resign ourselves to starting work without him.'

'In that case,' said Franzosi. 'I entirely agree with you, Highness. Let us adjourn to the rehearsal room and take a look at this challenging score.'

Cristabel hesitated. 'There are to be no more formalities?'

'Why should there be?' Prince Maximilian smiled savagely. 'The Prince has told his "loyal and devoted" subjects what his plans are. Now he is going back to the Palace to be spared the sight of them for another year or so.'

'Hush!' She put a warning hand on his arm. 'But you . . . Should you not be with the royal party?'

'The last thing my father wants. Why do I call him that? My "employer". And we must be thinking of our duties.' They were out of the crowd now, in the comparative quiet of the green room. He opened the rehearsal-room door, turned to Franzosi. 'Thank you, Signor. There are things, first, that I must discuss with Lady Cristabel. Wait outside, will you? I'll call when we are ready. There.' He closed the door on the surprised maestro. 'At last.' He turned back to Cristabel. 'I've thought I'd go mad, all winter, seeing you, working with you, unable to talk to you. I'm a free man, Cristabel. You heard what my father said.'

'I heard. Last autumn it suited him to make you engage yourself to poor Minette de Beauharnais; this spring he has changed his mind. You do dance to his tune, do you not?'

'No!' Explosively. 'You heard his tone when he spoke of me. Did that sound like the father of an obedient son? Oh yes, I agreed gladly to release myself from your "poor Minette". You'd hardly call her that if you knew how she used to speak of you and Miss Peabody last summer. She's no friend of yours, Cristabel, never delude yourself about that.'

'I am Lady Cristabel,' she said. 'And I choose my own friends.'

'Forgive me! I'm going too fast, and all in the wrong order. Idiotic! But I've been so wretched all winter, thinking of you, dreaming of you, listening to you sing better and better. And, Cristabel, don't pretend. You felt it too, that time, in rehearsal . . . If I were to touch you now, what would happen? Ah, don't!' She had moved a step away. 'You broke my heart with your Dido. But what could I do but stay silent. I was honour-bound. You don't understand.'

'I most certainly do not. And we should not be longer alone, Prince Maximilian.'

'How can you? Cristabel!' He reached for her hand. 'I won't believe you have not felt it too, the happiness growing between us. The chance of it. Impossible then. I was committed. Did I flatter myself that you felt it too, suffered too, but understood, being who you are, that I must do my duty? But not again. Not this time.'

'This time?' She had withdrawn her hand from his.

'Oh, yes! My father wants me to engage myself to a Russian princess now. He's not absolutely sure which one, but is hoping that my stepmother's influence will find someone who is close to the throne. Even my ambitious father does not look so high as the Tsar's sisters Catherine and Anna. But he thinks a Russian alliance our best hope now that he has defied Bonaparte.'

'Not an Austrian one?' Interested, despite herself.

'No. He's afraid of being swallowed, and I don't blame him. But what I am telling you, Cristabel, is that this time I was man enough to refuse. That's why I am in disgrace, out of the succession, his opera manager, nothing else. And free, at last, to offer you my hand. Cristabel, I love you dearly. I can offer you only the life you have already chosen for yourself, but shared! Imagine the happiness of it! The world at your feet, and I beside you, your guide, your friend, your lover. Surely we both knew this was our fate, all those years ago, when I stood back to let you shine as Orpheus. I want always to be beside you, Cristabel.'

'You're sure, now?' She faced him, head up, hands behind her back, a challenging pose she used on stage. 'Yes, I admit it, Prince Maximilian, there was a time when I did let myself begin to think we had a future together, you and I. Fated? Perhaps. A long childhood dream come true? Maybe. You wakened me rudely enough when you yielded to your father, without a word to me, and let me learn it, like the rest of the world, in public.'

'But what could I have said?'

'I don't know.' She admitted it. 'But something. A glance, a look?'

'Minette watched me like a hawk. She hates you.'

'Poor Minette.' She said it again. 'I suppose she fell under your spell too. That little lost boy look of yours . . . But I'm grown up now, Prince Maximilian. I shan't let myself be carried away again, infatuated as I was this winter, and I'm grateful to you for that. If I ever marry, which I doubt, it will be someone older, someone with power. And it won't be for a long time. I've my own way to make in the world, and I mean to do it on my own. You broke my heart for me, and I sang Dido the better for it. But I don't ever mean to suffer like that again. I can't afford to, it's bad for my voice. I've made you angry. I'm sorry.'

'Yes.' He was white with rage. 'Forgive me, Lady Cristabel, for troubling you with my ill-timed proposal. From now on, I promise, it shall be strictly business between us. I wonder, though, what you would have said to me if I had come to you, not as a young man with his way to make in the world, but as heir apparent to Lissenberg.'

'Intolerable!' She almost spat it at him. 'You insult me,

Prince. Make your own arrangements with Signor Franzosi and I will abide by them, but I think it would be best if we did not try to work together on this opera of Herr Wengel's.'

'But we must. You know we must. My father expects . . .'

'I'm getting a little tired of what your father expects, Prince Maximilian.' She turned away from him. 'Goodbye, Prince. Let us do our best to pretend that this unfortunate conversation never happened.'

'Miss Peabody!' Prince Maximilian found Martha and Lady Helen still in the theatre. 'Can you spare me a moment?'

'As many as you like, Prince. We are waiting for Lady Cristabel, who seems to have vanished.'

'That's just it!' He looked around the emptying theatre. 'If you would excuse us, Lady Helen? Over here.' He led Martha to two seats at the end of an empty row. 'I've made a complete fool of myself. I need your help.'

'Yes?' She had seen him single out Cristabel and was beginning to guess at what had happened.

'Idiotic,' he said. 'Taking it for granted. You heard what my father said, of course.'

'Yes,' she said again. 'I'm sorry about your opera, Prince.'

'Oh, if it was only that! I have high hopes of Herr Wengel's . . . But that's just it! I've made her so angry – rightly so – I've been such a fool. She says she won't work with me, Miss Peabody.'

'Ah,' said Martha, 'that's serious, isn't it? For her, as well as for you. No, don't tell me any more, Prince. I would rather not know.' She was pulling on her gloves. 'I suppose, in so far as she has one, I am her manager.'

'That's what I thought.'

'So I must talk some sense into her. It's her career at stake, as well as the celebration opera, which, I take it, you cannot trust Signor Franzosi to handle?'

'No! I've had a quick look at it. It's brilliant, Miss Peabody, I beg you to tell Lady Cristabel this. It's musically very advanced indeed, an immense challenge. As a success, it will be the talk of Europe. As a failure, it could be a disaster for us all.'

'Particularly for Lady Cristabel.'

'I'm glad you see that.'

'It's making her see it, or care about it, will be the problem. Very well, Prince, I'll do my best.' She rose. 'Any messages for her?'

'My abject apologies.'

'No,' she told him, 'those I won't deliver. There's always wrong on both sides in cases of this kind.'

'Thank you!'

'One thing.' She turned back to him. 'Herr Wengel. Is his illness real, do you think, or diplomatic?'

'Diplomatic? Why in the world should he choose not to come, today of all days?'

'You've never met him, have you? He's a strange man. It did strike me that now he has won the competition, he might make an equally diplomatic recovery. In which case, might not the answer be for him to take over the direction of his own opera?'

'Of course! Idiotic of me not to have thought of that, but my world has turned upside down, Miss Peabody. It's hard to think straight, with a broken heart.'

'I'm sorry.' She meant it. 'Will you bear with a piece of advice from a friend to you both?'

'Gladly.'

'Frau Schmidt is spending tonight in Lissenberg. You know her, of course.'

'Indeed yes, since she is related to my mother. But not so well as I would like to.'

'Improve the acquaintance then. Call on her. After all.' Smiling at him, 'You have defied your father once already today, you might just as well keep it up. So – call on her. She is an infinitely wise and reliable old lady. I think, if you ask her right, she will tell you if her grandson's illness is merely a pretence, as I strongly suspect. And if it is, get her to persuade him to make a surprise recovery and take over the management of his opera. And for you – may I speak like an old friend? – I would advise a trip abroad. To Russia, perhaps, to look at some princesses?'

'Miss Peabody, you will never cease to amaze me. Without committing myself, you mean?'

'Without committing yourself to anyone about anything.'

'Easier said than done.'

'So many things are.'

* * *

Every copyist in Lissenberg was hard at work for the next few weeks, getting out the parts for *Crusader Prince*. 'It's brilliant,' said Cristabel, when she got hers. 'But, Martha, you gave me no idea of how revolutionary the theme is.'

'Revolutionary?'

'Yes. Prince Brandt planning to lead his people against the tyranny of Charlemagne.'

'Good gracious. Let me see.' She read eagerly through the scene Cristabel indicated. 'This wasn't in the text I copied,' she said at last.

'You mean it's been changed? After the Prince selected it?'

'It must have been. Let me see the rest of it, Cristabel. Amazingly clever,' she said at last. 'It's just that one extraordinary scene between you and your husband, Prince Brandt, which proves him the intended liberator of his people, rather than their tyrant. Franz Wengel is a brave man.'

'Mad,' said Cristabel. 'And I'll tell you something else, Martha, Gian Carlucci will no more be able to sing Prince Brandt than the man in the moon. And even if he could, if you ask me, he'll be afraid to.'

'Will you?'

'Be afraid?' She thought about it. 'No, I don't think so. It's tremendous theatre, marvellous music, there are to be guests at the celebrations from all over Europe. However angry it may make Prince Gustav, if it's the success I expect, there will be nothing he can do about it, except smile, and congratulate us. I look forward to it! Yes?' She turned as a servant scratched at the door.

'Herr Wengel to see you, Milady.'

'At last!' She rose to greet him. 'You are recovered then, Herr Wengel? I am delighted to have a chance to congratulate you. We have been reading your opera. You're a bold man.'

'I'm an idiot! I gave strict instructions that none of the parts were to be sent out until I had discussed them with the principals. My illness kept me confined longer than I had expected, and my miserable copyists ignored my orders. I am come both to explain and to implore your discretion.'

'You can count on us,' she told him. 'I am sure I don't need to tell you how magnificent your opera is. Nothing will stop me from singing in it, and most especially singing the scene with Prince Brandt that is likely to cause the trouble. But, tell me, who else has seen it?'

'Only Carlucci, thank God, since only you and he are in the scene. He came straight to me to resign the part. He has his career to think of, he says. I agreed, in exchange for a promise of absolute discretion.'

'Can you trust him?'

'Oh, I think so. I am not without friends in the major opera houses. He knows I could do him harm if I wished to. We are thinking of a pretext that will allow him to leave without damage to his career.'

Cristabel laughed. 'Not easy. Since it is so obvious that your music is too difficult for him. Frankly, I'm a little nervous myself.'

'No need,' he told her. 'I wrote it precisely for you, Lady Cristabel. You will be superb.'

'I long to get started. But how are you going to find my Prince Brandt? There's not a moment to be lost.'

'No indeed. Fortunately my admirable grandmother saw the problem almost before I did. And Prince Maximilian has volunteered his assistance. You did not know that he is going abroad on a diplomatic mission for his father? He is to combine it with finding us a tenor, and in the meantime I am to have the pleasure of working with you, Lady Cristabel. I shall be a poor substitute, I am afraid, but I promise you I can sing the part, or I would not have written it. I intend to start rehearsals next week.'

'Good. Prince Maximilian is going abroad, you say?'

'He's gone. There are rumours in town of a disagreement with his father. I did hear it suggested that the talk of a diplomatic mission was merely a polite phrase for what is tantamount to exile. He's to be back for the celebration itself, I believe.'

'A sadder and a wiser prince?' suggested Martha.

'So his father doubtless hopes.' He turned to her smiling. 'The word, in town, is that he'll be forgiven if he brings home a suitable bride.'

'Suitable for whom?' asked Cristabel.

'Need you ask? His father, of course. Some foreign lady with outlandish habits and not a word of Liss. There's even talk of a Russian princess who would treat us as serfs, not subjects.

We all love Princess Amelia,' he went on, 'she's a neighbour, after all, and has done her best in her hard situation, but a Russian barbarian from the steppes would be something quite other.'

'It would certainly make your opera uncomfortably topical,' said Martha. 'Are you really sure you are not going too far, Herr Wengel?'

'Not the way I am going to produce it,' he told her. 'You'll see. But for the time being, that scene is to be kept entirely secret. You and I will rehearse alone, Lady Cristabel.'

'Throwing convention to the wind?' asked Martha drily. 'I think perhaps you had better begin by rehearsing here, where Lady Helen or I can act as chaperone, otherwise there will be more of the talk in town that you speak of, Herr Wengel.'

'Talk! Convention!' He turned his full attention on Martha as Cristabel moved away to pick up her score. 'We are making musical history and you talk about convention! I had expected better from an American rebel like you, Miss Peabody.'

'Oh, I'm all for freedom, and I'll defy the conventions any time I think it necessary, but why go out of the way to cause talk? There'll be enough when it comes to the performance.'

'You're right as usual.'

'How tedious of me! You really have been ill.' He was looking fine-drawn, she thought, his dark eyes deeper than ever in their sockets above the luxurious growth of beard that surely had now a faint hint of grey among the gold.

'You thought it merely a pretence? Well, I confess, I was glad enough to have an excuse to stay away. You know how I feel about pomp and circumstance?'

'Everyone is going to know after they've seen *Crusader Prince*! But, are you really better? Should you be here? What does your grandmother say?'

'She says I'm a self-willed young fool, and sends you her kind regards, Miss Peabody.'

'And mine to her. But, Herr Wengel, I have been longing to know what you think of your hero, Bonaparte, now. What kind of a liberator is it who stoops to judicial murder?'

'The Duc d'Enghien? A horrible business. I can only think that there must be more to it than has been made public. The trouble is, we know so little of what really goes on. If the conspiracy in which Pichegru and Moreau seem to have been involved really threatened the stability of France . . . If the Duc d'Enghien was a part of it . . . Miss Peabody, you can have no idea what the Reign of Terror was like in France. They have proved themselves dangerously, bloodily unpredictable. No wonder Bonaparte dares take no chances.'

'If . . . if . . . if. Special pleading, Herr Wengel? From you, who used to tell me about Bonaparte's reform of the law . . . the order and stability he was bringing to the countries he conquered – I beg your pardon, liberated – I wondered a little about it all when I got to Venice. I can tell you, it did not feel much like liberation there.'

'But that was the Austrians.'

'To whom Bonaparte had handed Venice.'

He threw out a hand. '*Touché*! But that was before he was First Consul.'

'True, but he was First Consul right enough when he re-established slavery in the French colonies. That whole wicked business of Toussaint l'Ouverture! I'm not sure I don't find his death even more shameful than poor young d'Enghien's. That hadn't happened either when you used to praise Bonaparte to me so, as a liberator, back in Paris.'

'And you thought him such a villain.' His smile transformed the drawn face. 'Just because he was rude to your English friends.'

'No, Herr Wengel, do me justice! It was because I scented absolutism in him, the thing we Americans most abhor.'

'Absolutism?' Thoughtfully. 'I do hope you are not right. I must admit this high-handed treatment of poor d'Enghien does smack of it.'

'High-handed? An odd description of murder, surely?'

He threw out a hand in surrender. 'It's disturbed me so much, I'm not thinking clearly. I had pinned all my hopes on him.'

'Hopes?' She saw that Cristabel was listening again. 'You used him as a model for your Prince Brandt?'

'The liberator of his people.' He flashed her a quick, considering look. 'Yes, I suppose I did.'

13

The cattle were up on the high pastures and the vines in full leaf on the slopes between the theatre and the town. The chorus forgot their lines less often, and Martha was getting tired of sitting in on Cristabel's rehearsals with Franz Wengel. Their great scene began with her revelation that she had been the devoted page who saved his life in the Holy Land, and in the passionate reconciliation that followed he was carried away to tell her his real plans for the future of their country.

It was the passionate reconciliation that Martha found hard to endure. Cristabel was putting her heart into the character of Princess Algisa as she had never done before and the scene grew more intense with each rehearsal. When she threw herself into her 'husband's' arms at last, Martha found herself studying the text, looking out at spring-green meadows, looking, in fact, anywhere except at the embracing couple across the room. Cristabel had never said a word about Prince Maximilian or his sudden departure. She had simply thrown herself into her work as if her sanity depended on it. Perhaps it did, but did it also depend on Franz Wengel's daily visits? And if this should prove the case, would he be able to resist her? Indeed, why should he?

'You're looking tired, Martha,' said Lady Helen one June morning. 'Let me chaperone Cristabel's rehearsal today. It's a long time since I have done so, and I'd enjoy it. If you don't mind, Cristabel?'

'Why should I? A change of audience will be good for us. It's true, Martha, you do look tired. Selfish of me not to have noticed, but this part is eating me up!'

'With marvellous results,' said Martha. 'I wonder when we shall hear from Prince Maximilian.' It was the question she had been expecting Cristabel to ask.

'And the elusive tenor,' said Cristabel. 'If only Herr Wengel's voice matched his acting, I would be inclined to snap my

144

fingers at our absentee director and urge that Wengel take the part himself. But I would sing better with a better singer,' she went on thoughtfully. Martha breathed again. Cristabel was merely throwing herself into the part like the professional she was. Absurd to mind watching it so much, and maddening if her desperate, sleepless nights were beginning to leave their mark on her daytime self.

'And Herr Wengel would have more time for rehearsing the rest of the cast,' she said now. 'He was fretting only yesterday about the way the chorus mangles his music.'

'He may find he has to make it a little easier for them,' said Cristabel.

'I doubt he'll do that. But he's looking exhausted, had you noticed? I think that illness of his took more of a toll than he will admit.'

'Or that he is burning too many candles at too many ends,' said Cristabel. 'If he didn't insist on rushing back to Brundt so often, we'd get on better. Nothing goes right when Signor Franzosi is in charge, poor man. He's losing his nerve a little, I think.'

'I don't altogether blame him,' said Martha.

She was glad to receive a visit from Ishmael Brodski that afternoon, just when she had put on bonnet and pelisse for a stroll through the vineyards.

'You were going out?' he asked, after the first greetings. 'Admirable! May I accompany you, Miss Peabody?'

'Delighted. I am tired of my own company today.' They had become curiously good friends in the course of the winter. She found she could talk to him about things that would not have interested Cristabel or Lady Helen.

'You look full of news.' She unfurled her parasol against the morning sun.

'I am! Bonaparte has proclaimed himself Emperor of the French. The Pope is even to crown him, giving an air of respectability to the business.'

'And the murder of poor young d'Enghien is to be forgotten?'

'It looks like it. The British have protested, and the Tsar put his court into mourning, as Prince Gustav did, but everyone else seems to be going with the tide, with one exception that will interest you: Herr van Beethoven had been writing a symphony dedicated to Bonaparte. When he heard the news, he defaced the title page. But he is the only one. Hardly surprising that Prince Gustav has gone off on one of his hunting holidays. He must feel the need of some very serious thought about his position.'

'You think he may bend the knee and apologise to Bonaparte?'

'We must learn to call him the Emperor Napoleon now,' he warned her, 'and, yes, I do. If I were Prince Maximilian, I'd be expecting the worst.'

'His father will want him to re-engage himself to Mademoiselle de Beauharnais?'

'Well . . .' He spread his hands in a characteristic gesture, 'what do you think?'

'I think it very likely.'

'And how are the rehearsals going?' He had followed her line of thought, as he often did.

'Superbly, but they need their tenor. Have you any news of Prince Maximilian's quest, Herr Brodski?'

'I did hear a rumour that he had given up hope in Italy and is on his way to Vienna. I also heard that it is not only the technical difficulty of the part that made Carlucci resign it.' He did not quite make it a question.

'You hear a great deal, Herr Brodski.' Time to change the subject. 'What news of the war?'

'The new Emperor is making great preparations for an invasion of England. All his energies are concentrated on his fleet and the invasion barges he is building on the north coast of France. Lucky for Prince Gustav, and all of us here on the Rhine. But it will be only a matter of time, I think, with that one. Today Emperor of France, tomorrow the world.'

'Never the United States of America, Herr Brodski.'

'You're right. His selling of Louisiana to you Americans last year does seem to prove that. When he has conquered England, he will turn east, for Russia and India. Follow in the path of Alexander the Great as he has always wished to do.'

'He'll come this way? Are we sitting on a powder keg, here?'

He shrugged. 'We always have been. Be grateful for the difficult road into Lissenberg, Miss Peabody, for yourself and for your companions. The worst that will happen here is starvation. I wish you had Prince Gustav's ear.'

'Oh, why?'

'Someone needs to persuade him to take some thought for the future, to lay in supplies, to try and make Lissenberg more self-sufficient. I am speaking to you as my trusted friend, Miss Peabody.'

'You know you may, and I'm flattered, but, alas, we three have not a jot of influence with the Prince.'

'But Lady Helen is a good friend of Princess Amelia, maybe the best she has.'

'That's true.' Thoughtfully. 'And I have sometimes thought that, disgracefully though he treats her, Prince Gustav listens to his wife's advice more than he lets appear.'

'Precisely. He may have a mistress in every capital in Europe – and very expensive they are too – but when his wife speaks, he listens. Can I persuade you to drop a word in Lady Helen's ear?'

'In the interests of not being starved to death? Certainly. Just tell me what to say.'

He made her a remarkably courtly bow. 'If they are all like you in your United States of America, Miss Peabody, I think the new Emperor is wise not to tamper with them.'

'I'll certainly say something to the Princess,' agreed Lady Helen. 'It's an unpleasant prospect, if true, but I am sure your Jewish friend is exaggerating the danger. For one thing, Lord Nelson's navy will never allow an invasion of England. This parvenu Emperor will waste his strength there in vain. But in the meantime, I wish there were news from Prince Maximilian.' Martha had thought something was troubling her. 'These rehearsals of Cristabel's – I had no idea – you should have told me, Martha.'

'Told you?'

'You know perfectly well what I mean! Throwing herself in his arms like that! What in the world would my brother say?'

'What in the world has your brother to say to anything?'

'He is her father.'

'He's never behaved like one. And Cristabel has played love scenes before.' Was she arguing as much with herself as with Lady Helen?

'Not like this one. There's something about that Franz Wengel . . . He's too handsome . . . They do it too well . . . I wish the professional would arrive.'

147

'But Herr Wengel is a professional.'

'Then he's too good a one for me. He behaves . . . like a prince.'

'He's acting a prince.'

'Too well, and I see no need for Cristabel to throw her heart into the scene the way she does. It's only rehearsal, after all.'

'She'd never agree with you about that.' But did Martha? She offered to chaperone Cristabel's rehearsal next day, telling herself that she did so because she wanted to hear what Wengel thought about Bonaparte's making himself Emperor.

She was shocked at his appearance. If he had looked tired before, he looked hag-ridden now. He actually missed his cue a couple of times, and Cristabel finally announced that she had had enough of rehearsing. 'We must hope the tenor comes soon!'

'Yes indeed.' He agreed with unflattering emphasis. 'Forgive me, Lady Cristabel, if I have seemed abstracted.'

'Abstracted!' Impatiently. 'Not here at all. In Brundt I take it, where the action is.'

'What did she mean by that?' he asked Martha anxiously when Cristabel had left them.

'Nothing, I think. Or, at least nothing that need trouble you.'

It was good to see him laugh. 'You mean, she thinks I've got a girl there?'

'I suspect so.'

'You know better than that.'

'Yes. I'm afraid this new move of Bonaparte's has hit you hard.'

'Hard! It's knocked me out.'

'You'll come about. I'm sure of it.'

'Thank you.' His smile stirred her heart. 'You're a woman in a million, Miss Peabody. You have never said, "I told you so".'

The tenor arrived the next day. 'An Irishman,' Cristabel reported. 'Would you believe it? A young cousin of Michael Kelly's. Prince Maximilian found him in Vienna, singing small parts and trying to learn German. He trained in Italy, so his Italian's good enough, if he can only sing.'

'You've not met him? What's his name?'

'Desmond Fylde. No, I have yet to meet him. He made the journey from Vienna in record time, arrived exhausted and went straight to bed. We are to have a first rehearsal in the morning. Martha, you'll come, won't you? I cannot begin to tell you what a blight my poor aunt cast on things today. I'm really a little anxious about her.'

And she about you. But Martha did not say it. 'Has Prince Maximilian returned too?' she asked instead.

'Not he. Enjoying himself in Vienna, no doubt, and will come back affianced to some eligible young cousin of the Emperor Francis.'

'Without consulting his father?'

'Why should he? Prince Gustav has been making it clear enough that he looks on the little Prince as his heir.'

'In which case Prince Max is hardly likely to find himself a very eligible bride. I wonder which career he really wants, that young man. Prince or musician.'

'I doubt he knows himself. He lets things happen to him.'

'Instead of making them? Well, he's grown up in a hard school. You ought to understand that, Cristabel.'

'Because I did too? But I've escaped.' She blushed. 'Thanks to you. Do I thank you often enough, Martha?'

'No need! Or, if you feel you should, try, for my sake, to be a little more sympathetic to poor Prince Max, who has no one to help him in his choice.'

'What choice?'

'Well, if he wanted to, he could simply end it all by withdrawing from the succession, just as you walked out on your father, but I think he's not likely to do so, and you should understand why. It's this sense of duty you aristocrats suffer from – the best of you. I wouldn't say Prince Gustav was overly afflicted by it, but I suspect that if you could see into Prince Max's heart, you would find that he feels obliged to be available so long as the little prince is so young – such an unknown factor.'

'Yes, he is, isn't he,' said Cristabel thoughtfully. 'Shut up in the Palace as he has been, an ailing infant, a backward boy by what one has seen of him.'

'Devoted to his older brother,' said Martha. 'Did you notice at the prize-giving ceremony how he wanted to run to him?'

'No, did he? Well, that's to Prince Max's credit at least. I wonder what his opera is like.'

'You've not seen it?'

'No one has. He took it with him. Good gracious, maybe that's what he's doing in Vienna!'

'Trying to get it staged? I wonder which version?'

'How do you mean?'

'Don't you remember? There was talk that Prince Gustav disapproved of the original libretto because the heroine outweighed the hero. Another good part for you, Cristabel, by the sound of it. I wonder he never showed it to you.'

'Well, the rules were very strict, the operas were supposed to be seen by no one but the Prince.'

'For fear someone should question his judgment?'

'Very likely.'

Anna came to Martha that evening. 'Fräulein Peabody, the porter-women have asked me to speak to you. They are worried; they've been comparing notes, working things out, they don't think fast, working as hard as they do, but some of the older ones, who have done the winter climb for many years, they got talking to each other. But it sounds crazy,' she broke off.

'What does? Tell me, Anna?'

'They think twice as much as usual went up to the castle last winter. Beans, lentils . . . smoked meats . . . Things that keep a long time. When they got talking about it, they started to wonder why. They just hope that the supplies in the valley will be sufficiently made up this summer.'

'And are they being?'

'That's why they asked me to come to you. It's not the kind of thing you can be sure of, but they don't think so. They thought, as you are such a friend of Herr Brodski, perhaps you could find out. Because if they aren't, we're going to be in trouble next winter, and no mistake. If only the old Prince hadn't died we'd have had a road through all year round by now. He had engineers talking about it, even decided where to blast through, then he died, sudden, and that was that. "Too expensive," Prince Gustav said after he bought us, but we think he likes things the way they are. He's almost God here, in the winter, when you think about it. I'm trusting you, Fräulein.'

'You know you can. But I had no idea there had been talk of a road through.'

'No, you wouldn't. He doesn't like it talked about, and what he says goes. But if you would have a word with Herr Brodski, Fräulein, ask him to contrive a look at the warehouses, both in Lissenberg, and in Brundt, make sure we're not imagining things.'

'And what if you're not?'

'Then something will have to be done, won't it? Or we're all going to be hungry next winter.'

'But why?'

'Probably just because no one thought of it. And, of course, everyone knows how deep the Prince is in debt. That's another thing we don't talk about. Why should he care if a few hundred starve to death in Brundt?'

'Monstrous! And it's half way through the summer already,' she realised. 'Wait a moment, Anna, I'll write a note to Herr Brodski, ask him to come and see me. I do hope he's in Lissenberg.'

'Oh yes, he is, Fräulein, that's why I came to you today.'

Brodski called next morning and listened impassively to what she had to say. When she ended by saying, 'But, surely, Herr Brodski, it's impossible; they must be imagining things,' he looked at her gravely.

'Nothing is impossible here in Lissenberg,' he told her. 'And, in fact, I had heard rumours myself of warehouses that are not so well-stocked as they should be for the time of year. But as I knew that the normal amount of supplies had been coming in, I am afraid I shrugged it off as just anti-government talk, of which lord knows there is plenty, in private. But what I did not know was that twice the usual amount was taken up to the castle last winter. I don't think anyone knows that. On that basis, there most certainly is cause for alarm.'

'But what's to be done?'

His smile transformed the dour, handsome face. 'I like the way you go to the heart of the matter, Miss Peabody. First, I shall confirm the facts of the case. Then I shall talk to some of my friends.'

'Not to the Lord Chamberlain?'

'What use would that be? He would listen politely, and push paper around, so that nothing got done for three years or so. Your nameless friend is quite right about Prince Gustav's debts. If I told you what he owes, just to me, it would shock your father's daughter to the bone. No, no. The merchants of Lissenberg will have to take their own action. I hope I shall be able to persuade them to do so. After all, if it does come to a crisis, they should be able to command their own prices – on paper at least – for what they manage to bring in. But just in case I am less successful than I hope, I think you should urge your porter-ladies to make what arrangements they can for their own families. A little tightening of the belt this summer, to lay down more than usual of their own produce for the winter. A little more poaching, maybe, than the menfolk usually risk, so that there shall be some salt meat too.'

'Their belts are pretty tight already,' she had been thinking while he talked. 'Herr Brodski, I insist on being allowed to help. You will put the most you think I can afford into the fund you are setting up, and I mean the most. I don't see why the poor should be the only ones to tighten their belts. Could you find a buyer for my diamonds, do you think?'

'Not in Lissenberg, nor do I propose to try. But I will gladly let you contribute what I think reasonable. And there is something else you could do, could you persuade Lady Cristabel to write to her mother?'

'But, why?' And then. 'Stupid of me . . . Count Tafur.'

'Just so. A powerful man. We need value for money in this operation, Miss Peabody. A word from him would help us to get it.'

'Then you shall have it.' How strange it was to know that Franz Wengel's planned revolution might change everything. But she tried hard not even to think about this for fear of betraying him.

'Write to Mama?' Cristabel had returned from a rehearsal of the whole company flushed with excitement. 'If you like; it's about time I did, but to say what, Martha?'

'Just a short casual message to Count Tafur. But, tell about your rehearsal, Cristabel. How is the new tenor?'

'Admirable! His Italian's not too good, but our Lissenbergers won't care about that, and his voice is just right for mine. And as for his looks – you just wait until you see him, Martha. We'll have the chorus swooning over him in droves . . . And Irish charm until you hardly know where to look!'

'No Irish brogue, I do hope?'

'Only when he wants. It's all part of the Irish charm, huge black eyes and hair worn a little longer than usual. And just the right height for me; Herr Wengel was a little tall, I had to play our big scene on tiptoe. Do you know, I really begin to have hopes for this production, Martha! He's a quick study, too, he tells me. We're to rehearse our scene this afternoon. You'll come and be our chaperone, won't you?' She smiled brilliantly. 'I might even need one, now it's Desmond Fylde and his Irish eyes.'

'Lady Helen rather thought you needed one with Herr Wengel,' said Martha a touch drily.

'No! Idiotic. My poor aunt must be going out of her mind. Herr Wengel indeed! Oh, he's got a brilliant future in front of him if *Crusader Prince* is the success I expect, but look at his past. What's known of it.'

'What do you mean?'

'You didn't know? There are some very curious stories about his birth. Oh, that formidable old grandmother of his carries it off with a high hand, but so far as one can make out her daughter was no better than she should have been. A very huddled-up affair of a wedding, and the baby born much too soon after it. No wonder he has a chip on his shoulder and some revolutionary ideas to go with it, that Franz Wengel. And my aunt was worrying about me and him!' Her tone was one of honest amazement. 'She should have known me better.'

So should I, thought Martha. 'My grandmother was a servant girl,' she said.

'Ah, but dear Martha, you are an American.'

And a rich one. Another of the things she did not say. There were getting to be too many of them. 'Who told you about Franz Wengel's mother?' she asked. 'And what became of his father?'

'I don't know.' Shrugging. 'As to who told me – one of the chorus, I think. They don't have much to do when they are off stage but gossip, and more of them than you would expect are native Lissenbergers.'

'Didn't Prince Max make a point of giving them the preference, where it was possible?'

'I believe he did. Franzosi grumbles a good deal about their

Italian. That's why I don't think it's going to matter about Desmond Fylde's accent not being exactly perfect.'

'I look forward to meeting him,' said Martha.

Fylde was everything Cristabel had said, but Martha could not quite like him just the same. Because she knew she lacked it, she had always fought her instinctive distrust of charm, but as she watched Desmond Fylde say exactly the right thing, in just the right tone, to Cristabel, to Lady Helen, even, occasionally, to herself, she felt increasingly that there was something about him that was altogether too good to be true.

But Cristabel had been right that he was the ideal partner for her. 'I begin to think we have a winner in *Crusader Prince*,' Franz Wengel told Martha one hot July afternoon at the end of a last act rehearsal. 'I owe Prince Maximilian a great debt for finding Herr Fylde. I look forward to telling him so.'

'If he ever arrives,' said Martha. 'But you're right. Fylde and Lady Cristabel are extraordinary together. It's quite un-believable how his voice brings out the best in hers. But, Herr Wengel . . .' She paused, searching for words.

'Yes? Something is troubling you?'

'It's the last scene of all. Forgive me, but I have the curious feeling of something not quite right, something missing. It builds so high, and then, nothing. Forgive me,' she said again, conscious of a rare, infuriating blush.

'Forgive!' With one of his quick, keen glances. 'For being too acute a critic? But don't worry, Miss Peabody, it will all come together on the night, I promise you. And, in the meantime, as my friend, I beg you not to mention this to anyone else. Lady Cristabel and Herr Fylde are too absorbed in each other to notice, and I doubt anyone else will.'

'No.' She agreed with him so heartily that she did not sleep that night. Just what was he planning for the first night of *Crusader Prince*?

14

The anniversary celebrations were to begin at the end of August, and culminate in the first performance of *Crusader Prince*, on the seventh of September the day Prince Gustav had actually entered Lissenberg, twenty-five years before. By the end of July preparations were going on furiously. Every inn in Lissenberg was fully booked, and a small army of women from the town were up at the Palace, scrubbing and scouring neglected wings that were to be filled with the Prince's guests.

'If they come,' Ishmael Brodski told Martha.

'Is it in doubt?'

'It must be, since Prince Gustav has not yet made peace with the Emperor. And the latest news is that Napoleon himself has started on a tour of the Rhineland and invited his allies to pay court to him at Mainz. If you were one of them, Miss Peabody, would you go there, or come here to Prince Gustav's little celebration?'

'The Prince will be furious.'

'Much good it will do him. Baden will send a high level representative, I expect, because of Princess Amelia, but I have no doubt that the Prince himself, and his grandson, will be at Mainz with the rest of the Rhineland princes. And even Prince Gustav will hardly expect the Holy Roman Emperor to come to little Lissenberg.'

'I wonder who he will send.'

'And whether Prince Maximilian will return with news of an Austrian alliance. You have heard the rumours that Prince Gustav will finally name his heir during the anniversary celebrations?'

'No! Who?'

'That's the question. I think everyone now begins to accept that the little prince is not likely to live to succeed even if he were to be named heir. Prince Maximilian continues in black disgrace.' He ran surprisingly aristocratic long fingers through thickly curling hair. 'May I treat you as a male associate, Miss Peabody?'

'Please.'

'You know, of course, about Prince Gustav's latest mistress, the Countess Bemberg? He makes them all countesses, but this one is at least a Lissenberger . . .'

'I had heard something.'

'Naturally. But had you heard that she gave birth to a healthy boy not long ago?'

'No! But, Herr Brodski, he couldn't . . . The Princess Amelia . . .'

'One would certainly think not. But, you know the saying, that whom they wish to destroy the Gods first make mad. I am beginning to wonder if that is not what is happening here.'

'You cannot be serious.' With a quick, anxious look at the door.

'Never more so. I asked Anna to wait outside.'

'For fear of eavesdroppers?'

'Yes.'

'What are you saying to me?'

'That I think the situation here is going from bad to worse. Something is going on, Miss Peabody, and even I do not know what it is. My usual sources of information have dried up entirely. I don't like it. We're sitting on a mine, in more ways than one. Frankly, I don't want to be here when it goes up. You'll think me a coward, but you know as well as I do that we Jews are always the first to suffer when things go wrong. I have written to my friends, the Rothschilds, to warn them that I intend to get out of Lissenberg before the roads are closed for winter, and I urge that you and your friends do likewise. Foreigners are apt to be targets too at such times.'

'But the opera . . . the company . . . Lady Cristabel would never . . .'

'She could ask for leave of absence after the celebrations are over. Go to Venice to see her mother . . . Wait things out there.'

'I doubt she'd do it.' Cristabel was full of plans for a season with Desmond Fylde.

'The new tenor?' As so often, Brodski read her mind. 'Very well then, leave her and her aunt, they're Palace servants after all, they should be safe enough. Your case is quite different. You have made yourself too well loved here in Lissenberg for the Prince's liking. First the women porters, now the money you have put into supplies. Don't think he doesn't know about that. And your country is a long way off. If an "accident" were to happen to you in the course of a disturbance of some kind, or if you were simply to disappear, what do you think would be done about it?'

'I don't know.' She said it slowly, thinking of those ice-cold cells behind the tunnel.

'Dead women tell no tales. Miss Peabody —' He rose, towered over her, hesitated for a moment. 'My mother was a noble Polish lady; my Jewish father ran the family estates. They ran away together, loved each other most devotedly; the happiest couple I ever knew. They brought me up as a Protestant, the world treats me as a Jew, always has, always will. But I'm a rich man. Not as rich as you, but rich enough. And I am tired of being treated as I am here, consigned to the Ghetto. I am going to look for a new life, in your United States. Come with me! I have loved you for a long time. I believe we could be as happy together as my parents were. I am asking you to be my wife, Miss Peabody.' He looked down at her, black eyes blazing.

'I'm more flattered than I can say.' For the first time, a proposal had taken her completely by surprise. 'I wish I could say yes. I truly do. But — I don't love you.'

'I've enough for two.' He took her hand. 'Give me a chance to make you love me? We could do so much together, you and I. And — children. I'd so much like your children. Ah — don't cry!'

'I can't help it.' She looked up at him, trying to smile, letting the tears fall, her hand still in his. 'It's so much what I've always wanted. And I can't.'

'May I ask why not? I don't think it's because I am a Jew.'

'Of course not! It's much simpler than that; it's because I love someone else. Hopelessly, I think, but that's not the point, is it?'

'It might be,' he said. 'You always face facts, Martha Peabody. It's one of the things I love in you. If you know it is hopeless, give me a chance? Let me be your escort back to America. I promise you shall be cherished, adored,

157

chaperoned, and not a word said of this until you are safe home in Philadelphia. Then, let me ask you again.'

'Safe home in Philadelphia?' She said it almost wistfully. 'I've been chaperoned enough for a lifetime, but cherished . . .' She released her hand, brushed it across her eyes. 'No, it wouldn't be fair. And, besides, I'm not going back to Philadelphia. I think my life is here in Europe now, whatever happens.'

He looked at her gravely. 'But suppose you lose it?'

'I'll suppose no such thing! But –' a shiver ran down her spine. 'You won't leave at once, Herr Brodski?'

'Not if you won't come with me. I told you I loved you. If you stay, I stay.'

'Oh!' Her hand went up to her mouth. 'I'm glad, of course. But if something happened, if you were hurt, it would be my fault.'

'Nonsense!' The black eyes sparked at her. 'Mine only, for being an obstinate dog of a Jew who still hopes to make you change your mind. Yes?' There was a scratching on the door.

Anna. 'It's Prince Maximilian,' she said. 'He's back, asking for Lady Cristabel.'

'Who is rehearsing,' said Martha, 'with Desmond Fylde. Send the Prince in, Anna.' She caught a long, measuring look from Brodski. Sympathy. He thought she loved the Prince. It would be comic if it were not all so sad.

'Then I must leave you,' said Brodski. 'Think of what I have said.'

'It's been a long time.' Martha held out a friendly hand to Prince Maximilian.

'Too long!' He looked exhausted, anxious, angry? 'I should have returned sooner, with or without leave. What's going on here, Miss Peabody?'

'You ask me that!'

He laughed angrily and she thought with a little shock of surprise that the charming boy had grown up at last. 'You are as likely to tell me as anyone else! My father won't see me, spends all his time with the Countess Bemberg –' A note of savage mockery on the title. 'My poor stepmother is ill and so is young Gustav. I don't like the look of him at all. The doctors

158

are baffled, they say. It couldn't be more unfortunate, just when the Prince is ready to name his heir.'

'He's really going to?'

'He's committed to it. And I came back with such hopes! I wanted Lady Cristabel to be the first to know, but she is busy rehearsing. At least *Crusader Prince* seems to be shaping up well. She and Mr. Fylde make a brilliant pair, I hear. Franzosi is delighted with them.' Was he himself less so? He was silent for a moment, lost in gloomy thoughts of his own.

'But your news, Prince Maximilian?' she prompted him gently. 'Your high hopes?'

'My opera is to be put on at the Burgtheater in Vienna. It's a great honour, the chance I had hardly dared dream of. They want me there for the production, of course. If you could have heard the flattering things Signor Salieri said! I had hoped that Lady Cristabel . . . But she is too busy rehearsing even to see me, and now, with little Gustav so ill, I am afraid the Prince will have no option but to name me Regent at least. And there go all my plans . . .'

'You'd feel it your duty to stay here?'

'Of course. There is so much needs doing. Naturally, I hope the Prince will live for many years, but he has never interested himself in Lissenberg's problems. Once I had some standing in the country, I think I could do a little . . . It's my duty to try . . . And so much for my plans for a life in music. This kind of chance doesn't come twice. I had even hoped . . . let myself believe that Lady Cristabel . . . But the time I've spent in Austria has made me see things more clearly than when I was shut away here in Lissenberg. We must have strong allies for the dangerous years ahead. I think I must resign myself to a dynastic marriage, the question is, which way?'

She thought he was taking a great deal dangerously for granted, but it was not her place to say so. One point though she did feel she must raise. 'The Lissenbergers,' diffidently, 'they have strong views, Prince Maximilian. Should they not be considered? There was a great deal of hostile talk, you know, when word of a possible Russian alliance got out. They don't much like foreigners.'

'You're well informed. So maybe you can tell me what has become of Franz Wengel, whom I expected to find here, putting the last touches to his opera.'

'He's not here? But I saw him only yesterday, he was delighted with the way things were going. He said nothing about leaving.' But when had Franz Wengel talked about his own plans?

'He's gone just the same. To Brundt, they say. Said he'd be back for the dress-rehearsal. What can be more important than *Crusader Prince* just now?'

'What is your opera called?' She thought it time to change the subject. 'What's its theme? Your duty of secrecy to Prince Gustav must be long over now.'

'Yes, of course. It's a German theme, Miss Peabody. One of our old legends. About a valkyrie – one of Odin's hand-maidens – who falls in love with a mortal and loses her own immortality as a result. I had hoped that it would be the first of a series, a kind of cycle of operas, about their fates and those of their child. The Prince detested it.' An angry laugh. 'Said it was a glorification of the female principle and that I should be ashamed of myself. It would be a wonderful part for Lady Cristabel. Well, I wrote it for her. They like it particularly in Vienna, feel it appropriate to this time of war, and rumours of war. Did you know that Herr van Beethoven is working on an opera too? I long to see it. A liberation theme, they say. Mind you, not everybody likes his music in Vienna. The old guard finds him too difficult. Not Papa Haydn, of course.'

'Did you meet him?'

'Oh yes, both of them. Both interesting men in their different ways. I can't tell you how stimulating it is to be in Vienna, Miss Peabody. But tell me about *Crusader Prince*. Is it really going as well as Franzosi says? His geese do tend to be swans. To be frank with you, I was not too happy about Wengel's libretto when I finally managed to see it. A terrible tailing off in the second half, I thought.'

'There's been some rewriting.' She could hardly say less.

'I'm glad to hear it. Including, I take it, this famous scene between Lady Cristabel and Fylde, that no one is allowed to witness. You must have seen it.'

'Many times, but not since Mr. Fylde took over. He's magnificent, Cristabel says.'

'A real find. I hope he is keeping up his German lessons. I'd like him for the tenor rôle in *Odin's Daughter*.'

160

'Your opera is to be sung in German?'

'Yes, indeed. Now that Austria and Prussia look to become allies at last, there's a great deal of all-German feeling building up in Austria. Herr Beethoven is working with a German libretto too, I understand. I think Wengel may find himself behind the times in clinging to the Italian. Is it really true that he insists no one see the last scene of his opera even at the dress-rehearsal?'

'I believe so.' She found herself wondering if Wengel had gone away to avoid further discussion of this.

'Lunatic! I must see him. Ah! Lady Cristabel!' He turned eagerly to greet her, his colour suddenly high. 'I hear you are surpassing even yourself as Algisa. I long to hear you. But what is this idiocy about the last scene? You must help me make Herr Wengel see sense. And you, too, Mr. Fylde.' Turning to the tenor, who had entered the room behind Cristabel.

'Ah, but you don't understand Prince.' Martha had noticed how subtly Fylde slid in and out of a touch of Irish brogue. 'It's a brilliant idea of Herr Wengel's. No one is to know how the opera ends until the first performance. It will raise public anticipation immensely, don't you see? In fact –' one of his ravishing smiles for Martha, 'even Miss Peabody doesn't know the ending, though she thinks she does.'

'You've changed it again?'

'Herr Wengel has.' He touched a finger elegantly to full lips. 'But mum's the word. We are all sworn to secrecy, and Herr Wengel is not a man one ignores.'

'Ridiculous,' Maximilian turned back to Cristabel, 'I appeal to your good sense, Lady Cristabel . . .'

'Mine? What would I be doing with sense, Prince? I'm your prima donna, remember.'

Did Maximilian recognise, as Martha did, the faint trace of Fylde's Irish brogue in her voice? 'I beg your pardon,' he said, colour higher than ever, 'I had mistaken you for the Lady Cristabel Sallis. A duke's daughter with some knowledge of the world.'

'Thank you.' She swept him a mocking curtsy. 'And so I am. And so I have. But Mr. Fylde has more, and you would be well-advised to recognise it. You talk of rank, Prince, so let me tell you that Mr. Fylde would be a prince in Ireland if we all had our rights. And I am proud to recognise him as such.'

She turned to look up at Fylde with such a naked blaze of adoration that the little group fell suddenly silent.

Martha watched the colour ebb from Maximilian's face, leaving him sheet-white. Someone must speak. 'Well, I'm nobody's daughter, in your terms, Prince,' smiling at Maximilian, 'but I value my own judgment too, and I believe there may be something in what Mr. Fylde says. You've never met Herr Wengel, have you? I promise you, he is no fool. He would not hold out for this secrecy without very good reason. And we do have to face it that the new Emperor Napoleon is holding court at Mainz just when the anniversary celebrations take place here. It would be a disaster to have a thin house for *Crusader Prince*, for all kinds of reasons, political as well as personal. You must see that. And this secret ending, if word gets about, which naturally it will, must be a great public draw.'

'For the wrong kind of public,' said Maximilian.

'That may be true. But any public perhaps better than none? Imagine your father faced with empty seats.'

'Oh very well,' Martha thought him so shaken by what Cristabel had revealed of her feeling for Fylde that he hardly cared what he said, 'have your great mystery then.' He forced a smile for Cristabel. 'And forgive my intrusion.' He made them a comprehensive bow which managed, somehow, to exclude Fylde. 'Good-day, ladies.'

'And good riddance,' said Fylde cheerfully when he had gone. 'But at least we have gained Wengel's point for him, thanks to you, Miss Peabody. He'll be grateful, I've no doubt.' He smiled at her knowingly, and she found herself very close to hating him.

'Lady Helen,' Martha had managed to find her alone in her room, 'I'm worried about Cristabel.'

'Oh?' Lady Helen looked up from her embroidery.

'When did you last sit in on a rehearsal?'

'Oh, some time ago. Now we have a professional singer, it's less important, and Herr Wengel has this great passion for secrecy.'

'I see.' She had been busy herself with arrangements about winter supplies. 'Cristabel seems to think Mr. Fylde is an Irish prince.'

'A what?'

'An Irish prince, if he had his rights. Could it be possible?'

'I shouldn't think so. The child is daydreaming again. He's a great charmer, of course.' Tolerantly. 'If it makes it easier for her to act with him, that she imagines herself a little into love with him, what matter?'

'I think it might matter a great deal. I wish you would talk to her about him, Lady Helen. Make her see him for the fortune-hunter I am sure he is.'

'But what fortune?' asked Lady Helen.

Tempers shortened and tension mounted as the celebrations loomed nearer. Princess Amelia and her son were still gravely ill. 'Not well enough to see me,' Lady Helen returned from the Palace looking anxious.

'And the little prince?' asked Martha.

'No change, they say. And look very glum when they say it. Poor little boy. I saw Baron Hals, the Chamberlain, while I was waiting. He looks positively hag-ridden. And no wonder, poor man. Lord knows what would happen if one of them were to die when the celebrations were at their height.'

'It doesn't bear thinking of,' said Cristabel. 'You can't mean they might be cancelled, Aunt?'

'They would have to be, my dear. You must see that.'

'*Crusader Prince*?' It was a wail of anguish.

'I think you should be steeling yourself for the possibility.'

'Surely to God the Prince would have the wits to keep a death secret if it should happen so inconveniently.' Desmond Fylde had called, as he frequently did, to escort Cristabel to their rehearsal.

'They say he is in a savage humour.' Martha had long since stopped being shocked by Fylde, though it still amazed her that Cristabel seemed unaware of his basic coarseness.

'Your friend Brodski, I suppose.' Lady Helen had a special tone of voice for Ishmael Brodski. 'He keeps you well-informed.'

Her tone reminded Martha of the short, sharp battle they had fought over her seeing Brodski alone. For a moment, she was actually tempted to throw his proposal like a bombshell into their midst. Tempted to accept it? 'Yes, Brodski,' she said. 'And Prince Maximilian, who called yesterday hoping to see you, Cristabel. He told me his father is furious at the low level of representatives who are being sent to the celebration. No potentates for your great night, I am afraid.'

'I'd rather have a few people who understand music and will really listen,' said Cristabel.

'Ah, they'll listen to you, Lady Cristabel.' Fylde's huge brown eyes, languishing at Cristabel, reminded Martha of a spaniel she had once had. 'As to cancellation, we'll not be thinking of it. But it's time we went to work, you and I, my princess. Poor Franzosi has worries enough without our being late.'

'His princess!' fumed Lady Helen when they had gone. 'The impudence of it! Oh yes, no need to tell me that's the part she plays in the opera, I know that as well as you do. But the way she lets him use it as a term of endearment! Martha, I begin to think you were right and I was wrong. But how could I dream that she would take that bold-faced adventurer seriously! I shall be glad when this opera is over! And in the meantime, I believe we should think a little about Mr. Desmond Fylde. He's a cousin of Mr. Kelly's, is that right?'

'So I believe.'

'It hardly sounds like royal stock.'

'No.' Martha smiled. 'If Mr. Kelly had had the slightest pretension to royal blood, I am sure he would have let one know it. But it could be on the other side, mind you.'

'Who could I write to?' Lady Helen frowned. 'The trouble is, I don't want to start tongues wagging about Cristabel any more than they do already, and any enquiry about Mr. Fylde would be bound to have that effect.'

'Yes.' Martha smiled at her, not without a trace of malice. 'Dear Lady Helen, shall I ask my good informant, Herr Brodski to put some enquiries in train for us?'

'Oh, my dear, if you would!'

15

Disconcertingly, Brodski had anticipated Martha's request for information about Fylde. 'I thought it was bound to come sooner or later,' he told her, 'when I saw the sheep's eyes he was making at Lady Cristabel. He's no more royal than you, Miss Peabody, and a good deal less so than I am on my mother's side. He's up from the Dublin slums, and not much of a cousin of Mr. Kelly's either, though I doubt Kelly would disown him. The Irish seem to stick together, especially when they are away from home.'

'Just an adventurer then?'

'A man with his way to make. Yes. A brilliant singer, a consummate actor in life as well as on stage. If I were you, Miss Peabody, I would use this information very cautiously. You don't want to drive the poor deluded girl into his arms.'

'I know. Best wait until after the performance to do anything, don't you think?'

'Absolutely. And after the Prince's declaration of his heir.'

'You think it may be Prince Maximilian after all?'

'For once in my life, I do not know what to think. When did you last see Franz Wengel?'

'A few days ago. I hear he has gone to Brundt.'

'Just when rehearsals of his opera are reaching their climax. Odd, isn't it?'

'Well, yes.' Even to this dear friend she must be careful what she said. 'Perhaps he has gone away to avoid further discussion of the secrecy surrounding the last scene?'

'Shirking his fences, they'd call it in England. It doesn't sound like Wengel to me.'

'But you and I have just agreed not to trouble Lady Cristabel with the truth about Desmond Fylde until the opera is safely over.'

'True enough. But there is something about Wengel that troubles me, baffles me . . . Something I can't put my finger on. It's not often I feel like this. But you – I think you like the man, Miss Peabody. Trust him?'

'Yes.' Here at least she could give unqualified assent.

'And I respect your judgment as my own.'

'Thank you.' Now she felt guilty because of all that she had not told him.

'Do you know a surprising thing?' Brodski said now. 'Those two dubious young men, Lodge and Playfair are back.'

'Back? But how can they be? After being asked to leave?'

'They have come as representatives of the Austrian administration in Venice. Not much Prince Gustav can do about that.'

'What a very odd choice.'

'Is it not? Hardly surprising Prince Gustav is not in the best of tempers. Which is putting it mildly, I understand. I think you three ladies should congratulate yourselves on the fact that you have not been invited to the celebrations at the Palace. There is a rumour that Countess Bemberg will be presiding, since Princess Amelia is too ill to do so.'

'Good gracious,' said Martha. 'How would Lady Helen take that?'

'Just as well she's not going to have to. But I think the Prince may be making a serious mistake. Even the Lissenbergers have their breaking-point, and the Bemberg might just be it. Her reputation was not of the best before the Prince happened on her. To put it mildly. I am treating you as a male associate again.'

'I like it.'

'Good. Well, the word in Lissenberg is that they were happy enough to have the Bemberg foist her bastard – forgive me – on the Prince for support – what's one more, after all? – but any suggestion that the child be legitimised would cause outrage.'

'You mean it's not his?'

'Precisely. He may delude himself, if he wishes to, that he is still capable of fathering a child. His doctors know better. The very fact that the Countess's brat is said to be healthy is an argument against its being his. Look at the poor little prince.'

'One doesn't get much chance to.'

'Exactly.'

*　　*　　*

Martha had just retired to her room that night when Anna came tapping at her door. 'May I speak to you for a moment?'

'Of course.' The girl looked distraught.

'It's Prince Maximilian. He came down the tunnel. He's in the women's hall. He asks that you come to him. It's urgent, he says.'

'Now?' It was very late.

'Yes. Tell no one, he says. He'll explain.'

'I should hope so.' But she had picked up a dark shawl and wrapped it round her. 'You'll come too, Anna? If we meet someone, it's a problem about the arrangements for next year's supplies.'

They met no one. The air of the women's hall struck chill since no fire had been lit there all summer. It was dark, too. Martha took the lantern from Anna's hand at the top of the steps down into the hall. 'Wait here. If someone comes, stop them.'

'Yes.' Her cold hand shook as she gave Martha the lantern.

'Thank you for coming.' Maximilian spoke softly from the darkness near where the fire should have been. 'I could think of no one else to turn to.'

'What is it?' She pitched her voice low, like his, so that even Anna, keeping watch for them, should not hear.

'It's Princess Amelia. I've managed to get her away. Hidden her in a disused dungeon I found when I was a boy. But she can't stay there. It's cold. And she's ill. Not as ill as they think, but ill enough.'

'What do you mean?'

'She was being poisoned. Her maid suspected something and came to me. She has eaten only what I managed to provide for the last few days, is better, but there is no way we can keep it up; the danger to her is too great; he might resort to more drastic measures.'

'Dear God. You mean, he –'

'Don't say it. Not even here. I could think of no one but you, Miss Peabody. Can you help her?'

'I must,' said Martha. 'But how?' She thought for a moment. Then: 'I trust Anna absolutely. She and I could get her up to my room, but how to explain her presence after that? Tell me, how close a check is being kept on the visitors who enter Lissenberg for the celebrations?'

'Not as close as the Prince had intended.' Maximilian's voice was dry. 'There's disaffection in the Civil Service. Well, their pay is in arrears, what does he expect?'

'So someone could have slipped through?'

'Yes. But – a woman on her own?'

'It doesn't seem likely, does it? I know! She came in with Lodge and Playfair, a friend of Cristabel's mother. A servant, perhaps? A messenger? Urging us to get out of Lissenberg before the winter.'

'You'd be very wise to do so,' he said soberly, then lowered his voice to a thread of a whisper. 'He's losing control, Miss Peabody. This proves it. He's dangerous. I should have come back sooner. I'm out of touch. I don't know what to do, whom to trust. I've never felt so inadequate in my life. It's terrible at the Palace. He has these rages. We shuffle our feet, try not to meet each other's eyes, say nothing. He grows more autocratic every day. Anything could happen up there.'

'The little prince? What about him?'

'Ah, poor little boy. He's dying, I'm afraid. And all his father's fault.'

'Not –'

'No, no, not poison, stupidity. Prince Gustav wanted him to make an impression on his guests. He insisted that he ride over the mountain with him to welcome the first diplomatic arrivals. It was too much for an ailing child. He lost control of his pony and was thrown. You hadn't heard?'

'Only that he was ill.'

'There you are.' A kind of savage satisfaction in his tone. 'That tells you how absolute Prince Gustav is! The whole court saw the child thrown, and no one has dared breathe a word of it. You had better not either. But how will you persuade Lodge and Playfair to back this story of yours?'

'I shall blackmail them,' she said.

'Dear me! I think I won't ask you with what. You should have been a princess, Miss Peabody. Or, better still, a prince!'

'I'm very happy as I am, thank you. So long as we all survive the next few weeks. But we had better rescue the Princess from her cold cell. There will be no one about in the hostel now. I think Anna and I can get her safe up to my rooms. She can walk, I hope?'

'Just. She's very weak, poor lady.' He reached down to

take the lantern from her. 'This way. We won't speak; the guard-room is too close.'

Summer made no difference here. It was ice-cold in the tunnel itself, and when Maximilian turned off down an apparent dead-end they met the damp. The flickering beam of the lantern showed it glistening on walls and ceiling, and Martha restrained an exclamation as a freezing drop fell on her face. In front of her, Maximilian had bent low under an arch. Following him, she saw a tiny cell, what looked like a heap of scrap metal, with a cloaked figure awkwardly perched on it.

'Highness!' she whispered, taking an icy hand. 'I've come to help.'

'Don't call me that! Call me Mary . . . One of my names. And, thank you!' The Princess raised huge hollowed out eyes to Martha's. Even in this dim light she looked ghastly, her own skeleton.

'Best be going.' Maximilian handed Martha the lantern and helped the Princess to her feet. 'And, not a word. Can you lead the way, Miss Peabody?'

'I think so.'

It was a slow, difficult business, the tunnel so narrow that it was hard for Maximilian to help the Princess, and, when they reached the vaulted women's hall at last, he picked her up and carried her over to where Anna was waiting. Putting her down, he asked: 'Can you manage from here?'

'I shall!' The Princess pushed back her concealing shawl, managed a ghost of a smile for him. 'I do thank you, Max.'

'Hush!' Martha put a gentle hand on Anna's to quench her exclamation as she recognised the Princess. 'We'd best be going, if you are strong enough, Mary. You'll call tomorrow, Prince?'

'Early. I wish you God speed, ladies.'

As they helped the Princess up the stairs to her room, Martha thought of all the things she should have said to Maximilian. Too late now. Settling the exhausted Princess in her own bed, she turned to Anna. 'Can you find me a pallet, Anna, anything? I'll sleep on the floor beside her.'

'I hope you know what you are doing.' Anna had looked terrified since she recognised the Princess.

'What else can I do? But I promise I'll not involve you further, Anna. Except for one thing.'

'Yes?'

'Could you get a message to Frau Schmidt for me? Ask her to come and see me as soon as she can.'

'She's in Lissenberg for the celebrations,' said Anna. 'I'll send first thing. And, Fräulein Peabody, of course I'll do anything I can to help. The poor . . .'

'My poor friend Mary.' She looked down at the Princess, who had fallen into the total sleep of exhaustion. 'Thank you, Anna.'

The thin pallet made it easy to wake early. The Princess was still deeply asleep when Martha left her to go and knock quietly on Lady Helen's door.

'Yes, what is it?' Lady Helen was an early riser, but did not like her privacy invaded until she had her face ready for the world.

'Trouble.' Martha plunged into her story, making it as brief as possible. 'I don't think we should tell Cristabel,' she said at last. 'She needs to concentrate on the opera.'

'Yes, indeed. But – do you really believe Prince Maximilian? Mad to have let him talk you into this! Are you quite sure? It seems incredible!'

'It's true, though. The Princess is asleep in my bed.'

'What will Prince Gustav do when he finds her missing this morning?'

'God knows! In the meantime, she is a friend of Cristabel's mother's, who accepted the escort of Lodge and Playfair to Lissenberg and got ill on the way. Too ill to see anyone. I shall look after her.'

'You can't possibly keep it up for long. If anyone should see her . . .'

'I know. We've got to get her away. I'm trying to arrange it.'

'Don't tell me,' said Lady Helen. 'I don't want to know.' She gave Martha a long, thoughtful look. 'You're absolutely right about Cristabel. She must not hear about it; you know what anxiety of any kind does to her voice. So – I had better not know anything either. I am ashamed not to be able to help you, Martha.'

'Don't be.' How rarely Lady Helen used her first name. 'All I need is your silence, and I know I can count on that.' How strange it was that everyone seemed to think her in love with

170

Prince Max. This led her thoughts to Brodski, but he was not the ally she needed now.

When she got back to her room she found the Princess awake and looking just slightly better. 'I'll get you something to eat.' She had given strict orders that her surprise guest was not to be disturbed.

'How can I thank you?'

'Too early yet.' With a smile. 'I'm afraid I shall have to leave you locked in here while I try to arrange things for you. I hope you won't mind.'

'Mind? If you just knew how good it is to be alive, to be hungry. But —' her face clouded, remembering. 'My little boy, my poor little boy, do you know how he is? I've heard nothing since I've been so ill.'

'I'll try and find out.' It was not the time to tell her Max's story.

It was very early still. She must find out where Lodge and Playfair were staying. She sat down and wrote them a note, thanking them for their kindness to 'Count Tafur's friend Mary Schnelling'. She thought for a minute, then added a careful phrase: 'What a delightful surprise — after our last meeting — to hear that you have been able to return.' That should be enough to make them anxious about what she might know of the background to that odd business at the masquerade.

Anna appeared. 'A message from Frau Schmidt, Fräulein. She is below in her carriage; asks that you take a turn with her.'

'Admirable woman!' Frau Schmidt must have recognised the urgency of the message. 'My bedroom door is locked, Anna. My guest is ill; no one is to go in.' She was in the hall now, shrugging into her pelisse, intending to be overheard by a loitering servant.

The closed carriage had drawn up a little way beyond the hostel entrance, clear of the bustle surrounding it. As Martha approached, the door swung open and a strong hand reached down to pull her inside. For an instant, she froze with terror. But she knew that hand. 'How very melodramatic,' she looked squarely at Franz Wengel.

'My abject apologies.' The carriage was moving forward already. 'But my grandmother is ill, too ill to come. She had the good sense to pass your message to me. I am here at your service, but I cannot afford to be seen so near the theatre –'

'That you are neglecting so strangely. I can quite see that. And I am grateful to you for coming so quick. But, Frau Schmidt, is she really ill?'

'I am afraid so. And since she has her heart entirely set on seeing my opera she has agreed to be very sensible in the meantime. Luckily I was in Lissenberg, visiting her, when your message came. You said it was urgent, so I'm here.'

'Thank you. I think you will agree that it is.' Once again she told her story as swiftly as possible, aware as she did so of a tide rising in the man who sat facing her. Of excitement? Of exultation?

'Poisoning his own wife,' he said at last. 'But no way to prove it, I imagine.'

'I don't know whether Prince Max thought about that. His only thought was to get his stepmother to safety.'

'And very sensibly he did so. He trusts no one at the Palace?'

'So he told me. He says he's been away too long, is out of touch.'

'Fatal. Poor lad, I don't think he had any idea what harm he did himself in the public eye when he agreed to that match with the Beauharnais girl.'

'But he did it for Lissenberg!'

'Lissenberg did not think so.'

'And he's not a lad.' She found herself defending Max. 'He's grown up a great deal this last year in Vienna. He risked his life last night.'

'And yours. So, what are we going to do for the Princess? I'll deliver your note to Lodge and Playfair. Wise of you to bring it. And see that they support your story.' He laughed and she thought what a pleasant sound it was. 'It was a good day for me when we all met at that masquerade. I've never thanked you. I think, but for you, I would be languishing in one of those dungeons to this day.'

'I think so too.' Smiling at him, 'I hope your arrangements are going to be more successful this time.'

'This?'

'Time. I'm not entirely a fool, Herr Wengel. I do not in the least want to know what you are planning, but in exchange for my continued silence I want two undertakings from you.'

'Yes?' She had taken the wind quite out of his sails. A

nervous hand went up to stroke the luxuriant beard that made it hard to read his expression.

'That you will look after the Princess and that you will see to it that no harm comes to Prince Max. And, by the way, I would not write him off too lightly, either, if I were you. But I have your word?'

'You trust me then? I wonder why.'

'So do I.' This was dangerous ground. 'Because of your grandmother, perhaps?'

'She's a great woman.' Now she thought he was troubled. 'I owe her everything. I think I owe it her to tell you that I am not her grandson.'

'Not?'

'Her grandson. I only learned the other day. Oh, I'd heard rumours; didn't believe them. Finally asked her: I wish I hadn't now. I'm nobody; a foundling. She was embarrassed even to talk about it. I remember boasting to you of my good Lissenberg stock! I am paid for it now. A child from the gutter. Nobody knows this. I am trusting you as you have trusted me.'

'You can,' she held out her hand. 'Thank you for telling me. You must know that it makes no difference. Whatever happens, I shall be silent, and wish you well.'

'Thank you.' He bent over her hand, kissed it, leaned back to look at her very straight: 'I have a duty to do.'

'I know.' He would never know what an effort it had been not to touch that bending, golden head. 'And I do wish you well.'

'Pray for us. I won't tell you where or when. Better for you not to know. As for the Princess, my grandmother will send the carriage tonight, after dark, when the rehearsal is in full swing. It will take "Mary Schnelling" straight to our house in Brundt. She has never been there. If we succeed, there will be no problem. And, I promise you, I will make arrangements to get her out of the country, in the confusion, if we fail.'

'You must not fail. Lissenberg needs you.'

'I know. Is it not strange?' They looked at each other for a long moment in silence. 'Whoever I am, Lissenberg made me. I owe it to her. Owe myself to her.'

'I respect you for it.' How much they were saying, without words.

'Thank you.' One long look and he turned to go.

16

Wengel had chosen his time well for fetching the Princess. The celebrations up at the Palace began with a great display of fireworks that night and everyone who was not rehearsing was up at the top of the road, watching them from a respectful distance.

'I do thank you.' The Princess leaned down from the closed carriage to kiss Martha on the cheek. 'I'll never forget this.'

'Take care of yourself.' But the coachman had already whipped up his horses and moved away.

Entering the hostel, Martha was aware of a commotion at the back of the building and went to investigate. 'What's going on?' she asked a manservant.

'It's the royal guard, Fräulein. They've taken charge of the tunnel. There's one on guard in the women's hall.'

Looking for the Princess? 'Do you know why?' she asked.

'They don't themselves. Prince's orders is all they say, until the celebrations are over. There's a guard on at the theatre, too, front and back. Signor Franzosi's in a proper rage. Oh, and, Fräulein, there was a man here from the Chamberlain's office asking some funny questions. Nobody told him a thing. It seemed simpler.'

'Much! Thank you.'

Was this why Prince Maximilian had not come to see her as he had promised? Was he perhaps under suspicion? Arrest even? She was relieved when Cristabel returned from the theatre in a towering rage about the guards and mentioned Maximilian in passing. 'If it hadn't been for him, I think they'd have insisted on watching the rehearsal! He soon set them to rights about that! Oh, he sent you his apologies, by the way. I don't know why. He's not in much of a position to do anyone favours. They're all at sixes and sevens at the Palace, with the Princess and the little prince so ill. I do pray that neither of them dies! Just think if we had to cancel *Crusader Prince* now. I don't think I could bear it.'

'I doubt you need worry about that,' said Martha. 'I believe the Prince quite capable of concealing a death in order to save his celebration.'

'I do hope you are right.'

So the Prince was concealing the Princess's disappearance, while having her secretly searched for. Martha thanked God for the instinctive way the Lissenbergers closed ranks against him. It augured well for Wengel's plans, too. Did she wish now that she had asked about them? She thought not. Anyway he would not have told her.

Gossip about the festivities at the Palace seeped up from Lissenberg town, where the minor guests were staying. The Palace fountains were running with wine; the Prince had entertained his guests with a medieval tournament, where knights in full armour (from the Palace Armoury) tilted at each other with lances they found hard to manage. There had been two banquets so far, the second even more lavish than the first, and an archery contest won by the Prince himself. 'After some judicious errors by his opponents,' said Brodski. 'The Prince is at explosion point, they say. There was a moment when it looked as if he was going to shoot his rival instead of the target, but the rival missed his aim, like a sensible fellow, and survived.'

'What's the news of the Princess and the little prince?' asked Martha.

'Both too ill to appear. The little prince is dying, they say, and there are some odd rumours about the Princess. Poor lady! No wonder if the treatment she has had and her anxiety about the little boy have turned her brain. No one is allowed to see her. The doctors shake their heads. Even her father's representative has not been allowed in. I suppose they are afraid of what she might say.'

'And the Prince's announcement of his heir? Has he said when it is to be?'

'He keeps putting it off. Can't make up his mind. Originally it was to be tomorrow, up at the Palace, his loving subjects summoned up to hear. But something changed all that! You know, of course, about the new precautions that are being taken.'

'I should just about think so. We have members of the Palace guard at the back of the hostel, and Lady Cristabel says they are swarming all over the theatre.'

'Something has frightened him,' said Brodski. 'I wish I knew what. A man who understood what was going on might make a great deal of money, I believe. But I am not he. Tell me, Miss Peabody, do you by any chance know more than I do?'

'Why in the world should I?' If they both knew it was not an answer, there was nothing in the world he could do about it.

Desmond Fylde brought the news. 'The announcement is to be in the theatre! Just before the performance.' Flushed with excitement, he looked more handsome than ever. 'There never was such a guarantee of a full house.'

'Just so long as the audience is in a mood to pay attention,' said Martha. 'Are there any rumours about who it's to be?'

'Not one, Miss Peabody.' He always treated her with an extra layer of civility, concealing, she thought dislike and distrust.

'But how will it affect the performance?' Cristabel thought of nothing else.

'Not the least in the world, my Queen. They are not clearing the house for standing listeners this time, as I believe they did when last the Prince made an announcement there. Instead, his speech will be read, while he is making it, by the Chamberlain, to the crowd, in the square outside.'

'He'll speak from the stage?' asked Martha.

Fylde laughed. 'Will he not? The scene painters are working like slaves to produce a special backdrop for him. You should just hear them curse, Lady Cristabel.'

'How ridiculous,' said Martha.

'Not entirely so.' With a knowing smile. 'A little bird told me that the sets were being specially designed so that members of the Prince's guard can conceal themselves behind them, covering the audience through hidden slits.'

'The guard on stage!' exclaimed Cristabel. 'Intolerable. I shall complain . . .' she stopped.

'Just so,' said Martha. 'To whom? Anyway, think a little, Belle, you don't want your opening cancelled because of an attack on the Prince, do you?'

'That's true.' She began to smile. 'It does turn our first night into a quite extraordinary event does it not?'

'But, dear Miss Peabody,' said Fylde. 'You do not seriously expect someone to be fool enough to attack the Prince?'

'Of course not. But you must have heard the talk from the Palace. From what one hears, he is in a very strange state, starting at trifles. And fear of assassination is natural enough in an absolute monarch.'

'You sound like a history book.' He turned to Cristabel. 'Tell me, my nightingale, this last scene of ours – if the Prince is really in the kind of temper Miss Peabody suggests – is it wise?'

'It's musically extraordinary,' said Cristabel. 'The best thing I ever sang. It makes the opera. The Prince is a man of taste – he chose the opera after all. He will see it in its context.'

'I do devoutly hope so. I think I will have a word with Herr Wengel, if he ever deigns to favour us with his company again, and suggest a few minor alterations. Not in the music, my songbird, but in the words. Of course,' smiling the smile he knew so charming, 'one could, at a pinch, be a little less intelligible than usual.'

'But might one not be doing oneself harm in front of so international an audience?' asked Martha. 'I have heard, Mr. Fylde, that your Italian is not, in fact, quite so easy to understand as it might be. You would not wish the word to go round that you have problems in Italian as well as, forgive me, in German.'

'How kind of you to warn me, Miss Peabody,' he said through gritted teeth.

I have made myself an enemy, she thought. No, he was my enemy already. I have merely brought it out into the open. And then, poor Cristabel.

The dress-rehearsal of *Crusader Prince* was held behind locked doors in an empty theatre. 'I am truly sorry,' Franz Wengel had called on his way to the theatre, 'if I allowed you in, Lady Helen, and you, Miss Peabody, it would open the door to all kinds of requests I cannot grant. I do hope you understand.'

'A lot of publicity-seeking nonsense,' said Lady Helen.

He smiled at her, and Martha's heart lurched. 'It's my duty

to seek publicity, Lady Helen, for myself, and for my brilliant cast, as well as for my opera.'

'You sound very confident,' said Martha. 'Are you pleased that the Prince is adding to the notoriety of your first night by making his great announcement before it?'

Now his smile was all for her. 'Miss Peabody, I cannot begin to tell you how delighted I am.'

'Even with the royal guard menacing your audience from behind the scenes?'

'You'd heard of that?'

'Yes, I had wondered if you had.'

'Desmond Fylde is a great one for the spreading of news.' His eyes met hers. 'I have to thank you, Miss Peabody, for putting it into his head that he cannot afford to swallow his words in my great scene.'

'It's great?'

'I think so.'

'It went brilliantly,' Cristabel returned from the rehearsal flushed with excitement. 'It almost makes me superstitious. You know what they say . . . But I really don't think it can fail . . . Martha, there's something . . .' By common consent they moved toward the window, leaving Desmond Fylde describing his own brilliant singing to Lady Helen. 'Herr Wengel wants me to change the wording of my last aria. The very last lines before the final chorus, without telling anyone. Do you think I should?'

'I don't see why not. He's the composer, after all, and the librettist. Surely it happens often enough? What does Franzosi think about it?'

'Wengel doesn't want even him told.'

'Oh.' She thought about it. 'What precisely is the change, Belle?'

'You remember the aria? After Brandt has told me how he intends to fight for Lissenberg's freedom from Charlemagne. It's my great song of rejoicing for the glorious future of my country. Frankly, I always did think the last line was weak, found it hard to give it the climactic feel it needed. Now he wants me to move down to the front of the stage and sing three words in Liss.'

'In Liss?'

'Yes. The Liss word for freedom three times. It sings wonderfully.' She glanced over to where Fylde and Lady Helen were still deep in talk. 'I won't demonstrate now, but take my word for it, it's a superb climax.'

'Then sing it,' said Martha. 'And tell no one.'

'That's what Wengel said.'

Martha did not sleep much that night. Had she really encouraged Cristabel to give the signal for revolution from the stage of the Opera House? She thought she had, thought she was mad, thought she would go on trusting Franz Wengel. What would happen? Would the final chorus ever get sung? The foreign guests, of course, at the front of the house, would not understand, but Prince Gustav surely would. And so would the Lissenbergers at the back of the house and in the gallery. What happened next must partly depend on what Prince Gustav had said in his announcement. Or must it? She remembered what Franz Wengel had said about Prince Maximilian's losing the affection of the Lissenbergers, and thought it understandable enough. He had seemed too much his father's puppet, must be identified in the public eye with the wild extravagance of the celebrations up at the Palace. Fountains running with wine while the grape harvest was neglected . . . Fountains running with blood? She fell asleep, and dreamed wildly.

It was going to be another of Lissenberg's brilliant autumn days. Already, when they got up, they could hear the murmur of the crowd beginning to assemble below in the great square. 'The guards are gone from the tunnel,' said Anna, bringing breakfast. 'I suppose they need them all for the theatre and the square.'

'Yes.' Abstractedly. She was wondering where the guards who were to be hidden on stage would go after Prince Gustav had made his speech. Could she have exposed Cristabel to actual danger? Surely not. She would hang on to her certainty that Franz Wengel knew what he was doing. She racked her brains for any imaginable thing she could do to help. Keeping calm was the first thing, and keeping Cristabel calm, the next. And for the first time, she found herself actually glad of Cristabel's infatuation with Desmond Fylde. Whatever today might hold for Prince Maximilian, it was no longer any concern of Cristabel's. She wished she had seen Prince Max since that strange night's encounter, but was hardly surprised that she had not. He must be walking on egg-shells, up at the Palace. There had still not been a word about Princess Amelia's disappearance, and presumably the search for her was still continuing, in secret. No one would be leaving the country before the end of the celebrations, to try to do so would be to court disaster. Prince Gustav must know that his wife was hidden somewhere in the tiny principality, be sure of finding her sooner or later if he continued to rule. She was actually praying for Franz's success today. I would do anything for him, she thought. How strange.

The day seemed endless. Impossible to go out, since the square was now packed with Lissenbergers, making a day of it, picnicking in the hot sun, served with wine and bread and sausages by dirndled girls from the inn. 'I think you had better plan to get to the theatre early, Belle,' Martha said when they had finished their light luncheon. 'If the crowd is as thick as this now, it will be impassable long before the time for the announcement.'

'Yes.' Cristabel looked white and drawn. 'Herr Wengel told us to be there early. He promised to come for me, see me through the crowd. He said there was sure to be one. I expect that's him now.'

'Frau Schmidt, what a delightful surprise!' Martha hurried forward to greet the old lady when she appeared on Wengel's arm. 'But how are you? Are you well enough for this long day?'

'That's just why I took the liberty of bringing her here,' said Wengel. 'She is not well enough, but she is also a very strong-minded old person. She insists on seeing my opera, but must not be exposed to the long wait in the theatre. I thought I would put her in your capable hands, Miss Peabody.'

'I'm so very glad.' Aware of disapproval from Lady Helen behind her, she leaned forward to kiss the cool cheek, and was instantly aware of the tension that held the old lady, like a clock overwound. 'You must rest,' she said. 'Until it is time to go.'

'There will be time to rest afterwards,' said Frau Schmidt. 'My guest sent you her greetings and thanks, by the way.'

'How is she?'

'Much better, but anxious.'

'Time to go.' Franz Wengel kissed his grandmother on both

cheeks. Not his grandmother? How strange; he looked like her. Like someone? Martha lost the thought as she kissed Cristabel and wished her luck, then turned back to Wengel, 'And to you, too. All the luck in the world.'

'Thank you.' He bent with one of the courtly gestures that always surprised her, and kissed her hand. 'I owe you so much, Miss Peabody. And now I am asking you to take care of my grandmother. I know you will.'

She met his eyes. 'Whatever happens.'

'Thank you.' Now at last he smiled at her and her heart dissolved within her. 'If I succeed today, may we talk tomorrow, Miss Peabody?'

'I hope to be the first to congratulate you.'

'I hope you will have cause to do so.'

17

'Time to go.' Watching from the window Martha had seen the palace guard begin to clear a way through the crowded square for the royal party's arrival. 'We must be in our places well before the Prince gets there.' She was relieved to see that the crowd was in a good temper, apparently on easy terms with the soldiers who were pushing them back. 'Three cheers for the Prince's guard,' shouted someone, and got them.

But should she be pleased? How did this augur for Wengel's plans? No time to be thinking about that now. As they emerged on the hostel steps, soldiers there moved to open a way for them and another voice shouted, 'Way there, make way for the women's lady.' The crowd began to shuffle back with friendly murmurs to let them pass.

'You seem to have achieved some kind of notoriety,' said Lady Helen drily. She had not pretended to enjoy entertaining Frau Schmidt.

The theatre was crowded already, liveried flunkeys busy showing people to their places. 'This way.' An usher hurried forward to greet them, addressing himself, Martha noticed, to Frau Schmidt.

'We are not to greet the Prince in the foyer this time?' asked Martha.

'No, he wishes everyone seated.' He led them up a short staircase that gave directly on to a single row of seats at the extreme right-hand end of the balcony. 'These are what you wanted?' Again he was addressing the old lady.

'Just right, thank you, Hans,' she smiled at him.

'A friend of yours?' Lady Helen asked.

'Everyone in Lissenberg is my friend,' said Frau Schmidt. 'And yours, I think, my dear,' to Martha.

A fanfare of trumpets blared outside. 'He's coming.' Frau Schmidt had taken her place at the end of the row with Martha beside her.

'He's here!' The audience rustled to its feet as the royal party appeared at the entrance to the centre aisle, and Martha, who had been doubtful at first about the angle from which they would see the stage, recognised the great advantage of the seats Frau Schmidt had chosen. They commanded a view of almost the entire house.

As Prince Gustav advanced down the aisle, the audience gave a little sigh at sight of his companion, Countess Bemberg, glorious in gold brocade. Behind them came Prince Maximilian with one of the ladies of the court. Too far to see his expression, but Martha did not think she needed to. The royal party moved left and right to fill the front rows while Prince Gustav came leisurely forward, smiled down at the orchestra, playing Haydn's Lissenberg anthem for all it was worth, and climbed crimson velvet steps, ready for him to the left of the stage. As he did so, the curtain rose, revealing the set that had caused such heartburning among the stage-hands. At first sight it hardly seemed worth the trouble, a receding vista of laurel hedges centering on a distant statue. But from her angled position, Martha could see a member of the royal guard, behind the scenes, musket to a hole among the laurels. She found she was clutching Frau Schmidt's hand, felt the pressure returned.

Prince Gustav was centre stage now. He raised a hand and the orchestra hiccuped to silence in mid-phrase. 'My people,' to the gallery. 'My friends,' to the stalls. 'I have left you too long in doubt about my plans for the future of our beloved Lissenberg.' He paused for effect, every inch the master of the scene. He had reverted, for this occasion, to the court costume of the previous century, and it suited him well. The wig that made him look like pictures of Louis XIV, the elegant court black and shining lace ruffles set off his tall figure and commanding presence. 'My friends,' he went on, treating them all to this address, 'I have done so because I was not sure what would be best for Lissenberg. It has taken much anxious thought, many sleepless nights, before I have been able to sacrifice my personal interest to that of my faithful people.' Another pause. Martha felt a stirring of interest in the audience, felt it herself. What could he be going to say? 'My dear friends,' leaning forward a little, 'I am going to talk to you now as father and friend, and I count on you to listen to me as the loving subjects I know you to be. I have married twice for your sakes, had two sons, two possible heirs. What shall I say to you? How tell of my deep disappointment? My eldest son, Maximilian does not wish to be Prince of Lissenberg. He wants to write opera, be a travelling player. He would give you up for that.' A deep sigh from the audience. 'And for the younger, little Gustav, I have to tell you that he is nothing but a sick child, to be nursed and cared for, never to be a ruling prince. And his mother, his poor mother, whom I have so much loved . . . My friends, she has taken leave of her senses. The doctors say there is no hope for her recovery. No wonder if her poor little son is not well either; it is a sad inheritance he has. My dear friends, I am laying my heart open to you here, as your loving Prince should. I have had, for some time, a comfort in these afflictions of mine, my good friend the Countess of Bemberg. She has a son, a little, healthy, promising boy. He is our future, here in Lissenberg. I have written to the Pope, there will be no problem. I shall divorce my poor, demented wife, send her home to her parents, and you shall have a Princess worthy of you, an heir to be proud of, a future assured. And now,' he went on without a breath, giving no chance for a reaction, 'it is time for our prize opera, the story of another Prince of Lissenberg who loved his country.' A commanding gesture as he moved to leave the stage and the orchestra plunged into the overture.

'Clever,' breathed Martha to Frau Schmidt. Clever enough? She thought not, and settled down to enjoy the opera with the rest of the house. No one in their senses would have ventured an instant protest to interfere with the production of Lissenberg's prize opera.

It was going brilliantly. If Cristabel had minded Prince Gustav's summary dismissal of Max, it had not affected her singing. She had never been in better voice than in her first act farewell-duet with her husband, off on his crusade, or the aria in which she planned to disguise herself and follow him. And when she reappeared, in tunic and hose, as his page, she got a round of applause that stopped the performance. 'She's in tremendous voice,' said Lady Helen as the curtain fell for the one long interval and the audience burst into a torrent of clapping.

'And so is Desmond Fylde. They are striking sparks off each

other. It's making for a formidable performance, I hope it doesn't mean . . .'

'Impossible,' said Lady Helen. 'A nobody like Fylde. What's happening?'

'The Prince hasn't moved.' Martha could see him from where she sat. 'He's just sitting there, talking to Countess Bemberg as if she was the only woman in the world.'

'And if he makes no move, nor can the audience,' said Frau Schmidt. 'Clever, that! Though maybe not very popular.'

'No. Look!' Half rising in her seat, Martha could see members of the palace guard on duty at the exit.

'And, look!' said Frau Schmidt as the curtain rose to reveal Franz Wengel alone on stage, his informal jacket and modern trousers in striking contrast to Prince Gustav's eighteenth-century elegance. He stood there for a moment, immobile, as the restless murmur of the trapped audience stilled gradually to silence. When it was absolute, he spoke. 'Fellow Lissenbergers, the square outside is so crowded that the Prince has decided we had best remain in the theatre. There will be time to talk to our friends outside when the performance is over. Meanwhile, we ask your patience and are making our interval as short as possible.' He nodded informally to Prince and audience alike and withdrew as the curtain fell again and a new volley of clapping and shouting broke out.

'What are they shouting?' asked Lady Helen. 'Deplorable to keep us shut up here like this!'

'I'm not quite sure,' lied Martha, and hoped that Prince Gustav was too absorbed in talk with his Countess to notice. Under the cries of 'bravo' and the individual names of the singers, Cristabel's the most prominent, was a kind of undertone, a leitmotif: the crowd was shouting 'Franz . . . Franz . . . Franz.'

Frau Schmidt had recognised it too. 'Just as well,' she breathed as the orchestra filed back into the pit.

'A short interval indeed,' agreed Martha, settling back in her seat.

The restless audience was soon gripped by the drama of the second half of *Crusader Prince*. Martha had always thought it unusual music, tonight she found it extraordinary as it built up from climax to climax, a great inexorable tide of song, sweeping the crowded house with it. During the short pause when the scene changed from crusader camp back to the Palace at Lissenberg, the audience hardly spoke or moved, and when the curtain rose to reveal an unmistakable replica of the throne-room at the Palace there was a great sigh of anticipation.

Fylde and Cristabel were singing, if possible, better than ever. Princess Algisa had just come, barefoot, back from proving her innocence by the ordeal of hot ploughshares. Now, as she threw off her loose penitential gown to reveal the page's tunic and hose, her doubting husband understood at last and fell on his knees before her. She put out a loving hand to touch his wiry black curls, then plunged into her final aria. It was the musical culmination of the whole opera, drawing together its threads, working up from peak to peak until at last, leaving Fylde on his knees, she moved forward, head high, arms wide, to give the last line straight to the audience in Liss: 'Freedom! Freedom! Freedom!'

And, 'Freedom!' It came back at her from the audience in a great roar of sound. 'Freedom and Franz!'

Pandemonium. Cristabel simply stood there, poised, waiting. The chorus had filed quietly on ready for the finale and Fylde had risen to his feet to stand as motionless as Cristabel, waiting for silence. In the pit, the conductor laid down his baton; in the front row Prince Gustav was speaking angrily to the Countess. But what could he do? The steps that had given him access to the stage had been removed before the opera began. He was helpless there, in full view of audience and stage.

'The guard!' whispered Lady Helen. 'Where are the guards?'

'Here they come.' Martha reached for Frau Schmidt's hand for comfort, but did not find it. Turning she saw that the old lady had disappeared, but a member of the Royal guard was standing at the doorway through which she must have vanished. Her own movement had caught his attention; without moving a muscle, he winked at her.

Looking down again, she saw that guards were now stationed all down the central aisle and across the front of the house. Guarding whom? There was another row of them behind the chorus, their scarlet uniforms contrasting with the black and white costumes. Cristabel had moved at last, turning instinctively to Fylde for comfort, and her place at centre stage had been taken by Franz Wengel. The shouts of 'Freedom and Franz' redoubled. Martha thought the orchestra had joined in now, only around Prince Gustav there was a patch of frightened silence.

Wengel took a step forward and the crowd hushed. 'Enough, my friends. And, thank you. I think you all understand that my opera was merely a prelude to what we must do now. We have sung of freedom for Lissenberg, now we must achieve it. We are going to settle our destiny here and now, and, by the way, in case any of you are anxious for friends and relatives outside in the square, I can tell you that our allies the royal guard have taken charge there, as they have here. The Lord Chamberlain is their unharmed prisoner; the crowd awaits the result of our deliberations.' He moved one more step forward, looked directly across the orchestra pit at Prince Gustav, and said, 'If you would be so good as to join us, Sir?'

Prince Gustav said something inaudible, but two members of the guard had stepped forward to usher him towards the velvet stair, now replaced.

You had to admire him, Martha thought, as he gathered his dignity about him to climb unassisted on to the stage and face Wengel. There was a hiss or two, quickly suppressed; the crowd was silent, waiting.

'What is the meaning of this outrage?' Gustav spoke past Wengel to the crowded auditorium.

'We are here to discuss the twenty-five years you have held Lissenberg, Prince Gustav. What you paid for our country years ago has been amply repaid in ruthless taxes, in extortion, and in neglect. We have no wish for violence, for a reign of terror as in France. For a long time we have held our hand, hoping for a peaceful solution, for the quiet succession of our friend Prince Maximilian. Hush!' He raised a hand as the crowd burst into a roar of 'No!' and 'Traitor!' 'Prince Max is no traitor, but he has been bred in a hard school. Perhaps he is not the man to lead Lissenberg in the fight we all see coming against Napoleon. As for the little prince, I am sad to tell you, my friends, that he died this morning. His father did not choose to tell you this. Nor did he tell you that, far from being mad, his wife, the Princess Amelia, escaped from his attempts to poison her and is here to give evidence against him. She is still not well, my friends, but if you wish, she will tell you her story in her own words.' As he spoke, Frau Schmidt had come on stage, leading a veiled figure. They paused, facing Prince Gustav. The Princess threw back her veil, gazed at him for a long moment with contempt. 'Do you recognise me, Sir?' she asked at last. 'The wife you tried to kill?'

'Bitch!' And then, 'They said you were dead.'

'They lied to you, Sir. Everybody lies to you.' She turned to Franz. 'May I go home to Baden now? There is nothing left here for me now my child is dead. Govern here better than he did. You have my blessing.'

'Thank you.' As Wengel bent to kiss her hand Prince Gustav suddenly lost control, exploded into a torrent of foul language, made as if to attack them, and was instantly, and not gently, restrained by his own guards. 'Take him away,' said Wengel. 'And do not hurt him.' He turned back to Princess Amelia. 'You shall have your dowry returned, and honourable escort home to Baden when you wish it. Yes? There is something else?'

'My dear Max,' she said. 'He saved my life. You will be good to him.'

'I shall treat him like a brother.' Wengel turned back to face the expectant house. 'My friends, Prince Gustav has proved himself unfit to rule. Now we must take serious thought for the future of Lissenberg. With your good will, which I know I have, I will take control until we can hold free elections for a democratic government. If Prince Maximilian wishes to stand, as I hope he will, no obstacle will be placed in his way. I do not think, by the way, that you should take what his father said about him any more seriously than any other of Gustav's lies. But what we have to face, my dear friends, is that Lissenberg is under serious threat. When I first began to plan – to dream of freedom from our twenty-five years of tyranny, I had hopes of help from France, from the man I thought the great liberator, Bonaparte. This year has proved those hopes the fantasy they were. If we want freedom, my friends, we must win it for ourselves, by ourselves. Luckily, my friends, in the army, have recognised this. As you see, they are on our side. It is lucky for us that they are. For Prince Gustav has done one good thing. Almost alone, he has stood up to the new Emperor who has paved the way to his throne with innocent blood. He has made Bonaparte our enemy, and we must be united as never before if we are to resist him. If you wish to unite yourselves behind Prince Maximilian, do so with my goodwill. He has a strong claim on Lissenberg and our love. Prince Maximilian?'

'Yes.' He was on his feet already. He took the steps with a couple of long strides and crossed the stage to face Wengel. Martha choked on a breath. Impossible! She was imagining things! No, the crowd saw it too. A gasp. Then a spellbound hush. Two young men. Identical? Twins? One fair, one dark, one bearded, one clean shaven, both dressed in black, Wengel in his modern trousers, Maximilian old-fashioned in knee breeches. Their beaky profiles matched like two sides of a coin. Their stance, as they faced each other was exactly the same, one foot forward, head up, enquiring, challenging. At the same moment, right hands went out, met, gripped.

'They've never met before,' Martha said it as much to herself as to Lady Helen.

'It's mad,' said Lady Helen. 'Impossible.' The crowd were beginning to talk, to exclaim, quietly at first. Now the two heads, so extraordinarily alike turned at a quiet word from Frau Schmidt, standing just behind them. Some silent message seemed to pass between them, and Franz Wengel spoke, getting instant attention. 'Frau Schmidt has something to say to us. Let us listen to her.' The two young men dropped hands and made way for her to step forward.

'Lissenbergers.' She hardly raised her voice but in the amazed hush it carried to the back of the house. 'I hoped it would happen like this, that you would all see the likeness before I explained it. Which I can. It is just another instance of Prince Gustav's tyrannical behaviour. When he bought Lissenberg twenty-five years ago his only shred of claim was through his Liss wife, my cousin. He insisted that she make the mountain journey in winter so that his child should be born in Lissenberg. She was taken ill on the way and gave birth in a mountain farmhouse, to twins, one dark, one fair. Their mother, my cousin, was dying. In the general confusion, no one could remember which boy was born first. When the Prince arrived, he was furious. He swore them all to secrecy, picked the dark child as the healthier-looking and arranged for the other to be adopted by a family in Lissenberg. They were creatures of his; he meant to keep an eye on the child; in fairness we should remember that. But that was the year the cholera hit Lissenberg; a judgment some of us thought. The adoptive mother was a friend of mine. When she and her husband knew they were dying, she told me the whole story, I thought it best to let the Prince think his son had died too. I smuggled little Franz back to Brundt with me and gave him to my daughter to rear. He has always been a most beloved grandson to me. I never told him this story; I have no proof of it. But, when I first saw Prince Maximilian, I knew the proof was there, for all to see. You have seen it today, my friends, and so have these two brothers. Now I leave it to you Lissenbergers to decide what to do about your two princes.'

The two young men were holding both hands now, deeply conferring with each other, apparently quite oblivious of the tumult of the crowd. Then, slowly, as one Prince, they turned forward to face the audience, Franz's right hand in Max's left.

Surprisingly, it was Max who spoke. 'No need of proof,' he said. 'It is here, within us. My brother and I know each other for brothers. There is nothing, ever, to be said again on this count. I recognise him, here, before you all, as my beloved twin, whose mind I read as I read my own. And I tell you all that it is he who should rule, here in Lissenberg. This is no sacrifice on my part. For once, the Prince has told you the truth. I have always wanted to make my life in music, with the woman I love.' Speaking direct to the audience, he did not see the instinctive way Cristabel leaned closer to Fylde, but Martha did, and her heart bled for him. 'The way is open for me in Vienna now,' he went on. 'My opera, *Odin's Daughter* is to be put on at the Burgtheater. I will always remain your loving Prince, but from now on, my life is there. And I tell you this, my friends, if it had been my magnificent opera being staged here, if I had written the masterpiece we have seen tonight, I could not have left its production in others' hands, not even to plan the brilliant, bloodless revolution my brother has achieved here tonight. Have your election, since he wishes it, but we all know what the result will be. I say, "Long Live Prince Franz".'

As the crowd took it up with a great roar of enthusiasm, he stepped back, turned to Cristabel and saw her strongly held in Fylde's arm. Anguish for him fed the cold tide of desolation that had flooded through Martha since that first moment when the twin Princes had stood facing each other, and the truth had hit her. Her dear friend Franz Wengel was Prince Franz, burdened with all the dynastic duties she found so hard to understand. Was he perhaps seeing it too? Was it deluding herself to have thought that he also had imagined a moment, when the plotting was over, when they two would have time to talk? Surely there had been something unspoken between them? Or was she merely a lonely spinster, imagining things? It made no difference. Franz would do his duty, she knew, and was proud to know it. And I shall go back to America. With Brodski?

'What are they saying now?' Lady Helen asked it for the second time, impatiently.

'What?' Coming up from a great depth of despair, she heard what the crowd was saying. Most of them were still shouting 'Long live Prince Franz', but some had changed back to 'Freedom and Franz'. These were male voices, and now, in a kind of descant above them, women were joining in with different words. 'Franz and his lady.' Could that be it? And, 'Where is our lady?'

Her eyes were suddenly veiled with tears, but she thought she saw some signal pass between Frau Schmidt and Franz, down there on the stage, so infinitely far away.

'Well, what is it they are saying?' Lady Helen asked it more impatiently than ever. 'Something about a lady? What lady?'

'I don't –' She turned at a gentle touch on her shoulder. It was the guard who had winked at her.

He was smiling now. 'You're wanted on stage, Fräulein. Time to take your bow. We all knew you were behind him, every inch of the way. Our Franz.' And then, handing her solicitously down the narrow stair. 'Only fancy him being a prince all the time! You won't mind it too much, will you, Miss?'

She was crying. She was plain Miss Peabody from Philadelphia, and she was about to make her first appearance on any stage. I can't do it. Of course I can. He's there waiting. But is he waiting for me? She brushed the tears away with the back of her hand as the friendly guard opened a door and pushed her gently forward. The chorus opened up a way for her, she caught the breath of a friendly whisper, was dazzled for a moment by light from the huge chandelier, moved blindly forward and saw Franz waiting for her. What could she do but walk straight into his arms?

'I thought I'd lost you.' His voice came muffled through her hair.

'So did I!' Now she could look up at him. 'What's that they are playing?' But she knew.

'I'm afraid it's the Lissenberg National Anthem. Time to take your bow, my love. We owe them that.'

'We certainly do. If they hadn't . . .'

'I'd have gone looking for a princess. Will you be my princess, Martha?'

'I'll be your wife,' she said, and looked up for his kiss.